A
DONOVANS
FRIENDS
NOVEL

FOR *Always*

A.C. ARTHUR

FOR ALWAYS

A DONOVANS FRIENDS NOVEL

Opposites attract...for better and for worse.

Fitness guru, Tyler West's life comes crashing to a halt with the news of his parents' death. Now, he'll be reunited with his brother on his family's land as they debate the fate of the ranch. And when the charming interior designer arrives to update the home before sale, the former stress of returning to his hometown takes a back seat to the passion he finds in her arms.

Gabriella Bennett's first career assignment has her nervous and excited. As the youngest of the prestigious Bennett family she's determined to succeed in spite of her family's doubts. But the moment the sexy cowboy hat-wearing owner kisses her, she knows that all is lost.

Desire sparks quickly and burns fiercely between them, so much so, that neither of them notice the threat to their lives... until it's too late.

Dear Reader,

It has taken me a while to get to Gabriella Bennett's story because I needed to find just the right time and place for her. As the youngest of the Bennett family, Gabriella has been through a lot beginning with her family's fight against jealous and vindictive people determined to bring them down (GUARDING HIS BODY) and leading up to when Adriana's relationship with Parker Donovan put her in the midst of yet another dangerous family situation (EMBRACED BY A DONOVAN).

Gabriella first began showing that she was ready to find love in her brother Rico's story (ALWAYS IN MY HEART). It was then that I started to feel like their might be someone out there for her. Tyler West living on a ranch in Hobbs Creek, Texas was the farthest thing from Gabriella's imagination. But once I had a clear picture of who Tyler was and where his story was going, I knew he was the one for Gabriella.

I truly hope you enjoy this next step into the Donovan Friends world. There is so much more to come!

Happy Reading,

AC

CHAPTER 1

*S*he dreamed of him. His arms held her close in a circle of warmth and comfort. His breath whispered over her neck as he dropped a kiss there and then moved slightly so that the next kiss brushed along the line of her jaw. She closed her eyes and let her head loll back, enjoying the streaks of desire shooting through her at his touch.

He pulled away, with a quick jerk as if she'd slapped him. She stumbled back in an attempt to keep herself from falling, but it didn't work. Her feet caught on something and she felt her body going down. Slamming onto the floor hurt worse than she imagined it would. Sharp, shooting pains ricocheted from her lower back to her abdomen. She cried out, but even that sounded more distressing than it should. But it was when she held her hands up to him that she received the shock of her life.

He didn't take her hands. He didn't do anything to help her up. And she couldn't get up on her own. The lower half of her body was still while she dropped her arms, flattening her palms on the floor, in an attempt to push herself up. Her legs did not move and her hands slipped on something warm. When she looked down, a strangled cry caught in her throat and she blinked furiously to keep the tears at bay. It was futile, the tears came anyway. In steady streams down her cheeks as she realized her hands were in a puddle of blood.

With a jerk of her neck she looked up at him once more. This time she opened her mouth to speak, to call his name, curse him for not helping her, something. Anything. Nothing. There was no sound. And he was gone.

Gabriella awoke with a start, sitting up in her bed, her eyes scanned the dark room for a sign. Of what, she didn't know. Or she did know, but didn't want to acknowledge her digression.

It was over between her and Austin. It had been for a while now. With a hand touching her chest where her heart still pounded, Gabriella closed her eyes and sighed. She was happy about the break-up and proud of herself for walking away and never looking back.

Even if the dreams continued to haunt her.

Two Days Later
Hobbs Creek, Texas
Westwind Ranch & Resort

Tyler grit his teeth and held back a curse. He was not in the mood for another one today. Or this month. Why couldn't they accept that he hadn't made up his mind yet and when he did, he would call them? This was beyond unprofessional.

And she was woefully overdressed. Westwind was a horse

ranch and resort. If she wanted to book a room, she was in the wrong place. The resort was down the winding path, closer to the road. It was a little after one so Dessie would probably be at the front desk right now. She would gladly book this woman—with the white painted toenails—a room. Or a weekend package, Tyler thought wryly. Her pedicure and the sky-high Manalo heels she wore looked expensive.

"Excuse me?"

And she speaks, Tyler thought with another sigh.

He made one last scrape against Golden Glory's hoof, holding the pick tightly in his right hand and her foot in the other. He was bent over in the stall with his back facing the entrance, that's how he'd glimpsed the woman's shoes before she spoke. He wasn't in a hurry to change his position or answer her.

"I'm looking for Tyler West," she continued.

Persistent.

GG whined and Tyler frowned up at the horse. Traitor. He didn't want to answer the woman and he didn't care if he was being rude. He was grieving and trying to take care of ranch business. He did not have time for another real estate agent poking their nosy little head into his business. When he decided whether or not he wanted to sell his father's ranch, he would contact an agent to do so. It was that simple.

When Tyler noted he'd been raised better, he eased GG's foot down and turned slowly toward the voice. Damn. This might not be as simple as he thought.

"I'm Tyler West."

Her smile was slow and as potent as three fingers of whiskey straight.

"I'm Gabriella Bennett. I'm the designer from The Proctor Group. Dessie Gwynne said I should come out to talk to you today. Is now a good time?"

"Dessie's down at the resort," he replied. "If you get back into your car and make a left instead of a right at the end of the driveway, you'll run right into the back parking lot."

She was tall, somewhere around five feet eleven inches in those heels. He was six feet four and a half inches, his height being a big part of the reason that fashion scout had approached him twenty years ago. The slim fingers of one hand clutched the straps of a Noe Saint Laurent tote, while the other rested confidently at her side.

"I've already met with Dessie and her husband Clyde, who I believe is the West family attorney." She stopped and lifted her free hand to tuck dark hair behind her ear.

Tyler followed each movement and took in each detail and then frowned because he couldn't figure out why.

"I was told to speak to you about a tour of the ranch house and how best to stage the place before the listing goes public."

"I haven't decided whether or not I'm selling the ranch," he snapped and turned back to his horse.

The horse he'd inherited three weeks ago when his parents were found dead in a burning truck. His fingers tightened on the pick as he struggled for composure.

"He's a beautiful Appaloosa. Do you get the chance to ride him often or is he part of the shows that take place at the resort?"

In response to her question Tyler looked back at GG's chestnut blanket coat. It wasn't strange that he knew what type of horse GG was without a second thought because he'd grown up on a ranch. As for the woman with the perfectly manicured nails and silky hair, well, she didn't look like the type to get dirty riding horses, let alone hanging out in stalls long enough to learn the names of the breed.

"They have quarter horses down at the resort. Nevil Snyder is the new head wrangler, he handles all the horses and other animals for the show. This is Golden Glory. He was my dad's horse."

"Oh."

The one quick reply wiped the smile from her face and simultaneously increased Tyler's irritation.

"Look, I'm kind of busy right now."

She nodded. "That's fine. Is there a better time for me to come back? Dessie and Clyde stated that they'd like to have the ranch on the market in the next month. Considering I'll be working on the staging of the main house, employee residences and the resort, I'll need to get started pretty quickly."

"What?"

She'd just said a lot, most of which he hadn't deciphered because he'd been stuck on the part where the ranch would go on the market for sale in the next month. That decision was his, and well, Jagger's. But who knew when, or if, his younger brother would decide to make an appearance. He hadn't been able to pull himself away from his "important business deal" three weeks ago when Tyler called to let him know about their parents' death. So Tyler had returned to Hobbs Creek to handle everything himself, just as he used to do when they were kids.

"No," he said when she looked like she was about to speak again. "I can't do this right now. Come back later."

"If you'd like to give me a specific time so I'll be sure to not interrupt you again," she said.

"Right," he replied with a curt nod. "Tomorrow. In the evening, around six I guess."

"That will work. In the meantime, I can draft some ideas for the resort and visit the employee residences. So when we meet, all I'll need to do is tour the ranch house. Then we can schedule another time to go over my thoughts and hopefully get started."

Again, she was saying a lot and Tyler just did not want to hear it. He didn't want to hear anything but the sounds of the ranch, the periodic whine of horses, the bleat of Spanish goats, squeal and grunts of the pigs. The Longhorn cattle would be out to pasture, releasing an occasional bellow or snort. And at night, after dinner when he sat on the porch, staring up to the starry sky the memories came. The ones he loved and would forever miss and the ones that still brought fresh pain.

"Fine. Tomorrow at six. We'll have some dinner and sit on the porch to talk about your plans," he said and waited for her to walk away.

She didn't and he wanted to frown or possibly yell. He did neither. Instead, Tyler did what he always did instead of asking the next question or waiting for uncomfortable conversations to run their course. He returned to the work at hand as if he'd never been interrupted.

At some point he suspected she'd left because by the time he finished all four of GG's hooves, had brushed him down and offered the gelding his favorite treat—apple slices—she was gone.

That was a relief. Tyler didn't want to be bothered with

people right now. Truth be told, he hadn't wanted to be bothered with anyone or anything since hearing of his parents' deaths.

Their bodies were found three weeks ago, each with an execution style gunshot to the back of their head, seated inside their F-350 while it burned to a crisp. A family on their way to the resort to check-in had stopped at the sight. They immediately called 911 and just four hours later, Sheriff Fred Alvarez called Tyler. It had been almost three o'clock in the afternoon for Tyler in Los Angeles that day, and he'd just finished a meeting with the marketing team for his new sportswear line. He didn't know how long he'd stood in the hallway of the office building trying to digest the news. But Bez, one of the guards Tyler's agent insisted he needed, had eventually led him to the SUV parked at the back of the building. A while later Tyler arrived at his apartment. He'd been texting his assistant Mellie, during the drive, so by the time he made it home, all he'd had to do was pack a bag and then he was back in the truck heading to the airport.

That's when he called Jagger.

"It's Mom and Dad," Tyler had said, his voice gruff with all the emotion he was trying to contain. "There's been an accident. The truck was on fire and they're...dead."

He hadn't known any other way to put it. George and Verna West, life-long residents of Hobbs Creek, Texas; owners of the Westwind Ranch & Resort; and, parents to Tyler and Jagger West departed this world on June 12th. That's how it read in the Hobbs Gazette and the obituary that had been distributed to the more than two hundred people who attended the funeral one week later. Jagger hadn't said much on the phone when Tyler called, just that he was in Paris about to close a big deal and would be unable to return to help Tyler with the funeral plans, or anything else.

Though this had been no surprise, Tyler was still disappointed and angry with his younger brother. For as long as he could remember, Jagger had left everything to Tyler. From the time Tyler was five years old he'd had chores on the ranch. They'd started with simple things like assisting the ranch hands with feeding the pigs and goats. By the time he was eight he'd been bumped up to feeding the chickens by himself and cleaning the horse stalls. Jagger was six by that time and was supposed to assist Tyler. But the first time George pulled one of his surprise check-ups and yelled at his youngest son for not closing the door to the chicken coop, set the stage for Jagger's life on the ranch. Nothing the younger West son did was right in George's eyes, which for Jagger meant, he never had to do anything. Tyler, who watched the ranch hands like a hawk because he didn't want to incur his father's wrath, did everything to George's satisfaction. So Tyler was the worker while Jagger became the playful West brother. The prankster and the star of the football team, Jagger was voted most likely to succeed in his graduating class. His brother went on to do just that after obtaining an MBA in marketing and landing a job at one of New York's most prestigious PR firms.

Tyler had achieved success as well, although if anyone from L.A. saw him walking out of the stable three hours after he'd gone in, they might not recognize him. His jeans were dusty in some places, caked with mud in others. The white t-shirt he wore looked more gray at this point, while the boots he'd just purchased a couple days after arriving in Texas, were now scuffed and splattered with a variety of animal fluids, dirt, mud and grass. He slapped the worn Dodgers cap he kept stuffed in his back pocket, down over his head as the late afternoon sun blazed as high and hot as it had early this morning.

This Tyler West was a far cry from the easy-smiling, charismatic model turned fitness guru that lived in a three bedroom townhouse in Chatsworth, California and had earned millions of dollars over the last twenty years. That Tyler wasn't a rancher by any stretch of the imagination, because he'd left everything about his childhood in Hobbs Creek the day after his eighteenth birthday when he'd packed a bag and flew to New York at the urging of Lorinna Holt, an agent at the KMC Modeling Agency that he'd met one day at the local mall.

Tyler hadn't fallen in love with modeling the way Lorrina had promised all those years ago, but he had enjoyed the money that he made doing the job. To stay in shape he'd spent a lot of time at the gym. Not ready to go back to Texas, his overbearing father and the ranch, he'd used the proceeds from modeling and everything he'd learned at the gym to fund his own workout video. That was when he was twenty-five years old. Now, thirteen years later, Ty-Fitness Inc. was a nationally recognized brand producing workout videos, meal plans and exercise apps, and in a few weeks a full brand of fitness wear for men, women and children.

Tyler was now a brand. He was not a rancher.

Yet, here he was, walking up the steps to the front porch where he'd broken his finger while wrestling with Jagger and Noah Windmyr, the former ranch manager's son. He was going to walk through those massive oak front doors and into the main foyer of the house and remove his hat and dust his feet on the rug just inside the doorway before moving any further. Because old habits die hard, if they ever died at all.

Despite how he felt or how he'd left, Tyler was back at Westwind. And he wasn't leaving until he found out who killed his parents.

"He's an arrogant jerk," Gabriella said into the phone as she plopped down on the bed.

Her suite at the Westwind Resort was lovely. From the gorgeous dark stained real hardwood floors to the heavy cherry oak furniture and the detailed stone fireplace, it was a vacationer's dream. In fact, from her walk around the interior of the resort, Gabriella saw very little that needed staging, a fact that made her wonder what she was doing here.

"Well, unfortunately, we've met a few of them in our lifetime," her sister, Adriana replied.

"And we'll probably meet more," Gabriella chimed in.

A king-size bed was way too big for her because it reminded her that she was in bed alone. A fact that used to be liberating. In the five months that had changed.

"At least you're at a resort. You can work and play, right?" Adriana asked.

Rubbing a hand over her closed eyes Gabriella took a second to re-focus herself. She spent way too much time doing that, but feared it couldn't be helped.

"There's a great outside pool, but the gym is on the small side. There's no spa. I think adding one would definitely increase the asking price. And there are horses."

She opened her eyes and stared up to the beige painted ceiling with its thick wooden beams.

"I visited the stables today and the horses there are beautiful," she told Adriana. "I can't remember the last time I rode a horse."

"Senior year of high school when you worked at the Lehigh Summer Camp," Adriana said. "That's the year Dad sold the two Thoroughbreds he'd let us ride occasionally. I believe they both went on to win races for several years after that."

"I never cared about the racing. I just liked riding. There was something really invigorating about it."

"And you were good at it. So why don't you book a horse ride while you're there?" Adriana asked. "I mean it, Gabs, you should take some time to relax."

Gabriella chuckled. "For the last seven years everyone in the family has been asking, 'When are you going to get a job?', 'What are your plans for the future?' Now that I have a job that I really enjoy, you're telling me to take some time off."

"No, I'm telling you to enjoy your life," Adriana said. "For the past five years I've watched nothing but turmoil erupt around the people I love most. It started with Roland Summerfield and his crazy daughter Larice nursing broken hearts and harboring grudges bringing all kinds of stalking and shoot-out drama to our family. Then Parker's family deals with their own secret son drama complete with more shoot-outs and murders. And, as if we're keeping some type of tit-for-tat going on, Rico and Eva were just re-visited by very emotional media coverage about the two-year anniversary of her brother being killed by that cop."

Gabriella recalled each situation and all the different

reactions each incident had stirred between members of her family and by extension, the Donovan, Lakefield and Desdune families. It had been a rough patch of years for all of them, she readily admitted that. Just as she reminded herself that keeping her own little drama a few months ago to herself was still for the best.

"I understand," she told Adriana. "I haven't taken a trip since your wedding last year. And I definitely have a nice vacation on the radar. But not until I finish this job. If all goes well I could land an exclusive design deal with The Proctor Group."

"They're a trading group, right? Explain to me again, how this works out for you and your interior design career?"

Sitting up now, Gabriella kicked off her sandals and tucked her feet beneath her. She loved talking about her work, especially to her family since it had taken them all so long to see how serious she was about her career choice. Gabriella had known immediately that she didn't want to work for Bennett Industries, a global communications company, alongside her father, Marvin, and brothers Alex and Rico. Her other brother Renny was a sculptor and her only sister, Adriana, had first gone into modeling, but was now starring in a popular television drama and two new movies next year. Waiting until she was twenty-seven years old to finally decide where she would work had been an ongoing source of frustration for her parents and siblings. But Gabriella knew that she needed to take her time figuring out what career would be best for her. Now, she knew she was doing what she was always meant to do.

"My degree in Design Strategy & Innovation allows me to be flexible in what jobs I take. The Proctor Group specializes in the sale of home/businesses, such as farms, wineries and ranches. My job is to meet with the client to ensure that their ultimate goal is to sell. In that case, I work primarily as a stager, getting the properties ready to secure optimum value for the client. On the off chance that there's a change of mind and the client decides to stay in their property, I'm still available with an assessment regarding interior design. It's a win/win situation."

"Okay, if you say so," Adriana said with a chuckle. "I'm just glad to hear you sound excited about something."

"I am excited." Gabriella admitted. "Even if the client was a rude brute earlier. I plan to wow him with my winning smile and charm tomorrow evening at dinner."

"You're having dinner with your client?"

"A dinner meeting, I suppose. He suggested it so I'm just going to show up and play things by ear. Which reminds me, I have to go. I want to do some more research and beef up my preliminary report on the resort."

"Okay, I'll let you go. But I want to tell you something first."

Gabriella stood from the bed and headed to the desk near the window where her laptop was already set up. "Sure. What's up?"

There was a pause and for a moment Gabriella became nervous. Was something else going on with Adriana and her new family? The Donovans had been through a lot in these last three years and because she was married to Parker, that meant Adriana had been in the thick of things. With the death of Roslyn Ausby, the woman responsible for the blackmail and murders that plagued the family, Gabriella and the rest of the Bennett family had breathed a sigh of relief that now, finally, all would be well.

"I'm pregnant."

Everything stopped. And then moved with a speed that made Gabriella suddenly lightheaded. The room was spinning and her hands were shaking. So much so, she almost dropped the phone.

"Gabs? You still there?"

"Ah, yeah. Yeah," she said after all her effort went into holding that phone tightly to her ear. She'd leaned against the desk and hoped her legs wouldn't totally give out and she crumbled to the floor.

"That's great. I mean, you're happy right? You and Parker wanted to have kids?"

Gabriella's throat was suddenly dry as she balled her other hand into a fist and pounded lightly between her eyes.

"We're ecstatic! We haven't told anyone yet. I wanted to call you before I called Mom and Dad because I know sometime during the course of that conversation they're going to ask if I've spoken to you," Adriana told her.

Gabriella shook her head. "Not with the news of another grandchild," she said dryly.

Renny and his wife Bree had two-year old triplets—Delia, Desirae, and Daniel. Those three currently held the hearts of Marvin and Beatriz Bennett. Adriana's baby would capture them next. And Gabriella was just going to have to accept that.

No matter how much it hurt.

CHAPTER 2

*H*obbs Creek hadn't changed much in the eighteen years Tyler had been away. The last time he'd been in his hometown had been five years ago when his mother had begged him to come home for Christmas. That thought didn't help Tyler's melancholy mood.

Main Street still looked like a flash out of that old Andy Griffith television show his grandmother used to love, with the police station on one corner, a barber shop on the other and across the street a general store and post office. He'd parked his truck in front of City Hall and walked to Clyde Gwynn's office, a block and a half away. The fact that he hadn't called first was a stark contrast to the lifestyle Tyler was used to in L.A. Nothing happened there without a phone call. But being back amidst the small town, slower and more laid back pace, Tyler had forgotten that courtesy. Therefore, he wasn't too upset to find that Clyde wasn't in his office.

The change in plan didn't bother Tyler much. In fact, it

allowed more time for him to pick up the things he needed from the store and to walk through the town where he'd spent his early years. He chose to walk the two additional blocks, stopping in the small shops that featured homemade goods he had forgotten while he was away and the new ones that had arrived. Tyler never did this in L.A. Shopping wasn't one of his favorite pastimes and he had assistants that would take care of that kind of stuff for him. There was staff at the ranch, but most of them were new. They were getting to know Tyler, the same as he was with them. It was weird because even though George was gone, Tyler still felt like Westwind was his father's domain and that he didn't belong there. That meant, asking the staff to do things for him personally was out of the question.

Inviting the designer to dinner was a calculated move. One Tyler hadn't been so sure of in the moments right after he'd done it yesterday. But during the hours that followed he had to thank his conscience for having the forethought. Sitting at a table with her would give him the opportunity to find out just what plans she thought were in the works. Whereas, Tyler wasn't sure Clyde was going to be totally honest with him. His father's friend was, of course, going to carry out George's wishes to the end. But what if Tyler didn't want the things his father had? He never had before. The vision George had for the land and the livestock never seemed to match what Tyler thought his future would hold.

"Well aren't you a sight for sore eyes? Tyler Walker West live and in the flesh."

To emphasize her words she'd walked right up to him, running her hand over his left pectoral and straight beneath the opening of the blue chambray shirt Tyler wore.

"Hannah Lynn Palmer," Tyler said, lifting a hand to slowly clamp his fingers around her wrist.

She arched one thick eyebrow and watched as he slowly, but purposefully, moved her hand from his chest and dropped it at her side.

"I've left you several messages," she said and brought that same hand up to fluff the tapered edges of her golden blonde hair. "But you probably aren't getting them. I know how hard it can be to hire good staff."

Tyler didn't immediately respond. As he recalled, Hannah loved to hear herself talk. Her father owned P&P Steakhouse, a few miles out from town. It was a premiere restaurant in the area and had been for as long as Tyler could remember. Ted Palmer often bought cattle from Westwind, and Hannah had gone to school with Tyler and Jagger. So it was safe to say Tyler and Hannah had a lot of history, even if he excluded the three and a half years he'd spent professing his love to her.

"Anyway, I'm glad you're out and about. I can understand the grieving process taking a while though," she continued. "When my momma died, I wanted to jump in that grave before they tossed the first shovel of dirt on her coffin."

She chuckled.

Tyler did not.

"So next Friday's the kickoff to the 4th of July celebrations. I thought it'd be great if we rode in the parade together. You know, like we did that year you won first place in 4H for that horse you loved to distraction. That was so much fun. Of course, I have no idea where my Junior Hobbs Creek Pageant crown is now, but I still know the wave."

She demonstrated. Right there on the sidewalk where cars

and trucks drove by and people walked past them, Hannah waved as if she were riding along happily in a parade. If old feelings didn't still cut raw with him, Tyler might have laughed at how silly she looked. Instead, he tipped the brim of the chocolate felt Stetson he wore back and gave her the best smile he could manage.

"No thanks, Hannah. I won't be attending the parade."

He made the mistake of thinking that would end the conversation, but when he attempted to walk around her, he felt her hand on his arm pulling him back.

"We haven't had any time together since you've been back. How about you come over to the restaurant tonight and we'll have a nice steak dinner."

His reply was quick and probably not what Hannah expected to hear. "I already have dinner plans for tonight."

"Oh." Her lips pursed. "Well, I hope you find some time to spend with an old friend while you're here. I mean, after all, our families are connected and have been for a very long time. I'm sure my father would like to speak to you about future business transactions."

Ted Palmer was the son of Judson Palmer, who had been the mayor of Hobbs Creek for thirty years before finally retiring. Judson had also played a big part in contributing financially to the rebuilding of a good portion of Main Street twenty-five years ago when a fire started at the church and burned from one building to the next until a three block stretch was destroyed. Because of this, Hannah knew the weight of what she'd just said, which only irritated Tyler more.

He moved so that he was out of her reach, being careful to keep his voice level and low. The one thing he hadn't forgotten while he was away from Hobbs Creek was how fast gossip traveled in small towns.

"When your father is ready to talk business he knows the number to the ranch office. As for any other connections, there are none. Good evening, Hannah."

With a slight nod, Tyler ended the conversation and turned to walk away once more. She didn't try to stop him this time, but Tyler knew it wasn't the last he would hear from her. Hannah did not give up easily, not when she set her mind to something. And whether he liked it or not, Tyler sensed that she'd definitely set her mind on something where he was concerned.

Gabriella stepped up onto the front porch of the main house at Westwind Ranch & Resort feeling as if she'd somehow been morphed from the 2017 Volkswagen Passat rental car into a 1950's John Wayne western movie. Her first impression was— there was an abundance of wood. An overabundance would be more like it. The wedge heel of her camel colored ankle boots, made a clunking sound as she walked toward one end of the wrap around porch. She'd changed into jeans and a white shirt for what she figured would be a casual business dinner. Now, considering the worn planks of this floor and the dust circulating from the dried dirt landscape, she wondered if she might still be a little overdressed.

She reminded herself that she wasn't in her hometown of Greenwich, CT or even in Manhattan where she visited her older brother Alex and his fiancé, Monica Lakefield, from time to time. This was Hobbs Creek, Texas, a small town in what was known as the Texas Panhandle region. And she was at Westwind Ranch & Resort, one of the most successful cattle and horse ranches in the area. The resort branch of Westwind was fairly new, being added on three years ago as a new business venture. It was the previous owners, George and Verna West's, step into tourism which was intended to become an economy booster in the area. According to Dessie Gwynn, the woman who'd hired Gabriella, it was slow going, but progressing.

"I've got dinner started around back."

The deep, but smooth, voice jolted her and Gabriella turned to see him standing near the front doors of the house.

Tyler West, oldest son to George and Verna. Fitness guru, model and in a few months designer of a new fitness clothing line. His Google bio said nothing about six feet plus of fineness personified. That may have been a bit much, she thought as she walked toward him. But then, when she stood only a few feet away she realized, no, it was actually an understatement. Blue eyes, that in the right light could look green, dark brown hair, close cut beard and naturally thick eyebrows that a woman would kill to possess. And he spoke French, which for Gabriella, was *the* sexiest language. Dressed in dark jeans, a dark blue chambray shirt, and chestnut colored cowboy boots, he was one tall glass of western deliciousness. If she were inclined to look at him that way. Which she was not because this trip was about work. Besides, neither her mind nor her body were ready for anything other than ogling good looking men.

"Great," she said and tapped a hand over the bag she'd just remembered she was carrying. "I have my notes and some preliminary design ideas we can discuss."

He didn't frown, but he didn't smile welcomingly either.

"Food first," he said and extended an arm toward the door.

Since he was the client, Gabriella nodded and followed. The entrance was two massive heavy oak doors with polished bronze door handles. Formidable, dominating, and like her host for the evening, not very welcoming. Inside was only a little better. Dark hardwood floors, western fabric vaulted ceilings, and, thick wood beam framed doorways, invited her in with soft golden lighting and plush cushioned chairs. The animal skin rug in the center of the foyer wasn't gorgeous, but the natural light she could see pouring into the room ahead filled her with optimism.

"We can go this way," he said from behind.

Gabriella turned to see that he was leading her to the left through another doorway. This room had dark paneled walls and heavy leather upholstered furniture. There was a fully-stocked bar with four stools that stretched along one wall, shelves loaded with books along another. The large fireplace fought with the bar as the room's focal point and the gigantic stuffed moose head hanging over the fireplace could go right into the same "must go" category as the animal skin rug in the foyer.

They passed through another room, with a little more light due to the wall of windows. Unfortunately, those windows were mostly covered by heavy plaid patterned curtains. The final room they moved through was more like a covered porch with screen in walls and dark wicker furniture.

Tyler pushed open a screen door and stepped out to the cemented deck area. Gabriella followed him, looking around at the new surroundings. More dirt packed landscape, outdoor lounge furniture that was a big step up from all the wicker she'd just seen, an open fire pit at the center of the chairs and a large stone grill built into the side wall of the house.

"This is a great space," she said before stopping at one of the chairs and setting her bag down. "We could open this up a bit. A pergola would look great down that way, with nice thin curtains in a cheerful color. Maybe an archway there, instead of the screen door, to soften the space a bit and alert guests that they're entering into a new space."

"Do you eat steak?"

His question shocked her into silence and Gabriella once again looked at her host for the evening. He stood near the grill and did not appear to be the least bit interested in what she had been saying. She took a quick breath and fixed her professional smile in place.

"Ah, yes. I do. Red meat is my favorite, much to my mother's chagrin. She insists I need to cut back or at the very least go for the leanest cuts of red meat I can find."

"We breed our own cattle here, in case you didn't know," he said. "And we don't use any antibiotics. We have mostly grain-fed beef, but a few years ago my dad started experimenting with the grass-fed method."

"I don't know the difference," she told him as she walked over to the grill.

He looked so natural standing there, holding the long handled fork. Next to him smoke billowed up from the grill, the delectable scent of cooking meat wafting into the air. He also had vegetables on one side of the grill—zucchini and red peppers. Wrapped in foil she suspected were baked potatoes.

"Most cattle spend the majority of their lives eating grass and other feed such as alfalfa out in pastures. Then they move on to a feedlot for grain finishing. These are called grain-fed. Grass-finished cattle stay on a pasture and alfalfa diet for their entire lives. There are few regions in North America that grow grass all year long, so the majority of grass-finished cattle are shipped from Australia and New Zealand. American organic farmers shelter their cattle in the winter and feed them hay and silage so they'll be grass-finished all year long. Grass-finished beef is leaner."

"Then why don't you raise your cattle that way here?" she asked.

He turned the vegetables over and then went to a table near the grill to pick up a plate.

"Beef cattle typically go to market weighing between 1,000 and 1,250 pounds. Grain-fed cattle put on weight more quickly than grass-fed, so they're ready for market sooner. Much of that weight is in the form of fat. So while leaner is good, grass-fed cattle won't have the marbling that makes the finer cuts of beef more tender and juicy."

"Oh," she said and watched him move the vegetables and potatoes to a plate.

He had a lean frame, but Gabriella knew that beneath those clothes were rippling muscles. She'd seen them during her Google search of him. Sculpted muscles that had made her reach out and touch her screen because her fingers had tingled with the urge to feel the cuts and bulges personally.

"How do you like your steak?"

She swallowed hard and gave a slight shake of her head to clear those silly, but enticing, thoughts from her mind.

"Well done, please."

He nodded. "That's how I like mine. My dad used to say I

was doing the ranch a disservice by overcooking the meat he worked so hard to create."

"My mom says she doesn't want to eat meat that's still mooing at her from the plate," Gabriella added with a chuckle.

He smiled in return. A real smile that she was certain gave his eyes a little glimmer. Her excitement was short-lived as he motioned for her to move to the table.

"Pour the wine and uncover the rolls. I took them out of the oven just before you arrived," he told her.

Again, she did as he directed, noting that he had gone through a lot to prepare a business dinner. The table was set for two, no candles or flowers, or any type of romantic frills which made sense. Still, there were cloth napkins, silver cutlery and wine glasses, as opposed to paper plates and Styrofoam cups which usually accompanied meals on the grill. She was overthinking this, she knew and she warned herself to stop. By the time Tyler came to the table with the plate of steaks in one hand and the vegetables in the other, Gabriella was sitting and placing her napkin in her lap.

He shocked her once more by bowing his head to say grace before doing anything else. The Bennetts were a blend of Beatriz's Brazilian heritage and Marvin's African American lineage. As far as religion went, that just meant that even though Beatriz had been raised Catholic, their family had been raised in a Baptist church, just as Marvin had when he was young. So the blessing of her food before she ate wasn't foreign, it was, on the other hand, not something she saw frequently when on dates. But this wasn't a date, she reminded herself.

"Why are you here?" Tyler asked after about three bites of food.

Gabriella had been just finishing another sip of wine. It was an excellent choice, she noted, full-bodied and spicy with a touch of oak.

"This wine is excellent," she told him as she set her glass down and looked at the wine bottle. "But I don't think I've heard of the vineyard before."

"It's local," he said. "Are you a wine taster as well as an interior designer?"

"No," she replied. "But I did attend a double wedding at Basset Banks Winery in Napa Valley. While I was there, I took a tour and learned some things about wine. Since then I've been tuned in to different pairings and tastes."

"I've heard of Basset Banks," he said.

"Oh really? Wade Banks married Brynne Donovan and Bailey Donovan married Devlin Bonner. The Donovans are my extended family through marriage. That's why I was invited. The scenery combined with the food and wine at the reception was glorious."

"And you still haven't told me why you're here," he said before spearing another chunk of steak with his fork.

"Yes. I did when I came by yesterday," she told him. "But I can start over. My name is Gabriella Bennett and I work for The Proctor Group. They specialize in the sale of ranches and wineries all over the world. I was hired by Dessie Gwynn to stage the house and resort in preparation for sale."

He set his fork down slowly as he finished chewing. Then he picked up his glass and took a sip. Gabriella sat back in her chair after speaking and now watched and waited for his response.

"My parents have only been gone for three weeks. Clyde Gwynn was my father's lawyer for as long as I can remember.

He read my father's will soon after I returned. Ownership of the ranch and resort came to me and my brother, Jagger. To date there has been no decision on whether or not we intend to sell."

That meant she shouldn't be here. Disappointed and a little irritated that this key point in the deal hadn't been hashed out before she flew all the way down here, Gabriella picked up her napkin and dabbed the sides of her mouth. She wiped her fingers and dropped the napkin onto the table.

"Thank you for clearing that up. I will be going now," she said and moved to stand.

"Wait," he said and stood as well. "I don't know why Dessie hired you. To tell the truth there's a lot going on around here that I don't know about. But I intend to get to the bottom of it."

"As I suppose you should. So I will just get out of your way and let you handle that."

"I feel bad that you came all this way for a job that doesn't exist," he said.

"It's fine. The company paid for the trip and the resort is rather nice. I may just stay another day to relax at the pool."

She picked up her bag and was heading toward the door when he touched her arm. She stopped immediately and looked down to see his hand on her bare skin. Actually, she was trying to figure out why that particular spot now felt so warm and that weird warmth was easing through her.

"I'll pick up the tab for the resort. Stay as long as you like," he told her.

He was looking at her intently as if there was something else he wanted to say. It was strange. This whole meeting, dinner, not date, whatever it was had been strange and Gabriella was ready to get back to normal. Actually, she'd been striving to get to that point for the past few months.

"Thanks," she said. "And thanks for dinner. It was delicious."

"You're welcome," he told her and walked her through the house once more.

It wasn't until she was in the car heading down the driveway that Gabriella looked into her rearview mirror. He was standing on the porch, hands thrust in his front pockets, watching her drive away. After a few moments he looked desolate standing there. Alone and confused, she thought as she continued to drive. It was none of her business. She'd stay at the resort for one more day and then she was going home. She'd just have to wait for another opportunity to prove her worth to The Proctor Group.

CHAPTER 3

*T*yler shut down his computer after reading all the email messages he could stand for the moment. His manager needed him to review contracts for international distribution of the last series of fitness videos he'd produced and there were three invitations for him to speak at various fitness conferences for next year. His career was blossoming, taking him in directions he'd never dreamed of. But he couldn't think about any of that at the moment. His mind was too wrapped up in what happened to his parents, the ranch and now, Gabriella Bennett.

This wasn't how things were supposed to play out. His parents had planned to grow old at Westwind. They'd also planned to hand it down to their sons—the two who hadn't worked the ranch at all in their adult life. But someone had altered that plan, someone Tyler wanted to see behind bars. In the meantime, Tyler needed to figure out what was going to happen with the ranch. He couldn't stay here and run it, not only because he didn't want to, but also because he had a life in L.A. He needed to get back to his career.

Gabriella Bennett could help with that. She said she was here to stage the house and the resort for sale. If he let her do her job, they could sell the ranch relatively quickly and Tyler's life could get back to normal.

The faces staring back at him from the picture sitting on the edge of the desk said otherwise. His parents. They'd loved this ranch and their sons. Waves of guilt washed over Tyler as he recalled how little he and Jagger had given them in return.

Sitting back in the leather desk chair, Tyler finished the bottled water he'd grabbed when he came into his father's office before the sun was up this morning. Now, blush-tinged light poured through the windows while he sat behind the old elm wood desk he remembered falling and gashing his head against as a child. It was just after seven and he still wanted to get a run in before he was scheduled to meet with the sheriff for an update on the case.

"Excuse me, Mr. West," a male voice said following a quick knock on the door.

Tyler hadn't closed the door because he was the only one in the house. So his frown should have been understandable when he looked over to the tall man standing there dressed in worn jeans, an equally as worn plaid shirt and beige vest. He had a dark brown complexion, broad shoulders and workman's hands which held his Stetson as he met Tyler's gaze.

"Come in, Stephen," he replied. "And call me Tyler."

Stephen Garret was the ranch manager at Westwind. He'd been in that position for two years and according to Clyde, was doing an exemplary job. George had no complaints about him.

Tyler wondered if that meant his father had complaints about the previous ranch manager, but hadn't found a moment to inquire about that as of yet.

"Mornin', Tyler," Stephen spoke as he came deeper into the office.

He stopped in front of the desk, between the pair of zebra pattern guest chairs. Tyler had been trying to figure them out since he'd arrived at the ranch, and decided they must have been his mother's idea. Stephen, didn't give them a second glance.

"We've got a problem," Stephen continued, his brow crinkling as he stared down at Tyler.

"What type of problem?"

"Down at the chicken coop and goat stalls. Latches were broken on the stalls and the door to the coop was wide open when I first came out. Nevil pulled in about half hour after I did and we've spent the last few hours wrangling all the animals back to where they belong. We were gonna fix the latches and get more netting for the coops, but then just on a hunch I walked down to check on the horses. There are some fresh muddy footprints in there and a pair of wire cutters were laying out on the ground. Could've picked up that mud from the goat stalls and tracked it all the way down to the equestrian center. It did rain a little last night."

None of this sounded good. In fact, Tyler thought as he slowly came to a stand, it was, just as Stephen had said—a big problem.

"Did you touch anything?"

"Not a thing," Stephen assured him. "Guess I was thinking just like you are right now."

Tyler nodded. "Good. Let's go have a look."

Minutes later Tyler and Stephen rode from the main house down to the equestrian center in Stephen's truck. It was a Westwind issued Jeep, one of their fleet of twelve used by staff when traveling around the twenty-five hundred acre property. They both jumped out of the vehicle and walked through the open doorway. Natural light poured in from outside but Stephen hit the switch to turn on all the interior lights. This was a relatively new structure, built just five years ago. Tyler remembered because his father copied him on all of the ranch's yearly reports and while Tyler didn't pay a lot of attention to them, he recalled the photographs of the new equestrian center when it had been christened. They'd always had a few horses on the ranch, but after a while George had thought to bring in more horses and offer riding lessons as well as some breeding services. The structure looked great with beamed wood ceilings, black iron and wood stall enclosures and cement flooring.

On that floor were unmistakable footprints.

"They go all the way to the back and then stop," Stephen said. "We checked and nobody's back there, but where the hell did he go?"

"Those back four stalls are empty," Tyler said. "Did you check them?"

"Nevil did. GG was antsy so I took him out and around a bit to calm him down. I don't know how long he'd been irritated, but I'm guessing since whoever came waltzing in here."

"Why would somebody come into the stables and then go out and open the chicken coop and goat stalls? Doesn't make sense," Tyler said more out loud than he'd actually thought.

"Not that I can see either. But then, things ain't been the same around here since your mom and dad died."

"You sure things were fine before they died, Stephen?" Tyler asked as he kept walking down the center of the dwelling. There were stalls on each side of him, but as they only had eight horses at the moment, they weren't all full. "I can't shake this feeling that something's been brewing here for a while. Like I'm walking into—"

"Into a heap of horse shit!" a voice yelled and followed with a hearty laugh.

Tyler looked down to make sure what was said was just a joke and then turned to see who had come through the front doors of the paddocks.

Jagger.

"What's going on big brother?" Jagger said as Tyler walked toward where he was standing. "Heard you're taking the fitness world by storm. Getting ready to launch that new clothing line. You should really hit me up about your marketing though. I can take your brand to the next level."

In true Jagger fashion the conversation shifted completely to him regardless of the fact that they were standing on their deceased parents' land.

"Glad you could finally make an appearance," Tyler said and accepted Jagger's extended hand for a shake.

"Did you want me to drop everything and fly here from Paris? Come on, man. You know how it is in the business world. At least you should, considering how good you're doing."

Jagger West was shorter than Tyler by two inches. His hair was black, but they both had close cut beards and blue eyes. They were also similarly built, even though Tyler sensed by the way Jagger's suit hung on him, that he was more on the muscled side than his younger brother.

"We have a situation here, Jagger," Tyler told him and turned to make the introduction. "This is Stephen Garret. He's the ranch manager. Stephen, this is my brother Jagger."

Stephen stepped up and Jagger shook his hand too.

"Are you about to go horse riding?" Jagger asked. "I expected to find you at the house, but I saw the truck stopped here when I was driving up so I pulled over."

"That's because something happened here last night," Tyler said.

"Actually, I think it may have been earlier this morning," Stephen interrupted. "I was here until around seven last night. I used to stay at the staff barracks, but I got married last month, so my wife and I have a place just fifteen minutes down the road."

"That's great," Tyler said. "Congratulations."

Jagger shrugged, his easy smile spreading across his face. "Yeah, congrats. Seems like wedding bells are in the air."

Tyler didn't get a chance to ask what that meant before they were joined by someone else. A woman, tall—probably near five feet six or seven, without the heels she was wearing—brunette, dark eyes and a pouting mouth that instantly shifted to a smile as she drew closer.

"Tyler, meet Brook Radison. Soon to be Brooke West," Jagger said.

Brooke extended her left hand to Tyler, turned upward so he had no choice but to notice the large diamond on her ring finger.

"Nice to meet you, Brooke," Tyler said and shook her hand. "I wish it were under better circumstances."

He looked to Stephen quickly then and continued, "The sheriff was scheduled to meet me out here later this morning. Why don't we give him a call and let him know we need him here now. I'll ride back up to the house with them and we can meet in the den as soon as the sheriff arrives."

Stephen nodded. "Got it," he said. "I'll get Nevil and let him know what's going on. Sheriff'll probably want to speak to him too. Staff's up and moving about already, so we've got coverage. I'll just make it clear we don't want any of them touching anything until the sheriff's had a chance to look around."

"Good. You have my cell number. Call me if anything changes," Tyler said.

"Will do," Stephen told him.

Tyler turned back to his brother and his fiancé. With an inward sigh he began walking toward the front doors. "Let's get back to the house."

"Yes. I can't wait to see it," Brooke said from behind. "We can get an idea of how much it'll make during the sale and plan from there."

Tyler remained silent until they were at the house. The moment he entered the living room and watched as Jagger and his fiancé came in too he said, "We're not selling the ranch."

"Of course we are," Jagger replied. "I live in New York and you live in L.A. Neither of us want anything to do with this ranch, or we would have come back to it before now."

Tyler didn't like that Jagger wasn't totally wrong.

"I was here five years ago for Christmas. You couldn't make it because you were...I don't even recall where you were. Anyway, this place has been owned and operated by a West for more than fifty years," Tyler told him.

"And look where that's gotten us," Jagger snapped. He'd walked across the room to the bar where he wasted no time fixing himself a drink. "I received the letter from the lawyer about the will. I'm here so he can read whatever my part is to me and then I'll be heading back. It makes more sense that we sign whatever needs to be signed to get this place unloaded as quickly as possible."

Tyler leaned against the back of one of two leather upholstered sage green couches. He crossed his arms over his chest and resisted the urge to yell at his brother for being an inconsiderate jackass. He knew a better way to deal with Jagger.

"5.6 million dollars," he began. "That's what this property is worth. But the business, it's pulling in close to a million dollars in profit every year." At least it had been for the last two years. Before that, they'd been very close to operating at a lost.

Jagger paused, the glass halfway to his mouth, and glanced at Tyler. "You're lying."

"For what reason?" Tyler asked with a shrug. "I've spent the last three weeks walking every inch of this place, reading every piece of paper here, talking to the staff, watching the day-to-day operations. Sales from the cattle alone could carry the place, but Dad was always thinking bigger. Expanding into horse breeding, offering riding lessons and training. And then there's the resort. All of these elements are boosting revenue. The place was doing extremely well."

Jagger took a gulp from his glass. His face contorted a moment while the sting of the aged whiskey he'd just swallowed made its way down his throat. A quick punch of sour, followed by a smooth glimmer of caramel. It was an interesting blend, one Tyler had become very familiar with in the weeks he'd been back. Liquor wasn't good for the body, especially not a body that was on display as much as Tyler's. But the moment he'd walked through those doors, Tyler had slowly begun to feel less like the man who owned Ty-Fitness Inc. and more like the young man who'd been desperate to get as far away from this ranch as he could.

Jagger finished the drink and looked toward the other couch. Brooke was sitting there, legs crossed, lips pursed.

"They created a brand and sold it for years," Jagger told Tyler. "I can see that becoming profitable. But we're not ranchers, Tyler. At least I know I'm not. So for my half, I say we're selling. Brooke and I are planning to get married later this summer and I'd like to show her a fabulous honeymoon."

"Your job at the PR firm not paying you enough anymore?" Tyler asked.

Jagger chuckled. "I pull in almost seven figures a year at Mason Partners. I made partner five years ago, one of the youngest in the history of the company. I have worldwide accounts. People and businesses that I've created and built a brand for, making them richer than they ever could have imagined."

Tyler nodded. Nothing had changed. Not one damn thing.

"I don't need to rundown my portfolio to you or anyone else. All I know is that Mom and Dad loved this place. They loved every inch of it and never wanted to leave. They nurtured and built this legacy for us and I don't know about you, but for me, it's not that easy to walk away from that knowledge."

"Sentiment has no place in business," Jagger replied.

"They're dead Jagger!" Tyler roared as he pushed away from the couch. "Gone! Their bodies were left to burn to a crisp in that truck. But that was after bullets were planted in the back of their heads. And you waltz in here three weeks late rattling off how much fuckin' money you make! What the hell is wrong with you?"

"Why don't we take a breath here," Brooke intervened.

Tyler turned his head sharply to stare at her. Up until this point he wasn't sure she was going to do anything other than sit and look pretty.

Now, she was walking to stand next to Jagger.

"There's some emotion to contend with. That's only natural when lives are loss, especially to some type of violence," she said.

Was she serious?

"But there's also business to be discussed. So why don't we—"

"Tyler?"

At the sound of his name being called, Tyler turned toward the doorway to see Stephen again.

"Sheriff Alvarez's out front. He wants to see the place first," Stephen said.

Tyler's jaw clenched before he nodded. "I'll be right out."

"As I was saying before being rudely interrupted," Brooke began the moment Stephen left. "We should sit down, have dinner and discuss this like adults."

Tyler didn't know why she was even involved in this conversation and so he ignored her.

"Some unauthorized person was on this land last night. I want to know who it was and why. If you're only worried about the money, stay here and count yours over and over again. I'll be back when I'm done."

Tyler left them, not giving a damn if they were there when he returned.

Gabriella picked up her phone to check the time. Her plan was to spend a few hours at the pool relaxing before heading back inside the resort to have dinner. In the morning, she would drive to the airport. Her bags were already packed, the email she sent to her supervising agent at The Proctor Group explained that Tyler West had not yet decided what to do with the ranch at this time.

Gabriella totally understood. There was no way she could sell her parents' house in Greenwich, nor did she think her brothers would ever sell or leave Bennett Industries. She suspected her family was quite different from Tyler's. Although she didn't know any of the West family well, she sensed that before his parents' death there was more than just physical distance between Tyler, his parents and his brother. That would explain Tyler's indecisiveness about whether or not to sell their property. As for the Bennetts, well, they were pretty close. So close that Gabriella hadn't even been out of town for two full days before Alex was ready to send in the troops to find her. Luckily for her, she'd had the forethought to tell Adriana where she was going and why.

But this wasn't about her family.

After noting the time, Gabriella ran her finger over the screen of her phone and watched as her list of text messages shifted.

It was gone.

She'd deleted it seconds after reading. It wasn't coming back. She just had to make sure. Yes, the message was gone. Just as

Gabriella had hoped to stay gone from Greenwich for a while. Distance would make it stop. All of it. She'd assured herself of this when she'd almost leapt with joy the day her mentor Mallory Klien of Klien Design Studios had called her with a proposition. Gabriella had done some freelance staging work for Mallory in the weeks immediately following her tumultuous break-up with Austin. There was no way she could have continued working with Austin's real estate team on their properties. So Mallory had thrown her a lifeline, then and now. It was Mallory who had referred Gabriella to The Proctor Group.

"It's the chance of a lifetime," Mallory had said as they had lunch on the deck of the lavish home Mallory shared with her husband Patrick and their two adorable sons. "If you do a good job for them, they've guaranteed to keep you on. You can travel and work in exotic locales and make a ton of money. It's perfect."

"It sure sounds like it," Gabriella had replied and two days later was packed and flying to Miami to meet with the top selling agents at The Proctor Group. Within a week after accepting the position and flying back to Greenwich, a courier delivered plane tickets, itinerary and preliminary pictures of the Westwind Ranch & Resort.

Four days later, Gabriella was in Hobbs Creek, Texas.

Now, just three days after arriving, she was packed to leave.

Dropping her phone into her bag she stood up from the lounge chair and sighed. No sense in sulking about a situation she couldn't change. It had taken her years to let that sink in. For now, Gabriella was going for a swim. She wasn't going to think about returning to Greenwich and possibly seeing Austin again. She wasn't going to think about the pain and confusion that would come with seeing Austin again. Dammit, she just wasn't going to think about Austin.

It was ninety-five degrees on this sunny summer afternoon and the water was cold and refreshing. She swam slowly and leisurely, eyes closed, enjoying every second. She didn't know how much time had passed, but when her arms and legs began to get tired, she swam to the edge of the pool and pushed herself out of the water.

He was standing there, holding a towel out towards her.

She accepted the towel and quickly wrapped it around herself. Tyler West was technically not a client. But Gabriella still felt off balance with him standing a few feet away from her fully dressed while she stood there in a very scant sapphire blue bikini.

"Just taking advantage of the pool before checking out in the morning," she said because they were the first words to pop into her head.

"As I said you can stay as long as you like," Tyler told her.

Gabriella shook her head. "This was a business trip. Now that the business is over, I'll be heading back."

No matter what she feared was waiting for her back in Greenwich.

He wasn't moving. In fact, he might have looked a little odd standing there in his boots, hat, jeans and t-shirt, when everybody else at the pool wore bathing suits and swim trunks. But truth be told he didn't. He looked handsome as hell. A fact which made Gabriella just a bit more uncomfortable.

She held the towel tighter around her body and moved to walk around him. She really hadn't expected him to follow her, but he did. And the next thing she knew, Tyler West was sitting on the lounge chair beside hers. She slid her feet into her flip flops and reached for her purse. He wrapped his fingers around her wrist to stop her movements.

"Give me a minute," he said.

She didn't want to sit with him a minute, not dressed like this and certainly not now since they weren't going to be doing business together. But there was something in the sound of his voice. Something in the feel of his skin against hers.

"Are you having second thoughts about selling the ranch?" she asked.

He looked toward the pool.

There was a family sitting on the side. Mom, dad, two little girls and a teenage boy. The boy had just tossed one of his sisters into the water while the other sister stood on the side giggling. The mother jokingly chastised the son, while dad chuckled. Gabriella could remember times when one of her three brothers would have happily tossed her and/or Adriana into the pool for laughs. Tyler watched in awe, as if this whole scene was new to him.

"My brother's back," he said eventually. "He didn't come when I called him about our parents' death. Didn't bother to ask me anything about the funeral. Hadn't even called to say he was heading down here. But just shows up this morning."

"When was the last time you saw him?" she asked.

He shook his head. His eyes looked different today, more green than blue. It was odd and yet, attractive.

"About six years ago. He was in L.A. on business and gave me a call."

"My brothers don't let me go six minutes without wondering where I am," she said with a chuckle.

Then she stopped because he still looked so very serious. Too serious, she thought.

"I have three brothers, older than me. Alex, Rico and Renny. And I have an older sister too, Adriana."

"You're the baby," he said.

"I'm the youngest," she replied.

The corner of his mouth lifted in a partial smile. She liked that much better than his serious look.

They were quiet a minute and Gabriella wondered what she should do or say next.

The arrival of a very pretty woman fixed that problem.

"Tyler, when you're finished, Jagger and I are waiting in the dining room. Clyde and Dessie are joining us for an early dinner."

She'd spoken in a very crisp tone, being sure to keep her gaze focused on Tyler. But before she walked away, she looked at Gabriella as if just noticing she was there. Gabriella almost laughed because that was impossible. The woman had come from behind her, which meant that in order to see that Tyler was sitting there talking to someone, she had to see the person he was talking to. Especially since he still held Gabriella's wrist in his hand.

"I spoke to Dessie already," he said.

"She mentioned that," the woman said as she continued to stare at Gabriella. "Jagger and I think it's a good idea for all of us to talk together. It saves time and will cut out any misunderstandings. We'll be in the restaurant."

His fingers tightened slightly, not painfully, around Gabriella's wrist.

"I'll be there in a few minutes," he told the woman.

She flipped her hair over one shoulder and raised a brow at Gabriella.

Easing out of his grip, Gabriella stood. She extended a hand and gave her most brilliant smile before saying, "I'm Gabriella Bennett from The Proctor Group. It's a pleasure to meet you."

With that came a look down to Gabriella's flip flops, and then up to her make-up free face as strands of wet hair stuck to the side of her neck.

"Brooke Radison, Jagger's fiancé," she replied and barely touched Gabriella's fingertips in the worst handshake ever. "Ten minutes, Tyler."

Brooke snapped those words to Tyler before walking away.

"Well," Gabriella said still grinning because she'd already deduced Brooke, Jagger's fiancé, was nuts. "I'll be going again. We won't bump into each other anymore because I'll be gone in the morning."

"Stay," Tyler said immediately.

Gabriella looked down to where he was still sitting on the lounge. "What?"

He stood, slowly and stepped closer to her. "Stay here. Go to dinner with me and tell them about your plans for the ranch."

Gabriella wasn't sure what was happening here. On the one hand she'd just met a very rude woman. On the other, was Tyler who had shown up out of the blue, handed her a towel and touched her wrist. Gabriella touched the spot where his fingers had been, while keeping her gaze on him.

"I thought you hadn't decided whether or not to sell."

"You're a designer. Re-decorate the house. It could use it whether or not I decide to sell."

"That's not what I came here for and it's different. The goals of redecorating and staging are different. I'd have to re-think, plan again, talk to you more about what you like, how you want the place to feel. It's a different job."

He reached out and touched her again. This time his fingertips lightly brushed her bare shoulder, before he pulled away.

"I want you to stay. I'll hire you. Sign a different contract or whatever you need. Just stay."

Why? What the hell was going on here? And did she really want to get in the middle of it? She'd left Greenwich because there was too much going on there. This was definitely not what she needed right now. But as she looked up into his now blue eyes and heard the bleak tone of his voice, she knew there was no other answer. Especially none that she'd be able to explain to Mallory or The Proctor Group.

"I'll be ready in ten minutes," she told him before grabbing her purse and heading up to her room.

CHAPTER 4

"This is a business dinner," Brooke said while Tyler pulled a chair out for Gabriella.

"And I'm all ready to discuss business," Gabriella said. She took the seat and looked over her shoulder to mouth a silent "thank you" to Tyler for pushing her up to the table.

"Well, this is nice. We can get a lot accomplished tonight," Dessie said as she lifted a napkin from the table and placed it on her lap.

Gabriella liked Dessie. She reminded her a lot of her mother even though their physical appearances were startlingly different. Where Beatriz Bennett had the same bronze complexion and dark brown hair as Gabriella, Dessie's deep mocha complexion and glossy black hair was a contrast. Dessie also had a boisterous personality and wide genuine smile. Gabriella had liked her from the moment she'd stepped into the resort and Dessie greeted her.

"Excuse me. Who is this?"

Gabriella smiled across the table to the man who was actually frowning at her. He had to be with the bitchy brunette because they shared the same sour disposition.

"This," Dessie said with a tilt of her head that warned he should fix his face, "is Gabriella Bennett. She is here to stage the house and the resort in a way that will bring exuberant buyers to our door. With her help we can get the most for the property. Gabriella, this is Jagger West and his fiancé, Brooke."

"*If* we sell," Tyler added.

He'd taken a seat beside Gabriella, so that Dessie was to her right and he was to her left. Dessie's husband, Clyde, sat on Dessie's other side. Gabriella had met him last night when she'd returned to the resort from her dinner with Tyler.

"The will said to sell the property. So that's what we should be doing." Jagger announced.

Brooke slowly placed her hand on top of Jagger's. She had a smile pasted in place and tilted her head toward Tyler and Gabriella before saying, "The purpose of a Last Will in Testament is to alert the living to the deceased's wishes so that those wishes might be carried out. From the way I heard it, George and Verna West wanted their sons to sell the Westwind Resort and Ranch."

They were a perfect couple. Almost too perfect, Gabriella thought. Brooke was as beautiful as Jagger was handsome. Each of them educated, no doubt, and ambitious.

Clyde nodded. "Yes, that is what George and Verna's will stated. And since neither of you boys have been here in a working capacity for almost twenty years, Dessie and I thought it was best to get things started for you. So Dessie contacted a company known for selling ranches and receiving the best price for them."

"That's where Gabriella comes in," Dessie said while patting Gabriella's hand. "Go on, tell them what you've come up with so far."

All eyes fell on her and she was ready. Clearing her throat Gabriella reached into the bag she'd hung on the back of her chair and pulled out her tablet.

But before she could speak, Tyler did.

"I met with Gabriella last night," he said. "She's going to give us options."

"Options?" Brooke asked. "Like blue curtains or black ones?"

The chuckle that followed was stilted and reached no one but Jagger, who grinned in response.

"Your options are to have the resort, main house and employee living spaces professionally staged to appeal to the buyers' market and thus, generating prime offers to purchase," Gabriella said.

She turned her tablet to face Clyde, Dessie and the two doubters sitting across from her. On the screen were preliminary staging designs she'd compiled for the resort. She'd only done a few hand sketches for the main house based off the pictures of the property that were on the Westwind website. But after her meeting with Tyler last night, she hadn't bothered to do anything more formal. And she had not seen the employee residences as of yet.

"Or, if the plan is to live on the ranch and make design updates to suit the new owners, I can compile information on style tastes and visions for the property and we can proceed from there. Whether you choose to stage or re-decorate, I am trained to handle both. I can provide references, but the stellar reputation of The Proctor Group speaks for itself. I am here in Hobbs Creek to complete this job and with your approval, could be ready to start first thing tomorrow morning."

"What type of profit do you and your company guarantee for a property such as this?" Brooke asked.

Gabriella noted the woman had barely looked at the tablet, but instead had kept her gaze focused on Gabriella. That was fine, Gabriella was used to being stared at. Her half Brazilian and half African American heritage gave her an exotic look that could be construed as different to those who looked for something to distinguish another person from themselves. She and Adriana had both endured a measure of bullying from girls in school as they grew up, and women in the social circles her parents traveled because they looked "different." Adriana had gone on to carve out a very successful career based on her "different" looks, and while Gabriella didn't base her business success on her appearance, she was proud of every part of her heritage. Even if it made others uncomfortable.

"We cannot guarantee a specific dollar amount. Our job is to create the best looking property possible and to present that property to the top buyers in the market," she replied.

"What's your success rate? Do you have a portfolio of satisfied customers? Statistical reports for cattle ranches in the Texas Panhandle? What makes you so sure we need you here to garner a good sale price?"

This barrage of questions came from Jagger and when Gabriella opened her mouth to respond, Tyler touched her arm.

After Tyler's invitation to dinner, Gabriella had gone to her room and quickly changed out of her bathing suit into a navy blue dress and tan sandals. She'd pulled her still wet hair back into a neat and professional bun and clasped tan and gold earrings to her ears. As it was so warm here in Texas, she hadn't bothered with the jacket that she normally wore with the dress, which left her arms bare. Tyler's hand—even if for just a moment—was warm and sent tendrils of something unexplainable up her arm.

"I think we need to be clear on a few points before we decide what should be done with the property," Tyler stated.

"What points? We're selling," Jagger interrupted. "Like Clyde just said, neither of us have been here working on the ranch since we were kids. We didn't like it then and I suspect we won't like it now. So, it's clear. We do what Mom and Dad wanted and sell the place. If she's going to help us do that for the best price, then we have a right to question her abilities or we can find another decorator for the job."

"You're being rude, Jagger, and that's not necessary," Dessie said, in what Gabriella thought might be the woman's most delicate disciplinary voice.

Jagger had the decency to at least look dutifully reproached.

"We own Westwind now," Tyler continued. "Fifty percent is yours and fifty percent is mine. As for my half, I want to take the time to decide what I think is best. So, while we're in limbo, I'd like to hire Gabriella to present her ideas for both options."

Jagger was shaking his head before Tyler finished. "That's a waste of time in my opinion because I already know I want to sell."

"Then I'll buy you out," Tyler added quickly. "Name your price."

There was a momentary stare-off as the West brothers traded intense glares across the table.

"I thought I'd find you here," a man dressed in a police officer's uniform said as he approached the table.

Gabriella wasn't sure if the man realized he'd just interrupted a very tense moment, but she used the time to close her tablet and quietly slide it back into her bag.

"Sheriff Alvarez," Clyde said and turned to shake the man's hand.

"Hey Clyde. Dessie," he added with a tip of his wide brimmed dark brown cowboy hat.

The color of the hat coordinated with the beige uniform shirt and chocolate brown pants. His badge was a brightly shined gold pinned to the left pocket of his shirt while the salt and peppered hair of his goatee could stand to be trimmed.

"I called out to the ranch and Clarice answered. She said she thought you were in town," the sheriff said to Tyler. "But I thought I'd stop by here first."

"What's going on?" Tyler asked.

Gabriella could hear the concern in his voice, but she wasn't sure what was happening.

"Just wanted to confirm with you that we're looking into things. After our meeting this morning, I went out and took another look at the crime scene where your parents were found," he told them.

Dessie waved her hand as if fanning herself. Gabriella could see tears forming in the woman's eyes and picked up the glass of water in front of her. She handed Dessie the water and kept a hand on the woman's shoulder while she took a slow sip.

"Do you have new leads on the murder investigation?" Clyde asked.

"None. At the moment. But we're still going through those lists of creditors, clients and suppliers. I don't want to intrude on your dinner," the Sheriff said with an eye toward Dessie. "But I just wanted you to know that I'm on top of this. George and Verna were like family to everyone around here. Somebody targeted them and I'm gonna find out why."

Tyler nodded. "Thanks, Sheriff. Please keep me posted."

"Will a murder investigation hold up the sale of the property?" Brooke asked the moment the sheriff walked away.

Nobody answered, but, in Gabriella's opinion, the look Dessie shot her way was a bit on the murderous side.

"I want to apologize," Tyler said as they walked down the stairs outside the resort.

Gabriella was walking quietly beside him after they'd finally finished the dinner from hell.

"For what? The crème brulee was fabulous," she replied. "And Dessie and Clyde remind me a lot of my parents."

She was being polite. He appreciated that, but would rather she just be honest with him. But he understood. She'd been tossed into this situation with people she'd just met, for the sake of a job. He definitely owed her an apology for dragging her into that dinner and his family's dysfunction.

"I'm sure this isn't how your jobs usually start off," he told her.

The steps had taken them away from the pool area and now

they were crossing the grassy stretch that led to the corral where pony rides, weekly rodeo and riding lessons were conducted.

"I'm sure this isn't how your dinner meetings usually go," she replied.

He looked over to her and she stared at him. Her features were dim in the dark of night but it didn't matter, he'd already committed them to memory. She had a slim nose and pert lips that made him think of strawberries and kisses. Her high cheekbones didn't overwhelm her face, but highlighted the slightest slant of her eyes and her long eyelashes. With her hair pulled back so tightly, everything about her face seemed more poignant. While that had been like a punch in the gut when she'd stepped off the elevator just before they moved to the restaurant, now, the sight of her had simmered to a slow burn in the pit of his stomach.

"I try not to have meetings over meals. I know that's hard to believe considering that's all I've done since meeting you," he said with a wry chuckle.

"Do that again," she said.

"Do what?"

"Laugh. It has a nice ring to it."

Of course he didn't, but he didn't stop smiling either.

"I apologize for that too. I'm not normally so, ah—"

She nodded and added, "Moody?"

Tyler waited a beat and then shrugged. "Yeah, I guess that's the word for it."

"No need to apologize. My brother Alex is like that sometimes. Mostly he's bossy and overprotective, but when something really bothers him, he can be pretty moody about it," she said.

So she was comparing him to her brother. Tyler didn't know if that was good or bad. What he knew for certain was that he was glad he'd asked her to join him tonight.

"I really appreciate you joining me and my family for dinner. I know it's not part of your job description."

"Well, if I end up redesigning and decorating I'll need to spend some time talking to each of you to hear about your ideas for the new style. But I understand what you're trying to say, so I'll just say, apology accepted."

Looking forward as they grew closer to the corral, he wondered if he should say something about his parents, or their murders, or that someone had come onto his private property and vandalized the premises. None of which was good date conversation. But this wasn't a date. If it was, he would have been more on his game. Because he did date periodically, and when he did, it turned out well and he wasn't ashamed to admit that. He could adequately romance a woman. He could also maintain a relationship—for as much as a person in his position could have a relationship—for a relatively good amount of time. About two months. After that it was on the road to serious and Tyler had done that before and never wanted to try it again.

"So tomorrow I'd like to give you a complete tour of the house and the employee living quarters," he said. "Then I promise not to rope you into anymore dinner meetings. I'll let you settle in and work on the proposals."

"It was no problem, really. I come from a big family and they married into bigger families, so I'm used to differences of opinion."

"Are you used to murder investigations too?"

He had no idea why he'd asked that question. Well, yes, he

did. There was no one else for him to talk to about this. Jagger didn't seem as interested in what had really happened to their parents as Tyler was and Brooke, well, Tyler didn't give a damn what she was interested in. Dessie and Clyde had been his parents' friends so they were far too emotional to look at things objectively. Tyler, on the other hand...where did he fit in all of this? The son who still carried around a ton of guilt because he was never good enough for his father, and the brother who, in Jagger's eyes, was always too good.

"Actually, yes," she replied to his surprise.

"What? Are you serious?"

Gabriella nodded.

"Years ago my family was targeted by a jealous man and his daughter. That ended in a shoot-out which involved my sister-in-law and her brother. My other sister-in-law's brother was shot and killed by a police officer. And my brother-in-law's family had a stalking, murdering woman terrorizing their family for the last two years."

Tyler stopped and turned to stare at her. "Okay, well in that case, I guess you can relate."

She nodded. "You want answers. You want to know who killed your parents. I'm assuming it's the murder investigation that the sheriff was talking about earlier."

"It was," he said and continued to stare at her.

He should say something, but words weren't coming. He found himself simply wanting to look at her. This woman that walked into his life yesterday afternoon wearing perhaps the sexiest pair of shoes he'd ever seen. Or maybe it was the white polish on her petite toes. He wasn't sure. All Tyler knew was that he had been intrigued by Gabriella Bennett from that moment on. And now he was standing here, beneath a starless night sky, wanting to…what?

"It makes sense," she continued. "And I hope you find the answers you're searching for. I hope—"

Her words were cut short as Tyler had already closed the space between them. With one hand clasping the back of her neck, he leaned in and took her mouth in one quick motion.

His tongue moved over hers in a warm duel that immediately sent heat spiraling throughout his body. She hurriedly clasped his arms before tilting her head and joining in the kiss. There were no sounds, not the crickets or any other animal in the vicinity. There was no breeze. No movement, except the dance of tongues. He couldn't think of anything else, didn't want to actually. He thought he needed to get closer, to touch more, and to taste more. Tyler just wanted more.

And then she pulled away.

"Sorry," he said the moment he looked at her face.

Her fingers were shaking as she lifted her hand and touched her now swollen lips. She backed away and Tyler felt like a complete jerk.

"I didn't mean to frighten you," he said and took a step toward her.

But she moved back another step, and then another.

"I should go," she said, her voice low and shaky.

"Gabriella. I apologize. It won't happen again. I won't overstep. I—"

She held up a hand and shook her head. "I'm going to go back to my room. I'll see you tomorrow, Tyler."

He wanted to say something else. He wanted to go to her

and walk her to her room. Assure her that he wasn't a jackass. Not normally. Something. Instead, he did nothing.

"Fine," he replied with a quick nod. "I'll see you tomorrow."

And then she was gone.

Tyler stood there watching her walk toward the resort. He stared until he could vaguely see her silhouette going through the glass doors of the facility. And then he sighed. He was messing up everything.

It was dark and starting to rain.

Gloved hands shook as they hovered over the door knob. It would be locked. It didn't matter. It wasn't time anyway. When it was time everything would fall into place. When it was time there would be pain. That was inevitable. Lessons that needed to be learned were hard and thus pain was a given. Stopping everything else to see this through was also inevitable.

It was destiny.

Gabriella stepped out of the shower and froze.

She'd left the bathroom door open because she was in the room alone and she'd started leaving doors open before she left Connecticut. She didn't like closed doors or tight spaces, or being alone. But she was an adult and she'd refused to be beat by another person's nonsense. Still, with her bravado firmly in place, she grabbed a towel and wrapped it around herself before heading out to the bedroom area.

And she heard it again. That same sound from just a moment ago.

Was someone at the door?

She stood there waiting for them to knock or maybe call out to here. She didn't know. She was being foolish. And so she moved, walking across the room to the bed where she'd set her nightgown and a bottle of lotion.

Dropping the towel, Gabriella sat on the bed and picked up the bottle. She poured jasmine scented lotion into her hands and began to rub it over her legs and thighs. The moment she touched her sensitive skin, thoughts of Tyler and the kiss they'd shared came rushing to her mind.

What had she been thinking?

It hadn't been of kissing him, she was sure. She didn't think like that, not anymore. Not in the last six months. Any type of sexual or intimate contact with a man had been the last thing on her mind as she'd gone through the most difficult time in her life. Yet tonight, she'd willingly kissed Tyler back.

Again, what had she been thinking? He was her client. A very big client whose project could take her career to the next level. Gabriella had so much riding on this job and already the brother and his fiancé didn't care for her. The last thing she needed was to let some physical attraction interfere with her last lifeline to this job. Because even though Dessie had been responsible for bringing her here, Tyler was clearly the one calling the shots at this point. Which was an even better reason she had for regretting that kiss.

No matter how good it had felt.

She rubbed the lotion up her bare arms, remembering the times during the dinner that he'd touched her. Three times total, she recalled. At the small of her back when he'd directed her to take a seat at the table, on her arm as he interrupted Jagger's questions and then when they'd been alone under the dark of night and his strong hand had clasped the back of her neck. There'd been a bit of force in that motion and while she should have detested that, should have hated that he would make the assumption that she wanted him to touch her without asking permission, Gabriella had liked it. She'd liked how instantly sexy it had made her feel. How just that touch had aroused her in the seconds before his mouth took over.

A loud thump from the direction of the balcony had Gabriella jumping on the bed. She hurriedly closed the top over the lotion and set it on the nightstand before standing and pulling the nightgown over her head. As the material fell down to her thighs she walked barefoot across the wood floor toward the patio doors. When she'd come in tonight she'd pulled the blinds closed. Now, she stood to the side of the window and tilted one blind so that she could peek through.

Nothing, but drops of rain on the glass and beyond that, darkness.

Sighing and only half believing this was her imagination this time, Gabriella double-checked that the patio door was locked. She went to the front entrance of the room and checked the locks on those doors as well. Then she moved back to the bed and removed her cell phone from the charger on the nightstand. Climbing into bed she tucked the phone beneath the pillow and turned out the light. She might not get any sleep tonight and she might also be overreacting, either way, the next noise she heard she was calling the police.

She wasn't taking any chances. Not again.

CHAPTER 5

*T*yler finished the sixty ounce tumbler of water he'd been drinking since waking at dawn. With his morning workout complete, the plan now, was to go for a run and check to be sure there were no more intrusions on the property. He wasn't sure when he would be returning to L.A., so he'd purchased a few pieces of exercise equipment and set them up in the room that used to be reserved for their boxes of off-season clothes. Tyler was staying in his childhood bedroom, sleeping in the full-size bed and reliving too many memories to count. The master suite was large and could have easily fit the exercise equipment along with the four post California King Bed and all the matching heavy oak furniture. But that was his parents' room. It always had been.

He'd just snapped the cap onto the tumbler and walked into the kitchen when he remembered that he was no longer alone in the house. Jagger sat at the glossed mahogany wood table across from the island in the spacious kitchen. Dessie was at the sink on the other side of the island washing apples and setting them into a bowl.

"She's silly acting and rude," Dessie was saying to Jagger as Tyler walked in. "Tell him Tyler. Somebody needs to teach his friend some manners. Verna would have never tolerated her sitting at a table acting that way."

"Mom's not here and Brooke is an adult," Jagger stated as he stared down at the newspaper on the table in front of him. "If you have something to say to her, say it to her face. She was up late touring the property, but she'll be down soon."

"Oh, don't think I won't," Dessie countered and then slapped the handle to turn off the water. "And don't you forget who used to help change your diapers and chase your little fast tail around the ranch either."

Jagger looked up as Tyler pulled out a chair and sat across from him. His brother shook his head and Tyler thought this scene was all too familiar.

"Maybe she was just saying what Jagger was thinking, Dessie," Tyler commented and then grinned as Jagger groaned.

"Probably. Or more like, what he put into her head about this family and this situation." Dessie shook her head and pulled out one of the side drawers.

Cutlery rattled around until she found what she was looking for and when she turned around again she was holding a pretty sharp-looking knife. She picked up the bowl where she'd set the apples and came to join them at the table.

"This is family business, Jagger. Now, I'm not trying to pick who you roll around in bed with, but just because she satisfies some physical need you have doesn't mean she can sit at the table and talk as if she knows what's going on around here," Dessie continued.

"I don't even know what's going on around here," Tyler stated seriously.

Jagger reached into the bowl and grabbed an apple. "Neither do I."

"Well, that's for us to figure out," Dessie said and started to peel one of the apples. "It's been so long since the two of you have been here you've forgotten how we do things."

"We still get up at the crack of dawn apparently," Jagger replied.

"Nobody came into your room and forced you to wake up," Dessie said. "You were probably trying to get away from that woman."

"That rooster crows much louder than my alarm clock back in New York, Dessie. And I'm going to marry that woman, so some respect might be due."

And because Tyler knew this was the point where the conversation was likely to take a violent turn, he reached out to touch the back of Dessie's hand. The one holding the knife.

"I think it might be more important to talk about what we think happened to Mom and Dad," he said to Dessie.

Her fingers were still clenched around the handle of the knife, her usually laughing eyes, now narrowed at Jagger. Seconds later her shoulders visibly relaxed and she turned her attention to Tyler. Dessie's usual warm smile spread across her face and she spoke as calmly as if they'd been sitting on the back porch talking about the sunrise.

"If you're going to ask who I think killed your parents, the answer is the same as the one I gave to Sheriff Alvarez, I don't know," she told him. "Everybody in this town loved George and Verna. They didn't have any enemies, no run-ins with folk or anything contrary like that."

"Did they owe anybody money?" Tyler asked. "I've been going back through my emails and printing out all the financial statements that Dad sent me over the years. There are no huge losses and no big debts listed. But that could just mean he kept them off the books."

Dessie had proceeded with peeling the apple. "I don't know anything about that. They had an accountant. Lucille Gangley. She's got an office down on Lange Street. Verna didn't talk much about the finances and since I was her friend, that means I didn't hear much about it. And if your father told Clyde, my husband wouldn't have told me. He's very careful about his attorney/client privilege information."

Tyler nodded because he knew that already. He'd asked Clyde some questions during the reading of the will and Clyde declined to answer them, citing the privilege.

"I'm just thinking there had to be somebody gunning for them," Tyler said.

Jagger finished his apple and placed the core on the empty plate beside his half full cup of coffee. "Why? Psychopaths kill random people all the time."

"But do they shoot them execution style and then burn the truck they were in just about twenty miles from their house?" Tyler asked. "It just seems fishy to me."

"Well, I disagree." Jagger announced and folded his paper neatly. "So for the record, my vote is to sell this place and move on."

"It's our legacy," Tyler told him. "That's what Dad used to say."

"He used to say that to you, Ty, not me. I was the one who could do no right, remember? So pardon me, if I don't give a damn about a place that never welcomed me with open arms."

"You could have done more, Jagger. You could have tried harder. Paid closer attention and applied yourself," Tyler stated evenly.

"Why?" Jagger asked with a shrug. "You were the favorite."

"That's childish," Tyler told him.

"It's true."

"Good morning," she said and all eyes turned to the doorway where Gabriella now stood.

"Well, good morning, Gabriella," Dessie said with a big smile. "Come on in. There's coffee on the counter and cinnamon rolls. You can pop one into the microwave and join us."

"No, I don't want to intrude," she said as she took a step toward the table. Tyler and I talked about meeting today to tour the property. We didn't set a time but I'm a morning person, so I'm here. Stephen was outside when I pulled up so he let me in."

"It's fine, you're not intruding," Dessie told him.

"You sure?" Jagger asked. "You don't think showing up at someone's house unannounced isn't rude?"

"She was invited," Tyler intervened as Jagger dared to glance at Dessie after his slick questions that were definitely aimed at Dessie's remarks about Brooke.

Tyler stood from the table and walked until he was standing in front of Gabriella. She smelled good. Like flowers and sunshine. Her hair was pulled up into a ponytail and her make-up was light and natural so that she looked more like a high school teenager than a businesswoman. But Tyler knew that comparison was deceiving. After the kiss they'd shared last night, there was no mistaken that Gabriella Bennett was all woman, with passion burning bright just beneath her very pretty surface.

"Grab some coffee and a cinnamon bun," he said to her. "I'll get cleaned up and then we can get started."

"Sure," she replied.

She met his gaze, but then looked down at her feet, before lifting her head and looking across the room toward the counter where the coffeepot was. Tyler hoped he wasn't making her uncomfortable. Just as he'd hoped all through the night that kissing her hadn't made their future dealings too uncomfortable to bear. As for the way he was feeling standing just a few feet away from her, well, never before had denim capri pants and a simple gray V-neck shirt turned him on.

When he realized he'd been standing there looking her up and down as well, Tyler shook his head.

"I'll just be a few minutes," he said.

"Right," she nodded and quickly moved away from the doorway. "I'll just get some coffee."

"Finally," Jagger said from behind them with an exaggerated sigh.

Was she really that intent on messing this up?

Gabriella set her bag in a chair and lay her sunglasses on the table, before crossing the room to stand in front of the coffeepot. She let her hands rest on the granite countertop and stared straight ahead for a few moments. The sun left a hazy golden glow over the land. Acres of grass stretched across the landscape until cattle looked almost like specks in the distance as they grazed. It was a soothing sight, one that helped in calming Gabriella from the panic attack she was certain would overtake her in the next few minutes. She breathed in slow, releasing the breath in measured beats, just like the online articles had advised.

Gabriella hadn't utilized the mental health benefits of her health insurance. She could have made an appointment with a psychiatrist and received medication to deal with her trauma and the stress and anxiety that had engulfed her since that day. And she could have called a psychotherapist to help her sort through the emotions that raged through her like a tsunami. She could have had help working through these past months and then she probably wouldn't feel so overwhelmed with the thought of failing at this very moment. But she hadn't. She'd decided she could handle it on her own. And she'd done pretty well. At least she thought so.

"Fresh cream is in the refrigerator," she heard Dessie say and was jolted from her self-treatment.

"Verna used to run this house like a well-oiled machine but I figured in the past few weeks things had been left alone. If the plan is to keep this place, hiring a house manager might be good. Stephen's wife, Naomi, is a delight. She worked here a couple summers while she was in college," Dessie continued.

Gabriella poured the coffee into her cup and went to the stainless steel sub-zero refrigerator to retrieve the cream. She poured some in her cup and decided to forego the sugar. She didn't need that additive to make her feel anymore jittery than she already did. And she didn't know if the coffee was decaf or not.

When she turned again and headed for the table, it was to see that Jagger had left as well.

"He doesn't like me very much," Gabriella said as she took a seat and set her mug on the table.

Not that it bothered her. She was good with people not liking her. It was their problem, not hers. But Jagger was a client too. So there was that.

Dessie shook her head. "He's not sure if he likes himself," she said. "The thing about death is that it can be eye-opening for some and soul-searing for others. I've known this family since Verna and I were young girls in high school together. I've changed those boys' diapers, put bandages on their scars, yanked them up when they were out showing off, and cried with my best friend when each of them moved away because Verna knew they had no intention of coming back."

"Until now," Gabriella said sadly. "They only came back because of their parents' death."

Dessie peeled another apple and set it in the bowl. The full lips, painted in a natural color lip gloss, sank into a frown and she shook her head faster, breathing in deeply. She didn't want to cry and Gabriella felt bad that she was bringing on a conversation that made tears well into the woman's eyes.

"I'm sorry," she said and reached over to touch Dessie's hand.

"No," Dessie said and sniffed. "Don't be. Death isn't always a sad occasion. Sometimes the good Lord calls his laborers home. George and Verna did all that they were meant to do on this earth. It was their time."

Even if someone else chose to take them out? Gabriella

wasn't certain she believed Dessie's words, but if it made the woman feel better, then she would let it be.

"So you're here with your designs and ready to tackle this project I see," Dessie said after clearing her throat.

"Yes. I did a little research last night after dinner and I think I'm ready to get a better idea of the job," Gabriella said.

She could hear her phone buzzing from her purse and after taking a sip from her cup, she reached over to the chair beside her to grab the phone.

"It's a great ranch. George was really good at working the land he had and raising the best cattle in this region. His father and grandfather taught him well. And then what he started doing with the horses. That was Verna's idea. She loved horses. But that even started to pick up. Westwind was also becoming known for its budding stud farm. George forked over some good money to purchase prized studs. They were getting ready to…what, wait a minute, are you okay baby?" Dessie asked.

Gabriella could hear her speaking but she didn't respond. She couldn't. Her gaze was fixed on the message on the screen of her phone and her heart was pounding loudly. She read the message again:

I WANT YOU BACK. I'LL DO WHATEVER TO MAKE IT HAPPEN.

She closed her eyes, but when she opened them, the message was still there. Until she felt the hand on her shoulder. Then, Gabriella moved quickly, erasing the message and dropping the phone back into her purse.

"Oh, sorry. That was just something about work," she stammered. "Another client that I need to follow-up with."

Dessie was now standing over Gabriella, staring down at her with her brow creased.

"All right, then, if you say so," Dessie said. "Drink your coffee. It'll settle your nerves."

Yes, Gabriella thought, she definitely needed to settle her nerves. So instead of continuing the conversation with Dessie, she sat at that table sipping her coffee and telling herself that it was just words. The words didn't mean anything. Just like those sounds at her door last night hadn't meant anything. Except this morning when she'd finally gotten out of bed after her restless night, she'd gone out onto the patio and had been slightly bothered to see that one of the chairs was overturned. That, didn't mean anything either. She prayed desperately that it didn't.

"I'm going to stick around here today," Dessie stated after a few moments of silence. "Audrey's filling in for me at the resort, so I'm going to get some cleaning done and cook a nice meal for everybody. It'll be a big Sunday dinner, just like Verna used to have."

"My mother loves cooking and hosting family dinners," Gabriella said. She'd been thinking about her family and how she prayed none of what was going on in her life now, would ever touch them.

"Then you'll join us too. It's nice to have everyone gathered around good food. Brings people closer together. And that's just what we need around here if we're gonna face what happened and what we need to do going forward," Dessie said.

"We're not only going to face what happened, we're going to find who killed my parents," Tyler said when he stepped back into the kitchen.

Gabriella looked over to where he was standing and had to take another sip of her coffee. As if he hadn't looked delicious when she'd first arrived wearing basketball shorts and a black tank. The muscles in his bare arms bulged and when he'd stood, the trim narrowing of his waist had her mouth watering as she recalled the pictures of his perfect eight pack that she'd seen online. Now, showered, his hair still wet and wearing khaki shorts and a white t-shirt, he looked neat, athletic and sexy as hell.

Dessie stood from the table. She carried the bowl and knife to the island before replying, "And in the meantime, decisions have to be made."

"I'm going to make them," Tyler told her. "You ready for the tour?"

"Ah, yes," Gabriella managed to say after she finished gawking at him. She stood and picked up her mug, about to take it to the sink, but Tyler took it from her.

She retrieved her bag, slipping the leather straps over her shoulder as she turned to smile at Dessie. It was just in time to see Tyler lean in and kiss the woman on her cheek. Dessie smiled and patted Tyler's hand that rested on her shoulder. And Gabriella sighed. If Tyler West loved his mother half as much as he seemed to love Dessie, he was a damn good man, even outside of his good looks.

They'd seen the employee residences first and he'd watched while she took notes and measurements. They rode in the Jeep along the paved roads of the ranch after that, stopping so that she could see the areas where the animals were housed. She took more notes. From a distance, they'd watched the cows grazing in the early afternoon sun. She'd asked a few more questions about their feeding and selling process while she took even more notes. But it wasn't until they came back to the equestrian center that Tyler noticed the light in her eyes.

She stepped right up to the paddock door and extended her hand to the Arabian bay. The horse, in return, dipped his head and let her run her hand down his forehead and muzzle.

"You're a natural with them," he said before he could stop himself.

Today she wore flat gray tennis shoes and had to go up on the tips of her toes to reach the horse. She looked adorable when she turned her head and smiled at him. The way the end of her ponytail shifted with her movement and her eyes lit up with the smile. It reminded Tyler of when he was a teenager and they'd first started having monthly rodeos at the ranch. He was always in charge of the pony rides and the children who were brave enough to climb up on that pony always smiled and looked over to him as if that were the best moment in their life. As he'd concluded earlier, Gabriella was no child, but she did look extremely happy at this moment.

"My dad had a vision for this place," he said, thrusting his hands into the front pockets of his shorts.

He didn't know why but he'd been talking a lot about his parents on this tour.

"I know you're probably tired of hearing about them by now," he added.

She shook her head. "Not at all. The background of this place is great information. If you decide to re-decorate, then knowing the visions and feelings of the people who lived and will continue to live here is imperative."

She was still rubbing her hand along the horse's muzzle. This one was named Brown Eyes, for obvious reasons.

With a slight shrug, Tyler moved a little closer to where she stood and continued. "When I turned fourteen we started hosting two rodeos per year. The people in town seemed to like it and when word began to spread, tourists started stopping by when they were in town, asking when the next rodeo was scheduled. So my dad decided we would begin to host them once a month. I was sixteen by then. We only had four horses at that time. I left two years later and, another two years after that, Jagger was off to Harvard."

"I think it's a good thing for people to branch off in their own direction, to see the world through their own eyes at some point," she said as if she knew the guilt he still harbored over leaving.

"Is that what you did?" he asked, suddenly more curious about her than his own guilt-ridden past.

Her hand slowed and Brown Eyes nudged his muzzle against her palm, as if telling her to keep going. Tyler smiled because the bay must have been reading his mind.

"I went to college right after high school. The University of South Dakota was my choice and after the first year and a half, I finally decided to study photography. But that didn't really work out. I took a year off and traveled to Pirata."

"Where is that?"

"It's a small village in Brazil where my mother is from. Well, actually, she's the princess of Pirata. There are approximately two thousand people living in the town and her older brother governs them, so she was free to leave and marry my dad."

"Oh." That was all Tyler could manage because he would have never guessed she was related to royalty. Although now, with the slight tilt of her head and the way she held her chin up, he could easily imagine her wearing a crown. "So you traveled. For how long?"

She shrugged. "Two years. When I left Brazil I went to Paris for a while with my sister Adriana."

"Adriana Bennett-Donovan," he said.

"Yes! Do you know her? I mean, did you two run into each other while you were on modeling jobs?"

"No," he replied. "The modeling industry is like its own universe with many types of models circling one spotlight. Your sister did more fashion and runway work than I ever wanted. I did mostly print modeling, magazines and billboards, things like that. Then I got into fitness modeling and the rest is history."

"History as in you filmed your first fitness video when you were just twenty-four years old. From there, you created the Ty-Fitness brand, building it into a multi-million dollar business that now features fitness videos, public speaking and a new fitness fashion line debuting this fall. There's also talk of you opening your first Ty-Fitness Center in Beverly Hills some time next year," she said.

Tyler thought she sounded like an infomercial.

"You did your research."

She nodded. "As did you."

"There's more information circulating about your siblings, than on you personally. Two of your brothers work for your father's company. Another one is an artist. And then there's Adriana. But nothing about you."

"I'm the baby. The flighty and misguided one. My parents always said had I been their first, I would have also been their last. I'm blunt and argumentative and I don't know what slowing down, committing and finishing something means."

"What was that? Your impromptu bio?"

"No. That's what any member of my family would say if you asked them about me."

"Somehow," he said and closed the last gap of space between them, "I don't think that's totally accurate."

"You don't know me that well," she said.

She blinked and stood a little straighter, but she did not move. No, she was not the type to back down, or to run for that matter. She was going to stand and face whatever came next, regardless of how she really felt inside.

That thought should have stopped him, but it didn't. It urged him closer, until he was lifting a hand to tuck the strands of hair that had fallen free of her ponytail back behind her ear.

"I know that I'm attracted to you," he said, glad he could manage to be completely honest about at least one thing he was feeling these days.

She inhaled deeply, and let the breath out slowly, before speaking. He knew what the effort cost her as she carefully considered her words.

"We're working together, Tyler. So I don't think there should be any type of personal entanglements between us."

"I understand," he said. And he did. But a big part of him, just didn't give a damn. "But answer me this one question. Are you attracted to me?"

Tyler couldn't help himself. Yes, he'd heard her words and if she demanded he step back and stop anymore advances toward her again, he definitely would. He was well-versed in the no-means-no rule. But there was something here. He could feel it between them as if it were a living thing, breathing and... possibly growing.

"Yes," she answered. "I'm not going to deny that. But in addition to our working relationship, I'm really not trying to be attracted to any guy, or involved with anyone at this time."

"That's cool," he said, practicing Herculean restraint as his fingers tingled to touch that spot on her neck where her pulse had just picked up pace. "We'll steer clear of any personal entanglements. After this—"

His lips were on hers once more. He couldn't stop it and he prayed with every ounce of religion his parents had pounded into his childhood mind, that she wouldn't want to stop it either. Not this time. Not this kiss. The one he felt he needed, more than he needed to breathe.

CHAPTER 6

*G*abriella had no idea what the dress code was for a "big Sunday dinner" at the Westwind Ranch and when she'd called Adriana to get her advice, she'd received her sister's voice mail. So she was on her own, which was actually fine. She was one of those people who believed that packing more was much better than packing less. Therefore, she had four dresses that were suitable for cocktail parties and formal business dinners. She decided on the purple one with the ruffle sleeve and tight fit, purple and black peep toe platform pumps, gold and purple bangle and black jeweled clutch.

It wasn't until she was climbing out of her car and walking up the dirt path to the front porch of the house that she thought maybe she was a bit overdressed. That was also about the time that she recalled the kiss with Tyler. The second one, because it was hotter than the first. Which was saying something because last night she'd thought that kiss they'd shared outside the resort was a scorcher.

But this afternoon, her lips had parted before his made contact because she'd been ready. More like, because she'd wanted that kiss. She'd wanted his hands to grasp her shoulders and pull her so close, so quick that she came up on the tips of her toes to meet him. And she'd definitely wanted his tongue to stroke alongside hers until she was breathless. She'd wanted these things so much that when he did them, she'd lifted her arms and wrapped them around his neck. He'd groaned as she'd pressed her aching breasts into his rigid chest. His hands had moved from her shoulders to palm her bottom as he made his burgeoning erection unmistakably known to her.

She'd loved how hard and thick he felt pressing against her, so much that she heard herself moaning. She wanted to stop it, to chastise herself for doing what she knew she shouldn't be doing. And what she definitely should not be enjoying. But she couldn't. Because it had felt too good.

He'd been the one to pull away this time. He'd stared down at her as his hands finally came unglued from her cheeks. She'd let her arms slide slowly down from his shoulders, her fingers trailing lightly along his chest, before dropping to her side.

"It won't happen again," he'd said solemnly, as if he were definitely making a pledge of some sort.

"Right," she'd replied, nodding her head to cement her agreement.

And then the tour had ended. Gabriella had touched Brown Eyes one more time before telling Tyler she had to get back to her room to take a scheduled conference call. It was a lie, but he didn't need to know that. She'd needed the space to breathe and think, and hate herself just a little for being so damn complicated.

Now, hours later, she was dressed and ready to see him again. Lord, she hoped she was ready to see this man again without jumping on him and begging for hot, sweaty sex.

Luckily—or maybe not—before she could be faced with that scenario, the front door opened and Brooke stepped out.

"Well, you finally arrived," she said and pulled the door closed behind her.

Gabriella held her clutch with both hands in front of her and waited. She knew that after last night's dinner, this moment was going to come. Women like Brooke needed to lay down the law first when faced with other professional and intelligent women. Gabriella didn't mind, she just hoped that Brooke was prepared, because Gabriella just might have some law of her own to lay down.

"I thought Dessie said dinner was at seven-thirty," Gabriella replied.

"Oh that's right, only family needed to be here at seven to greet the guests."

Brooke gave a triumphant smile. But Gabriella was not impressed. Still, she gave Brooke a brilliant smile of her own.

Brooke wore a classy one shoulder black dress and black patent leather pumps. Her hair was bone straight, hanging to her shoulders in a dark curtain. Her lips were red, plump, perfect as was just about everything else about her. Still, Gabriella wasn't impressed. Her sister was a gorgeous model. Her mother was a princess. She had a sister-in-law who was an ex-marine and another who was an ex-exotic dancer turned artist. So Brooke Radison, junior marketing executive, did not intimidate her in the least.

"And since we're on the subject, let me just make a few

things clear," Brooke continued. "This is a job. It's a job that you don't even officially have as of yet. There is no romance waiting to happen here. I saw how you looked at Tyler last night and I know that he went on a starry-night walk with you after dinner. But, please know that he's above you. Even if your father managed to make some money and your mother escaped that dirty town she's from. You are just a designer. And not a very experienced one, I recently learned. So stay in your lane or hit the road. Do I make myself clear?"

Well, Gabriella thought, as far as laying down the law that was pretty good.

"You are crystal clear, Brooke. Now, let me just add one tiny, little, thing," Gabriella said as she took a step closer to Brooke. "I am here to do a job. I come from a family of hard workers who pride themselves on keeping their word. I told Tyler and Jagger that I would provide detailed proposals for them to review and that's what I plan to do. As for who I intend to be romanced by, or even, take to my bed, that's none of your business. Not tonight, without a signed business contract. And not tomorrow, when I guarantee I'll be officially contracted to do this job."

As expected, Brooke was shocked. Gabriella wasn't supposed to reply. She was expected to cower and apologize and walk away. But Brooke's research was faulty. She had no idea that of the Bennett clan, Gabriella was known as the fighter. And that didn't mean she would physically assault someone— not unless it was necessary—it just meant that she didn't take crap from people, especially not primped and bourgeois women with control issues.

"Now, if you'll excuse me, I have a dinner to get to," Gabriella said.

She walked around Brooke who was standing there with her lips clamped tight and opened the front door of the house.

As good as she felt about knocking Brooke down a peg, Gabriella was in no way prepared for the sight that greeted her in the foyer.

Tyler with his arms full of some blonde whose laugh sounded like someone was killing a chicken.

He saw it the moment their gazes locked. The questions and then the dismissal.

"Hello, Tyler," Gabriella said as she came closer to where he stood with Hannah.

Tyler had already dropped his hands from Hannah's waist. Seconds before Gabriella had opened the door, Hannah had run into him, wrapping her arms around his neck as if she were actually in danger of falling. He knew it was a lie, but hadn't wanted to make a scene. Not tonight and not here with some of the ranch's biggest customers in the other room.

"Good evening," he said.

He had to lift his hands to take Hannah's wrists and untwine her arms from around his neck.

"Gabriella Bennett, this is Hannah Palmer. Hannah's father owns the P&P Steakhouse. He's also a long-time family friend and customer of Westwind." Tyler didn't have to look at Hannah to know she hadn't liked the way he introduced her.

Gabriella stepped forward, extending her hand. "It's a pleasure to meet you, Hannah."

Hannah nodded and shook Gabriella's hand gingerly. "Hello. You aren't from Hobbs Creek? Are you a tourist?"

"Gabriella is a designer. She's going to do some work here at the house and at the resort for us," Tyler replied.

He didn't want Gabriella to feel she had to defend herself to anyone, least of all Hannah. But he also knew women. More importantly, he knew Hannah.

"In fact, Gabriella and I need to go over some of the details for the project, so if you'll excuse us, Hannah."

Tyler didn't wait for Hannah's or Gabriella's response. He took Gabriella's hand and led her through the foyer and into the living room. He kept walking, nodding to a few people he'd already spoken to and leading her to the bar in the corner of the room. He stopped walking and released her hand. Then he grabbed a glass and fixed himself a drink.

"Hannah is a handful," he said after the first gulp.

"I could see that," Gabriella replied. "You had both your hands full of her."

Tyler cursed. His hand clenched the glass tighter and he looked at her.

"It's okay, Tyler," she told him. "You don't owe me any explanations. We don't owe each other any explanations."

"Because there's nothing to explain," he said.

She nodded. "Because we're not sleeping together."

"Well, glad we've gotten that out of the way," Jagger said coming to stand behind Gabriella. "Otherwise I might be concerned about why my brother is so intent on keeping you around."

Gabriella spun around quickly to face Jagger, while Tyler scowled over her shoulder at his brother.

"I was going to wait until tomorrow to suggest a time for us to meet," Gabriella said to Jagger. "But let's go ahead and set our meeting for tomorrow afternoon. I can be here at three. Does that work for you, Jagger?"

The bite to her tone was obvious. The look on Jagger's face was a cross between surprise and irritation.

"That time is good for us," Tyler answered.

"Fine," she replied with a quick look over her shoulder to him, before she walked away.

Tyler took another swallow of his drink while watching her walk away. That dress fit her perfectly, molding the curve of her ass in a way that made his dick twitch.

"She's a—" Jagger began before Tyler abruptly cut him off.

"Don't," he said, slowly lowering his glass from his mouth. "She's doing her job and you need to stop trying to press her buttons about it."

"She's an outsider," Jagger replied.

"And so is Brooke, so we're even."

Jagger picked up a glass and began fixing himself a drink. "Brooke is going to be my wife. We've scheduled the wedding for December 1st because she wants to honeymoon on Grand Serenity Island in the Caribbean. They're having some type of anniversary holiday celebration there she keeps going on about."

Tyler had been following Gabriella's procession across the room, but was sidetracked by a very interesting sight.

"You sure about that, little brother? Looks like she's becoming pretty chummy with someone else."

He nodded in Brooke's direction when Jagger only looked at him quizzically. The frown on his brother's face as they watched Brooke toss her head back and laugh, while rubbing a hand up and down the arm of a guy dressed in black denim jeans, black boots and a gray shirt with sleeves rolled up to his elbows. That made the tattoos on each arm visible, even though Tyler couldn't make out what the tattoo was specifically or what the words beneath it stated.

"That's Noah Windmyr," Jagger said through clenched teeth.

"Who?" Tyler asked. He looked at the guy's face again, studying the five o'clock shadow at his jaw and the disheveled mud brown hair.

"Noah. Jessie Windmyr's son. Remember Jessie used to work here on the ranch."

Yes, now Tyler did remember. Jessie Windmyr was a stout man with a bald head and a gold front tooth.

"He'd been a ranch hand when we were kids. But when I came home for Christmas that year, he was in the house a lot. When I asked Dad about it, he'd just said that Jessie had been promoted. He never said to what position."

"Noah was in the same grade as me, that's probably why you don't remember him," Jagger said.

His brother threw his head back and swallowed the scotch he'd poured before starting across the room. Tyler followed Jagger, because this was Dessie's dinner party and the last thing she'd planned for was a brawl in the middle of the living room. He'd lost sight of Gabriella and wondered if she'd gone into another room. And if so, who was she with?

"Hey, Noah," Jagger said, tapping the guy on the shoulder.

When Noah turned his attention from Brooke to Jagger, Brooke dropped her hand from Noah's arm. Tyler tried not to frown at her when she looked past Jagger to him. In that moment Tyler knew her type. She was an opportunist. But why had she set her sights on Jagger? Before their parents passed away, Jagger made a good living, but he wasn't obscenely wealthy. At the reading of the will Clyde informed Tyler that his parents' estimated worth was somewhere around nine million. This included property, stocks that had been passed down from his grandfather, treasury bills, and investment accounts. Cash-on-hand totaled eight hundred and ninety-five thousand. That was already divided between Tyler and Jagger. At Jagger's written request—because he was in Paris during that first week after the murders—his portion of the cash had been transferred into two separate accounts.

Brooke couldn't have known what Jagger would inherit. Not unless she'd already researched the ranch and their parents' holdings. Which, Tyler realized with a start, he did not doubt was possible.

"Jagger West," Noah said and extended a hand for Jagger to shake. "It's been a long time."

His brother looked more confident now that Brooke had moved to stand beside him, threading her arm through his.

Jagger accepted the hand and kept eye contact with Noah. Their father had taught them to look a man in his eye at all times —whether he be friend or foe.

"Eighteen years ago," Jagger said, releasing Noah's hand.

"And Tyler," Noah added as he looked away from Jagger. "You're back too."

"Hey Noah," Tyler spoke. He did not extend his arm to shake Noah's hand, and noted that the guy hadn't either.

"The West boys are back at Westwind," Noah said. "Bet nobody ever thought that would happen."

"Oh we won't be here long, will we Jagger?" Brooke asked.

"We're just wrapping up the sale of the property and then we'll be heading back to New York."

Tyler didn't reply because he didn't want to discuss the status of the ranch in front of Brooke, or Noah for that matter.

What he really wanted was to talk to Gabriella. But he still had no idea where she'd gone.

Gabriella needed some air.

She probably needed to catch the next flight out of this town and head back to Connecticut, with the mess she feared was going on around her. How had she walked into this confusion? Technically, it wasn't her fault. She'd been hired to do a job and she'd come here to do it. Simple. Right?

No.

Now she was being low-key threatened by a primped and pampered bitch. And if that wasn't bad enough, a washed up Barbie look-a-like was giving her the sharpest side-eye Gabriella had ever experienced. It was a wonder she wasn't cut up and bleeding at this moment, after the way Hannah Palmer had watched her crossing the living room. If there was one thing Gabriella hated it was catty women, with issues they always tried to blame on someone else. Hell, she had enough issues of her own, she didn't need to inherit or share any with others.

With a sigh she leaned against the edge of the outdoor stove and looked up to the sky. When she was inside, she'd looked through the wall of windows that were steadily becoming her favorite feature in the entire house, and saw that the sun was just going down. Now, she was outside enjoying the sight and trying to clear her mind of what had happened in the first few minutes of her being here, when she was joined by someone else.

"Hi. I'm Naomi Garret, Stephen's wife. I just wanted to meet you before we sat down to dinner."

Gabriella smiled and shook the woman's hand. "Hi Naomi. It's a pleasure to meet you."

"Oh no, it is definitely my pleasure," she said. "When Stephen told me you were an actual designer, I couldn't wait to get over here to meet you."

"Really? Are you interested in design?"

"Yes! I watch HGTV all the time. I was so excited when Stephen and I moved out of that little trailer we were staying in before the wedding. We'd been saving for a while so the trailer was cheaper than having to pay anybody rent. Mr. George let us park it on the grounds, back behind the employee residences. There's no couples allowed in that building, so once Stephen and I became engaged we had to figure something out."

"I see," Gabriella said.

Naomi had a pretty smile and a lovely cinnamon brown complexion.

"I hope you don't mind but once you get started working on the house, could I stop by just to see how it's really done?"

"Sure," Gabriella told her. "I mean, it's okay with me. I'm not sure if you'll need to get Tyler or Dessie's approval as well."

Naomi chuckled. "Dessie's the one who suggested I ask you. She knows I've been into designing for a while now. And when she told me she was going to hire a professional to help get the ranch together for sale I was so excited. Not that the ranch might fall into someone else's hands, but because someone trained in design would be here."

"Well then, if Dessie is encouraging you, you must be good," Gabriella said. "If and when I get started, I may need some help finding the best spots in town to pick up a few things. I use a lot of online vendors but I'm definitely planning to incorporate some local flavor. This place is already brimming with it, but I'd want to class it up a bit."

"Definitely," Naomi squealed. "Thank you so much! And yes, I know exactly what you mean. Ms. Verna had good taste, but it was an older taste. Tyler and Jagger are younger, so I think bringing the house into a more contemporary western setting would be good. But, I mean, you tell me. I know you're the professional and I'll do whatever you ask."

"Then we have a deal," Gabriella said. "I'm meeting with Jagger and Tyler tomorrow, so let me get your number and I'll call you afterward to let you know which way we're going with the project."

Gabriella had a good feeling about Naomi. Not just because she desperately needed to feel good about somebody on this ranch tonight, but because the woman had been referred to her by Dessie. Of everyone she'd met in Hobbs Creek so far, Dessie seemed to be the most genuine and Gabriella was determined to steer clear of the foolishness while she was here.

Including Brooke Radison and Hannah Palmer. Those two women definitely had plans for drama in their midst and Gabriella had already endured her share of that.

CHAPTER 7

*T*yler touched Gabriella's shoulder and when she turned, said, "Walk with me for a minute."

She hesitated and he held back a frown. "No touching or kissing or anything this time. I just want to talk to you."

"We talked before dinner," she said, folding her arms over her chest. "And tomorrow at three we'll be meeting to talk again."

"We won't be alone tomorrow at three."

"Anything you have to say to me, can be said in front of Jagger. This is a professional relationship, remember?"

"This is...something," Tyler agreed. "Look, we both survived a pretty tense dinner party and now the guests are gone. The night is clear and nearly as sweltering as it was earlier in the day. I just want to take a few minutes to walk with you. Is that so wrong?"

She didn't immediately reply, but Tyler knew she was mentally ticking down a list of everything that was wrong about going for a walk with him. He'd gone through that same list in his mind throughout dinner. And still, he'd decided to approach her.

"For just a few minutes," she replied finally. "I don't want to return to the room too late."

They'd been standing on the front porch and Tyler had already started down the steps before asking, "Why? Is somebody there waiting for you?"

"No," she answered quickly.

Too quickly.

"Not that it matters," she continued as they started walking toward the side of the house.

"It matters if there's a security issue or something else going on at the resort. If there's a problem, let me know and I can take care of it. Or you can just stay here."

The suggestion had come easily and Tyler found that he actually liked the idea of her being on the ranch with him. It was odd, but he'd already said it and couldn't take it back.

"My room at the resort is just fine. Thank you."

She was still irritated. He'd known that throughout the entire dinner. Dessie had put place cards on the long cherry wood table in the main dining room. Gabriella was seated beside Tyler on one side and Ted Palmer on his other. Ted had pretty much talked to Tyler the entire time, trying to get some confirmation on whether Westwind would remain the primary supplier for his steakhouse. Tyler had been as non-committal as possible, but still kept the conversation flowing in the direction of continuing their long-standing business relationship.

So he hadn't been able to assure Gabriella that there was nothing between him and Hannah. Somewhere between dessert and after-dinner drinks Tyler wondered why it even mattered. Gabriella had been stern in her position that they were only professionally involved. She wasn't interested in any type of entanglements with a man. And Tyler had agreed, about three seconds before he'd kissed her again. After that second kiss, Tyler had been pretty certain that he wanted Gabriella Bennett in his bed. But he wasn't going to force her there. He wanted her to come to him willingly.

"You and Naomi Garret seemed to hit it off," he continued as they moved further down the stretch of the house."

"She's really nice and she's interested in design. So if I end up working here, I'm going to hire her as a part-time assistant."

"Really? Just part-time?"

"Yes. She told me that Dessie had talked to her about possibly taking the position as house manager if the decision is to keep the ranch."

"Really?" Tyler asked again.

"Oh. Maybe I wasn't supposed to say that much. I just assumed that you knew," she said.

Her feet moved steadily over the grassy path. Tyler continued to look down as they walked because her heels were really high, maybe five inches. He'd seen many women who couldn't manage that well. Gabriella not only walked steadily in the heels, she seemed oblivious to how sexy those shoes made her legs look. For as lovely as Gabriella was, she never appeared to know it. Unlike many woman whom Tyler had crossed paths with. He liked that about her.

"No. It's fine. Dessie did mention something about hiring a house manager now that my mother is no longer here to run this place."

"So your father took care of all the ranch stuff and your mother managed the house? Then when they decided to open the resort, she hired her best friend to manage that. There seems to be a lot of love and loyalty surrounding Westwind."

Tyler looked over to her. They were still walking and she was staring straight ahead, holding her purse under her arm.

"It used to be that way," Tyler admitted. He hadn't thought about that aspect since he'd been back, but Gabriella was absolutely right.

"My parents where childhood sweethearts. They married at seventeen and started their life here. I saw my dad doing everything from milking goats to mucking stalls. And my mother could clean a bathroom better than any housekeeping staff I've had in all my adult life. She could also cook a fantastic pot roast and smoothly negotiate half off the price for a piece of furniture." Tyler rubbed a hand down the back of his head. "They were great people."

"And now you're wondering if you can be as great as they were if you choose to run this place?

Her question came as they approached the entrance to the garden his mother had fondly tended. Suddenly, Tyler wanted to know if Gabriella liked the garden too. He led them under the trellis covered in ivy.

"I know absolutely nothing about tending a garden," he said when he watched her looking around."

"This is beautiful," she said and walked ahead of him. "I love how the colors blend seamlessly together. It's probably vibrant and cheerful in the daylight."

"It is. And the cattle are large and healthy. The horses sturdy and from good bloodlines. Everything around here works the way it should. But I bought in exercise equipment because that's how I function. Back in L.A. I spend the bulk of my day either in my home gym or filming at a studio gym. So, yes, I guess you're right," he told her. "I don't know if I can run this place. I don't know if I have what my parents did."

She turned slowly until she faced him. They were a few feet apart because he'd been following behind her.

"Then you make it what you want. You run this place the way you want to. Not the way they did."

"What if I can't?" he asked the question that had been on his mind since the moment he set foot back on this ranch.

"But what if you can?" she proposed instead.

"Stay with me tonight," he said and slipped his hands into his pockets to keep from reaching out for her.

Her reply was immediate. "No."

"Why?"

"Because I'm working for you."

"Not because you don't want to?" he countered. He needed to hear her say it.

"Tyler," she started and then sighed. "We've gone over this already."

"You're right," he told her with a quick nod. "We've gone over the fact that you came to Hobbs Creek to do a job. So let's not rehash that. What if you weren't here to work? What if you and I just met? Would you stay?"

She held her bag in front of her, fingers clenching it tightly.

"I don't know."

"Yes, you do." He took one hand out of his pocket and ran a finger along his chin. "You're a decisive woman. You were offered a job, you accepted and you showed up. You were told to leave because there was no job. You said okay and you packed up. You were told there might be a chance again at that job. You said fine and you stayed. Not once did you say you didn't know, or that you had to think about it. You decided and you acted. That's what you do."

"You don't know me," she replied quietly.

"But I'd like to get to know you," he said. "I'd like to find out what your favorite meal is. Mine used to be shepherd's pie. Are you right-handed or left-handed? Do you snore? Electric toothbrush or regular? Autobots or Decepticons?"

She smiled.

"I kind of like Megatron," she replied.

He grinned, loving the fact that she actually knew who the Transformers were. "It figures."

When they stood in an oddly comfortable silence surrounded by the scent of flowers for a moment, he decided that was enough for the night. If he stood here with her any longer he would be tempted to pick her up and carry her to his bedroom. And while that sounded good, it wasn't her coming to him willingly.

"I'll walk you to your car," he said and turned to head back to the entrance.

When she called his name and touched his arm, Tyler stopped. He looked over his shoulder to see her standing at his side.

"I am attracted to you," she said and then cleared her throat. "I don't know why or how because it wasn't my intention. But there it is."

"There it is," he said and nodded. "So what now?"

"Now I go to my car and head back to the resort. I have a

meeting to prepare for. And you should probably go inside and wash Hannah's lipstick off your cheek."

Tyler instantly recalled Hannah's goodnight kiss and rubbed his left cheek. Cursing he looked at his fingers and saw the smudges of red.

"It's not what you think," he began. "Hannah and I went to high school together. I haven't seen or talked to her since I left Hobbs Creek twenty years ago."

She was nodding now and grinning at him. "It's fine, Tyler. As I said before we don't owe each other any explanations. Besides, I know what Hannah's intention was. She left her mark so I would stay away. I understand."

"But I'm not hers to mark. It's ridiculous and—"

His lips clapped shut when Gabriella rested a hand on his shoulder and leaned in to plant a kiss on his other cheek.

"There," she said. "Now Hannah and I are even, so we can drop this."

Tyler was going to say something else, but Gabriella had walked ahead of him and as he followed, he lost his train of thought because he couldn't keep his eyes off the tempting sway of her ass.

"I'm keeping the ranch," Tyler said the next day when they were all seated in the office on the first floor of the main house.

Gabriella had set up her laptop and turned it to face Jagger, Tyler, Dessie and Clyde who sat two on each side of the table. She stood at the head of the table, pressing the button on the remote she held as she'd gone through every slide with a picture of her design idea and gave a step-by-step explanation of the re-design and staging processes. Dessie had been the only one to ask questions regarding timelines, cost and staff required to see the project through. Clyde was on hand to comment on whether or not the funds for the project would come from the estate as they continued to liquidate some of the older assets George had acquired, or if the brothers' would provide the capital. Jagger leaned back in his chair with his hands clasped behind his head, watching with absolutely no interest at all. Until Tyler made his statement.

"Oh come on, man. You've got to be kidding me." Jagger complained with an exasperated sigh. "She's milking us for cash with this project and there's no guarantee we're going to recoup it in the sale."

"It is a proven fact that updated properties bring higher purchase prices," Dessie said. "Even I know that and I'm not a rancher."

"It doesn't matter because I'm not selling," Tyler told them again. "I want to keep the ranch. It's always been in the West family and I don't plan to be the one who changes that tradition."

"You're a fitness model, Tyler. You're not a rancher. Even though you jumped through hoops to prove to Dad otherwise," Jagger continued.

He was sitting up now, his elbows resting on the glass topped table as he glared at his brother.

"I did my best to learn everything I could from my father," Tyler replied. "I'm not going to apologize for that."

"You haven't been here for twenty years. You have no idea how many changes have been made to this place or how to even run it," Jagger continued.

"Stephen is a great ranch manager. I plan to sit down with him and talk about a permanent position which will give him even more responsibility around here."

Jagger nodded. "Oh, ok. So now you're going to just leave the staff to run the place."

"I'm not going anywhere," Dessie stated. "Audrey and I have done an outstanding job with the resort. We've been turning a steady profit since we opened. And with Gabriella's ideas to refresh the style of the rooms and add a full service gym and spa, we're bound to book even more rooms. I'm excited." She rubbed her hands together and smiled, but Clyde gave her a solemn look.

"You two have to agree," Clyde said. "The ranch was left to both of you, equally."

Jagger sat back then, tossing a smirk toward Gabriella. "I'm selling."

"Then I'll buy your half," Tyler replied without batting an eye. "Name a price. I'll get you a check and you can get back to New York. I know you have a wedding to plan."

Silence fell over the room.

Jagger stood quickly, pushing the chair back so hard it fell over. Dessie jumped at the sound and Gabriella took a retreating step back. Tyler got to his feet slowly, keeping eye contact with his brother.

"I want top dollar," Jagger said pointing a finger at Tyler. "You better hope you can pay it, muscle man."

Tyler looked as if he wanted to jump across the table and punch his brother in the face. Gabriella wouldn't blame him if he did. Jagger West was a certified ass.

Clyde stood then. "Maybe you two should cool off before we finish with this business."

"No," Tyler said. "I've made my decision. Now, you come up with a price so I can pay it and get you off my property."

"Gladly!" Jagger yelled. "I never wanted to come back to this stinking place anyway! And if they hadn't gone and gotten themselves killed—"

He moved so fast Gabriella thought she was watching a movie. Tyler's legs came up and he slid across the table, landing on the other side and taking a swing at Jagger all in one smooth stuntman-looking move. The punch connected with Jagger's jaw and a loud crack echoed throughout the room. Jagger stumbled back and then took a swing in retaliation, but Tyler was once again faster. He blocked Jagger's punch and landed another one in his brother's gut. When Jagger bent forward in pain, Tyler punched him again on the other jaw. Then he pushed Jagger back into the chair that Clyde had vacated.

"I want your offer first thing tomorrow morning and then I want you and Brooke off my land by noon. Do I make myself clear?"

Gabriella's heart was beating wildly, her legs shaking as she stood there watching this all unfold. If Jagger was going to have a smart comeback or attempt to hit Tyler again, everyone in that room knew how this was going to end. Jagger would be carted off to the hospital.

"Fine," Jagger said through a bottom lip that was bleeding and already starting to swell.

"Sorry," Tyler said in a huff as he turned away from his brother and pushed past Clyde and Dessie.

He didn't even look at Gabriella. Which was fine. She wasn't a part of this.

She began packing her stuff as quickly as she could, ignoring the sound of Jagger cursing as Dessie tried to help him.

"Come on into the kitchen to get some ice. You two boys always used to play so rough when you were little," Dessie was saying.

"I don't think Tyler was playing this time, Dessie," Clyde said as he pulled out his phone and stared down at it. "Jagger, you and I can meet in my office in two hours to talk about what you want to offer. I'll prepare the agreement and have it ready for you and Tyler to sign in the morning."

"He needs to lay down and get some painkillers in him, Clyde," Dessie continued.

"No, I think he needs to take care of his business and get out of his brother's way. They're too old and too big for roughhousing now. This is serious. And before I have to bury any of my friend's kinfolk, I'd like to do what I can to keep the peace."

Clyde moved to the other side of the table after speaking and then came down until he stopped near Gabriella.

"I'll need a copy of your proposal and budget for the redesign and decorating to submit to the estate. Congratulations," he said and then touched a hand gently to her shoulder. "I believe you'll do a great job here."

Gabriella smiled, even though she wanted to say there was no way she was working at this emotionally dysfunctional ranch. None at all. These people were crazy. They were volatile and, they were family, she thought finally. She had to grin as she slipped her laptop into her bag. How many times had she watched Renny and Rico fight? Or Alex and Renny? Renny always seemed to be involved in the fighting for some reason.

Jagger grumbled as Dessie continued trying to help him out of the room, leaving Gabriella alone. She sat heavily in the chair and closed her eyes.

She got the job!

She was going to re-design the Westwind Ranch and Resort.

A part of her wanted to jump up and do a happy dance. Another part said a silent prayer that she could do a good job.

"Sorry about that."

Gabriella jumped at the sound of his voice.

He was walking towards her, his black slacks and navy blue shirt making his hair and eyes appear darker. The beard—which she normally didn't like—was very sexy on him and Gabriella sat up straighter in the chair and cleared her throat.

"About giving me the job?" she asked jokingly.

Tyler stopped right beside her. He leaned back against the table and stared down at her with a smile.

"About trying to beat my brother's ass in front of you," he said. "It was unprofessional and probably unbrotherly, or something like that."

"It's okay," she said. "It's not the first time I've witnessed brothers fight."

"Yeah, but it's the first time I busted my adult brother's lip. My mother would be very upset about that."

"And because you're such a good guy, you're upset about it too," she told him before standing again. "It's over. Give him a few hours and Jagger will be saying that too. That's what brothers do."

Tyler shook his head. He reached out and grabbed her wrists before she could move away.

"I don't think so, but I also don't want to think about that right now. I'd rather spend some time with you."

"I can't," Gabriella replied instantly. "I have to get the proposal and budget over to Clyde, then I need to make contact with my account manager at Proctor to let her know what we're doing here. And I should meet with Naomi to go over all the specifics of the project."

He was rubbing his thumbs over the back of her hands, a very distracting action that had her warming in places she should not be warming in, while standing in this office with him.

"Are you saying that because you just watched me slug someone? Or are you running from me again?"

Damn, she so wanted to run. Long, hard and fast! But that wasn't in her nature.

"I'm saying that because even though you could probably toss me on this table and have your way with me at this very moment, I do still have a job to do." She took a deep breath and let it out slowly. Why were his eyes so alluring? And why did looking into them at this close range, make her want to wrap her arms around him and hold him close?

"You're right," he said finally. "I've got some things to take care of too. But I want to go riding with you. In the morning is the best time, riding along the land as the sun's coming up."

"That sounds really nice," she admitted.

"Then it's a date."

A date?

"We're going riding, Gabriella. That's all. So you don't have to look like I just stole your cat," he said with a chuckle.

"I wasn't looking like anything." At least she prayed she wasn't.

He shook his head. "It's cool. I told you I want to get to know you better. I'm also very attracted to you. But I won't do anything you don't want me to do. So in that regard, I'll wait until you come to me and you're ready."

Gabriella didn't see herself ever doing that.

"For now, I'll let you get back to work," he told her and then kissed her quickly on the lips before leaving the room.

Gabriella fell back into the chair again, closing her eyes and wondering what the hell she was doing. Here in this place? And with this man?

CHAPTER 8

*G*abriella had been taking pictures of the rooms on the upper level of the house, getting measurements and letting her ideas settle before she started purchasing materials. And she really intended to walk right past that open door and head down the steps, but her feet wouldn't move. Not after she saw him, legs spread while he lay back on the weight bench, muscled arms moving up and down as his hands gripped the bar holding the weights.

It was crazy because she'd seen men workout before. She belonged to a gym and used to work out religiously before... Anyway, she was no stranger to the sight of a sweaty male body. But this one was different. He was shirtless and when he finally placed the bar back onto the bar catchers and sat up, she had to suck in a breath. His bare chest looked so much better in person than it had in the pictures online. The ones she'd looked at too many times to be considered normal. He spotted her and smiled.

She was wet. In that instant moisture coated her lips and

seeped into her panties. Her breasts felt full, heavy and ready for whatever Tyler wanted to do with them. With a shake of her head she walked towards him.

"Looking for something?" he asked.

His voice was so deep, but smooth as it rubbed along her already sensitive skin.

"I was taking pictures." Gabriella realized how silly that sounded, but was unable to take the words back.

"Then please, continue," he said and stood from the bench.

Gabriella took a step back, lifted the camera and pointed it at him.

He was a model, so striking the perfect pose was nothing new to him. To Gabriella, snapping a picture of every angle of his perfect body was like taking another seductive step closer to him.

He stood with his arms straight down by his sides, fingers clenched into fists. She took the picture of his abs so flawlessly molded. He turned to the side and she pointed the camera downward, snapping a shot of his calves beneath the loose fitting shorts that fell to his kneecaps. Strength. She pressed the shutter button on the camera once more, and could only think of that one word. Every part of his body depicted a level of strength that he so easily displayed. When he turned so that his back was facing her she took another picture of his shoulders, the muscles in his back, and his taut ass. By that time her hands were trembling, her fingers aching to touch.

"I'm waiting on you," he said.

Just a he'd told her on each occasion they'd been together in the last few days.

Gabriella paused because she wasn't ready. She couldn't be.

This wasn't for her. *He* wasn't for her. Hadn't she continued to tell herself that in the almost two weeks that she'd been in Hobbs Creek? She wasn't looking for a romantic connection, or even just a sexual hook-up. She'd sworn off both since January and had no intention of backsliding.

But…he was waiting.

And she was here, looking at his chiseled back and veiny arms. She licked her lips slowly and felt her fingers going lax. The camera fell to the floor soundlessly and she stepped closer to him. They were so close now she could smell him. That all-man scent that had her already swollen vulva lips pulsating.

"Whenever you're ready," he prodded.

Was she ready?

Her arm was lifting as she watched her darker fingers touch the paler skin of his back. The muscles were hard, the skin taut, the sheen of sweat covering him cool to the touch. She put her other hand on him, fingers exploring every contour from his shoulders down to the curve of his torso. She stopped at the ban of his shorts, her heart thumping wildly in her chest. Her lips were dry, or was it her mouth? No, she thought as she licked her lips again, her mouth was watering. Her hands were moving again, tracing a path up both his arms, loving the feel of his corded veins and rigid muscles.

"Gabriella," he whispered.

She was ready.

Her arms went around his waist, her hands flattening over the cool material of his shorts. She gasped when her fingers stumbled upon his thick erection. Before she could stop herself she was wrapping her fingers around him, pressing her breasts to his bare back. He moved, making an adjustment, and then her hand was wrapped around the heated length of his naked dick.

Warmth flooded through her and she leaned in, resting her forehead against his sweaty back. She moved her hand up and down, faster and faster. He pumped into her hand, groaning and whispering her name.

Gabriella had never been this aroused before. She'd never felt this liberated and exhilarated in her life. She nipped the skin of his back as she continued to stroke him and when he hissed out a breath, she licked over the skin where she'd bitten.

"You're gonna make me come, baby," he was saying as he continued to thrust into her hand.

"Yes," she whispered, "I want you to come. I need you to—"

Tyler went still, his dick pulsating in her hand as warm liquid oozed down her fingers.

Gabriella sighed as if she too had come from this little tryst. She kissed his back again, pressing her now tight nipples against him in an effort to continue this gloriously aroused feeling. She wanted it to last forever, to carry her to a place she'd never before dreamed of being.

Tyler wasn't the kind of man she'd ever thought of being with. He wasn't a suit and tie professional and they had nothing in common. Nothing but this passion that had been steadily brewing between them since day one.

"I was ready," she admitted to him. "I was ready for you and so I came to you. Just like you asked."

She waited a moment, letting her own words sink in, before realizing he hadn't replied.

"Tyler?"

He didn't answer.

She slid her hands from around him and was about to call his name again, but she looked down first. Her hands were wet, sticky and covered with blood.

The scream ripped from Gabriella's throat and she sat up so fast in the bed that for a second she felt dizzy. Then she felt sick to her stomach and humiliated that the dream had found her, even as far away as Texas, it had still found her. She ran to the bathroom, ripping off her clothes and stepping quickly into the shower. As the hot water ran over her skin she prayed it cleansed her completely. She prayed for this nightmare to be over and to finally be set free.

A week later, Gabriella sat astride Brown Eyes, her hands comfortably holding the reins as she leaned forward to rub his forehead and whisper to him that she intended to have a nice ride.

"You two finished bonding over there?" Tyler asked.

"We're just getting to know each other," she said. "When I learned to ride my instructor said it was good for rider and horse to be on the same level regarding expectations."

Gabriella had only expected a nice leisurely ride this morning. She wasn't so sure she was going to get it since she hadn't gotten much sleep in the last week. Her days had been spent working with the construction crew she'd hired to knock down a couple walls in the main house, and completely re-configure the employee residences to afford them more privacy. In her opinion, the fact that a husband and wife weren't allowed to bunk together because the current residences were set up like a college dormitory was ridiculous. Dessie and Tyler had agreed once they'd read the memo that Gabriella wrote and emailed to them. She was also supervising Naomi who was a great help and full of ideas.

That kept her busy during the day. At night, it had been another story entirely. She'd had dinner with Tyler each night as a way of going over what was being done and what else would be required. At least that's what she told herself. It wasn't because they were dating. That would have been silly. Especially since Tyler hadn't tried to kiss her or even mention the attraction he'd declared was brewing between them. In fact, Gabriella could safely say that Tyler was being a perfect gentleman.

It was her traitorous body and warring thoughts that had Gabriella tense and distracted. That was why she'd decided to stop putting off the morning ride with Tyler. She was hoping this would give her some quiet time and that the fresh morning air would provide some sort of balance to the upheaval her life had been for far too long.

And that was partly Tyler's fault. He was riding the horse she'd seen him with the first day they'd met, named GG.

"I thought we'd just ride along the line of the property today," Tyler was saying.

Gabriella tightened her thighs against Brown Eyes and guided the horse to fall in step beside Tyler and GG.

"That's fine," she said keeping her gaze straight ahead.

Tyler looked great sitting astride a horse. As if he didn't look great doing everything else. But this morning particularly she'd already noted he was the sexiest cowboy she'd ever seen. His brown boots were scuffed, jeans faded, light blue t-shirt snug against his chest, and dark brown hat, pulled low on his head so that he'd need to tip the brim back to look at her directly. He'd done that the moment she'd walked into the equestrian center and Gabriella had all but lifted a hand to fan herself. This intense attraction had only been magnified by the explicit dreams she continued to have that featured him. Every night since that first one, with them in different scenarios, but pleasure being their foremost objective. And yes, the dream ended with pain, terror, screaming and most often crying. Just as all the others had. That was the part she hated. That she could not separate the before from the now. Because she knew it was unfair to herself and to Tyler.

"You seem a little distant. Is everything okay?"

She'd been looking ahead at the line in the horizon where treetops gave way to the sky with seamless perfection. Clouds that looked like cotton were already floating above, while the sun's bright gold rays had just begun to reach down and land in dramatic slashes along the ground.

"Ah, yeah. Everything's going according to schedule. The crew has already done some demolition and most of the staff have been relocated to the resort for now. Later today, Naomi and I are going to look at some fabric swatches for the upholstery in the den. She has great ideas and Dessie really has a feel for the house since she was so close to your mother."

Gabriella felt like she was talking too much, so she stopped. She noted Tyler nodding his head as she stole a quick glance at him. He was looking to his right, which was a stretch of land leading to the steel gate of one of the cattle corrals on the property.

"I meant, is everything okay with you?"

"Sure. I'm fine. Why would you ask?"

Because she didn't sound fine. Gabriella almost cursed her

own foolishness. One of the keys to actually making someone believe a person was doing just fine, was for that person not to say they were "fine".

"No reason," he said.

Of course there was a reason, but Gabriella wasn't about to press the issue. If he was going to let it go then so was she.

They rode a little further in silence. "You ever think about owning a horse?"

"No," she replied. "I live in a condo in Greenwich. There's a rooftop deck offered to residents for parties and lower level garage parking. But nothing to accommodate a horse."

"Your parents have land. You could build your own paddock. Or there are farms in the area that would board for a fee. I was just thinking that if you enjoy riding and being with horses so much, that you should have one when you go home."

Gabriella hadn't thought about going home. At least, she'd tried her best not to think about it.

"Trying to get rid of me already, Mr. West?" she asked with a chuckle.

His initial response was a smile that packed the punch of a lightning bolt searing straight to her chest. Dammit, she shouldn't have been staring at him. She quickly looked away.

"Just want you to have something that makes you happy."

"What makes you think I'm not already happy?"

"You make me think that," he said solemnly.

Gabriella's fingers clenched on the reins and she looked over to him slowly.

"I never said I wasn't happy."

"Happy people normally talk about their home life at least a little when they're on a work assignment. I know this because my manager and my assistant are always talking about their kids, their dogs, the cleaning service being subpar and a host of other things whenever we're on the road."

"Is that so?" she asked as they came to a small rise and the horses slowed their steps. "What do you talk about when you're on the road?"

He shrugged. "Work."

"But you're working when you're away."

"Seems like I'm always working."

"Not now," she said.

"Yeah. You're right. Now, I'm—"

Gabriella never heard what Tyler said next because gunshots rang loud and clear, crackling in the air and frightening her horse.

Brown Eyes took off, galloping in a different direction, rattling Gabriella until she thought she heard her teeth chatter. She tried to hold on, to keep a grip on the reins, but they were slipping through her fingers. Probably her fear response because her heart was hammering in her chest the faster the horse moved. More shots rang out and Brown Eyes went up on her back legs. Gabriella screamed. She was falling. She knew it because she remembered that feeling all too well. There would be pain. It was coming soon. And there would be...no, there wouldn't be blood. Not this time.

She hoped.

Tyler had waited for the Jeep. He hadn't wanted to. He'd wanted to pick Gabriella up off the ground and put her on his horse to race her back to the house. But he'd thought better of that idea. She was unconscious and therefore he had no idea how extensive her injuries were. Moving her could make them worse.

He had tried to get to Brown Eyes when he saw the horse rearing off. Things had happened pretty quickly. GG hadn't taken kindly to the gunshots either, but Tyler had been able to rein her in. He'd tried to get to Brown Eyes, to help Gabriella take control of him, when the horse went up on its hind legs. He knew then what was going to happen and he'd cursed. Jumping off GG he'd run to where she'd fallen to the ground. She was lying on her stomach, half her face on the grass, arms and legs spread.

"Gabriella!"

Tyler had called out to her he didn't know how many times, but she hadn't responded. He'd touched her face, pushed her hair back and felt along her neck for a pulse. It was there.

Thank God.

That's when he'd yanked his phone from his back pocket and called the house. Stephen was on his way.

There were gunshots. Six of them. Tyler cursed and looked around. Nothing. About twenty feet to the west there was a copse of trees. Easy enough for someone to lay in wait. But nobody knew that he and Gabriella were riding this morning. There was no one on the ranch except staff and the new security system had been installed a few days ago. Yet, someone had been out there, shooting at them.

The Jeep's tires screeched across the grass as Stephen arrived. The ranch manager was out of the truck and running over to them in seconds.

"What the hell happened? You said someone was shooting?" Stephen asked.

Tyler nodded. "Yeah. We need to get her back to the house and call a doctor."

"Dessie was dropping off some curtains when you called, so she was on the phone with paramedics as I headed out."

"I want to get her off this ground," Tyler said.

Stephen touched a hand lightly to his shoulder. "We should wait."

The ranch manager had come down on his knees too and was looking down at Gabriella until now, when he looked up at Tyler.

"It's safer to let the paramedics do it. They'll be here in a few minutes."

A hawk screeched and circled above them. Tyler and Stephen looked up. But Stephen reached behind his back and pulled out a gun.

"You think they're still out here?" Stephen asked Tyler.

Tyler looked around, going back to that copse of trees and narrowing his eyes. "I didn't see anybody running away."

Then again, he hadn't really looked. He'd been much more concerned with watching Gabriella fall off that horse. In those moments time seemed to stand still, something clenching in his chest and constricting his breathing until the moment he'd felt her pulse.

"I'm gonna go and have a look," Stephen said. "You stay with her."

Tyler wanted to find who had done this. He wanted to go back to the ranch, grab his father's gun from the safe and get out on the land just like Stephen, to find the bastard. But he wouldn't leave Gabriella.

Moments later an ambulance drove over the grass, stopping with its flashing lights and blaring siren about ten feet from where Tyler still knelt beside Gabriella. He was quickly shuffled out of the way by a woman and a man who moved efficiently and had Gabriella's neck in a brace in seconds. They moved her gingerly, getting her onto a stretcher just moments before her eyes fluttered open.

Tyler immediately went to the side of the stretcher, taking her hand in his.

Her fingers didn't move and she didn't try to find him with her gaze. She simply stared up to the sky and whispered, "Austin."

"She's staying here tonight," Dessie said matter-of-factly.

They'd just returned from the hospital with Gabriella. She was walking on her own and looking much better than Tyler recalled seeing her six hours ago. That's how long they'd been at the hospital while Gabriella underwent blood tests, head and body scans and exams by a general physician as well as a neurologist. It had seemed like so much for a fall, but they'd needed to be sure. Tyler had to be sure. Whoever was shooting was doing so because of him. His ranch. His problem. With Jagger gone, it was all on him.

"Nonsense. The doctors said I'm physically fine, just a little traumatized which is why I lost conciseness for a few minutes. But there's no reason why I can't go back to the resort," Gabriella argued. "It's probably best if I don't drive myself, but if Stephen or one of the other ranch hands can give me a quick lift, I'll just go and get out of everybody's hair. I've already taken up your whole day."

"Now, that's the nonsense," Dessie continued. She moved closer to Tyler and slapped him on the shoulder. "Help her upstairs. Put her in the guest bedroom and I'll be up in a few minutes to run her a nice warm bath."

"I'm standing right here, Dessie," Gabriella said.

"You are but you're recovering from a fall, so you're not talking sensible right now. Tyler do what I said," Dessie snapped before leaving them standing in the foyer.

Gabriella rolled her eyes at Dessie's retreating back.

"She's bossy," she said with a frown.

Tyler chuckled. "You don't know the half of it. You should see her when she's trying to get you to take some godawful medicine."

He shook his head. "It's not a pretty sight."

She cracked a small smile and replied, "I'll bet it's not."

They were only a couple feet away from each other but it seemed like miles. Tyler hadn't touched her since she'd whispered another man's name. It was probably his fault. When he'd asked her about being happy this morning, he should have just come right out and asked if she were seeing someone else. But during her first tour of the ranch when they were at the equestrian center, she'd told him she wasn't interested in getting involved with any man. He'd taken that to mean she was single. If that were the case, then who the hell was Austin?

"Well, I'd better get you upstairs," he said and moved toward her.

She moved back. "I can manage. Really, Tyler, I'm sure you have things you need to get done around here."

"Nothing more important than making sure you're okay," he said truthfully. "Once you're settled I promise I'll leave you alone."

For a moment he thought he saw sadness flicker across her face. But he was wrong, he was certain of that. He went to stand beside her, wrapping an arm around her waist and said, "Let's go, Ms. Bennett. You're officially a patient at the Westwind Rehabilitation Center."

When she looked up at him and smiled, Tyler felt that constriction in his chest again. He also felt like punching anyone named Austin.

CHAPTER 9

Tyler stood at the window, staring out into the darkness and lifting a glass to his lips. This was his glass of whiskey for the day. It had been added to his daily routine since returning to Hobbs Creek. In return, he ran an extra mile each morning. Except this morning. He'd been doing something else this morning.

"Who knew you and Ms. Bennett were going out for a ride?" Sheriff Alvarez asked.

"No one," Tyler replied without turning around.

He knew everyone closed in the office with him tonight. The sheriff, Stephen and Clyde—people whom Tyler assumed he could trust.

"Who got the horses ready for the ride?"

Tyler didn't want to answer any more questions. The answers weren't getting them anywhere. But the sheriff had a job to do and Tyler could respect that.

"I did," he said solemnly. "I went down to the equestrian

center at four. Gabriella arrived at a little after five. We set out around five-thirty and were only going to ride around the line of the property. We were going at a steady pace, out for no more than forty-five minutes before the shots came."

"From which direction?"

"I don't know."

"Found some shell casings behind those trees," Stephen said.

Tyler turned then. He hadn't seen Stephen since the man had walked off when they were down in the field. By the time they'd returned from the hospital, Stephen was out taking care of more ranch business. Dessie had taken Gabriella dinner in her room and Tyler had closed himself down here in his father's old office.

"So that's where he stood waiting?" Tyler asked, his fingers tightening on the glass.

The sheriff had taken off his hat. Tyler saw it sitting on the edge of the desk. His hair was still mostly black, with the tufts of gray staying cooperative at his ears. He scratched his head and raised a brow as he stared at Tyler.

"Why do you think it's a man?"

Tyler shrugged. "I don't know if it's a man or a woman. I don't know who it is, sheriff. That's the problem. Somebody killed my parents. Then somebody vandalized my property. Then somebody took shots at me and my…a guest on this ranch. Male or female, something is definitely going on here."

"He's got a point," Stephen added with a nod. "We've never had problems like this here at Westwind. After the vandalism we tightened security around here. Added the electronic gate with the call-box entrance and attached security monitors at measured intervals along the perimeter. Nobody gets onto this property without going through security."

"So this shooter has to be someone you know personally, or someone who has the credentials to get onto this property," the sheriff stated evenly.

"There's fifteen year around staff here—ranch hands, wranglers and such," Stephen stated. "And ten summer interns. They come on board early April and stay on until October. They all passed background checks."

Alvarez was scribbling as Stephen talked.

"They all stay on property in the employee residences," Tyler added. He'd made it a point to meet with Stephen for at least an hour each day to learn more about the ranch and the business that went on here. It hadn't been as foreign as he'd first thought it would be, with so many things, memories—good and bad—rushing back into his mind.

"Anybody have security clearance that doesn't stay on the property?" Alvarez asked without looking up from his notepad.

"Everybody's got a security badge now," Stephen spoke.

He was sitting in one of the guest chairs, elbows resting on his knees.

"The vet has one and his assistant. The project manager at the construction company Gabriella hired. That's all. Everybody else has to be buzzed in. Suppliers didn't like that change, but they're getting used to it."

"What about at the resort?"

Alvarez looked from Tyler to Stephen for the answer to that question.

"You can access the resort from the roads winding east behind the ranch. Could be someone staying at the resort, drives right over to the ranch and doesn't have to go through the security gate," he continued.

Tyler shook his head.

"We thought about that when we had the security specialists out here right after the vandalism. We drove the entire property looking for weak spots. There's a new security gate at the road a couple miles out after the resort. We thought about making the resort room keys able to access it, in case guests were just out to see the views, but we decided that would cast too wide a net of unknown people on the property," Tyler told him.

"So only the executive level employees at the resort have security passes to access that gate," Clyde added.

He'd been sitting on the couch near the fireplace, staring down into the untouched gin on the rocks he'd asked Tyler to fix for him.

"Dessie and Audrey are the only ones from the resort that have passes," Clyde finished. "I have a pass because Tyler kept me on as attorney for Westwind. Nobody else has access to the ranch."

"What about your brother?" Alvarez asked.

Tyler frowned. "Jagger left three weeks ago. He's probably enjoying his Jacuzzi in his Manhattan penthouse."

Tyler hadn't liked parting ways with his brother on such a sour note, but, in addition to the tension surrounding the ranch, Jagger hadn't been open to Tyler's suspicions about Brooke. Of course, telling his brother that he thought his fiancé was a manipulating gold digger might have come across better before he'd given Jagger a black eye and a busted lip. But there wasn't much Tyler could have done about that at the time. Jagger always did run his mouth too much.

"Jagger left before the security systems were installed. So we never got a chance to give him a badge," Tyler stated.

"But you would have given him one?"

Tyler didn't like the question any more than he liked the way Alvarez was glaring at him at the moment. "Of course I would have. He's my brother."

"It's no secret that you two had a run-in and you bought out his share of this ranch. Maybe there's some hard feelings. A grudge to settle," Alvarez continued.

"The West boys were raised better than that," Clyde said, coming to a slow stand.

"Jagger is my brother, regardless of whose name is on the deed for this property. We've had many spats in our lifetime, but nothing changes the fact that we're blood," Tyler replied through clenched teeth.

Alvarez nodded. "Gotta cover all the bases."

Tyler would have appreciated it if the bases didn't include his brother, but he took another gulp of his drink instead of replying.

"Now, what do we know about this Gabriella Bennett?" Alvarez had moved on.

"She's been on the ranch for three weeks now. Checked in to the resort on June 24th. Works for The Proctor Group, a national company."

"Dessie hired her to help fix up the ranch for sale," Clyde stated.

"And I hired her to re-design the ranch when I decided to keep it," Tyler added.

"Is that all we know about her? What's on her resume?"

Tyler tried not to frown because he knew Alvarez was paying particular attention to his reactions to the questions.

"I know that she's good at her job. She spends the bulk of the day here at the ranch or down at the employee residences. And at night she returns to the resort," Tyler told him.

Clyde spoke up again. "Sometimes she walks around the resort taking pictures and measurements. Dessie says she's determined to do a good job."

Alvarez nodded. He hadn't written down anything Tyler or Clyde had said about Gabriella.

"Word around town is you've got a personal interest in her," the sheriff said after a few moments of silence.

Tyler did frown then. He hated gossip. It was a part of the culture in Hobbs Creek and in L.A. Seems no amount of running or growing up had afforded him an escape from that fact.

"Word around town is not my word," Tyler replied.

"So she's not upstairs sleeping in one of those rooms?" Alvarez asked. "She's not going to spend the night here on your ranch?"

"She was shot at here on my ranch," Tyler told him.

He emptied his glass and set it on the desk in front of him.

"Could that be because of a jealous lover? You've got a pretty good following with your videos and pictures and stuff," the sheriff continued.

Tyler spoke in as calm a voice as he could muster, considering he wanted to punch the sheriff for reinforcing the guilt Tyler already felt about what happened to Gabriella today. "I wasn't involved with anyone before I came here and I'm not involved with anyone now."

"That's not what Hannah Palmer's saying," Alvarez persisted like a dog with a bone.

"Now, really, sheriff. Are you going to stand here and start bringing up all the town gossip? Or are you going to get out there and find out who was shooting at these kids this morning?" Clyde asked and then walked over until he was standing face-to-face with the sheriff.

"This session is over. Tyler has given you all the information he has. And so has Stephen. If you need to speak with these men about what's happened on this ranch today and the day of the vandalism, you can contact my office to schedule an appointment."

Alvarez tilted his head. "You sure that's how you want to play this, Clyde? I get the impression you don't know much of what's going on out here these days. George is gone so you're not in and out the way you used to be. There's a new West in town and he's doing things his way."

"He's doing things the way his daddy taught him," Clyde continued. "And I'm doing things the way my law school degree taught me. Now, again, this session is over."

Alvarez took his time flipping the cover over his notepad and sliding the pen into the holder on its side. He tucked that pad in his back pocket and then picked up his hat from the edge of the desk. Placing the hat on his head, Alvarez tipped it back and looked at Stephen, then Clyde, and finally to Tyler.

"I'll be going now," he said. "But I'll be back."

"Hopefully with news that you've caught the person responsible," Tyler told him.

Alvarez nodded before leaving.

When he was gone, Tyler sat heavily into the leather office chair.

"He's going to keep digging until he finds something," Clyde said.

"Good." Tyler nodded. "Let's hope he finds something fast. Before I have to take matters into my own hands."

Gabriella's cell phone was broken. It was on the dark wood floor in a million little pieces. So she reached over to the night stand to pick up the land line. She pressed the TALK button and put the phone to her ear.

He was laughing.

The way he used to laugh whenever they watched a stand-up comedy special. His favorites were Kevin Hart and Katt Williams. She preferred to watch an actual movie, but she'd compromised for him. Because that's what one was supposed to do in a relationship.

He continued to laugh as her hand shook. He was mocking her, again. And Gabriella couldn't stand it another minute. She tossed the phone across the room. It crashed through the window. The noise was so loud, she woke up.

With a hand to her heaving chest, Gabriella screamed in frustration. And then she remembered where she was. She clapped a hand over her mouth and sat in the middle of the queen-size bed willing the tears not to fall. She was so sick of this! She'd just let her chin drop to her chest and closed her eyes when she heard the door to the bedroom open. Jumping off the bed quickly, she grabbed the first thing she saw. Because it was the middle of the night and the only light in the room were the slithers of moonlight coming through the partially opened blinds, that was the pillow off the bed.

The light came on and Tyler ran over to where she stood.

"Are you alright? Did something happen?"

He was asking questions, his concerned gaze raking over her. She felt bare in a way that far surpassed the fact that she was wearing a nightshirt that barely covered her butt.

"I…ah…I'm—"

"Here, let me take this," he said coming closer and easing the pillow out of her grasp.

She'd still been holding it above her head like she was ready to hit him—or whoever was coming into the room—with it.

"I just," she started and then stopped. Gabriella let her arms fall by her sides and fought for the composure she always displayed in business situations. In fact, she made a point of displaying a carefully composed and often exuberant persona at all times, in front of all people. It was how she'd always been able to cope.

"Had a bad dream, I guess," she said with a shrug. "Sorry to have wakened you."

"No need to apologize," Tyler said. "I can go down to the kitchen and fix you some hot tea, or if you want to stay up for a while, I can stay with you."

His tone was low and soothing and almost put Gabriella at ease. Almost, but not quite. She'd been down that road before and had sworn she wouldn't travel that path ever again.

"No," she said adamantly.

He tossed the pillow on the bed.

She sighed.

"I'm not being a bitch," she said. "Or maybe I am. But I don't mean to be."

She cleared her throat. "I'm fine. I've had bad dreams before and I survived. Thanks for coming to my rescue, again, but I'll be okay."

He gave her a curt nod, and said, "But you're not okay right now."

She wasn't. She was anything but okay. Her stomach was doing some weird flip-flopping, her temples were throbbing from trying to forget the latest disturbing dream and the air conditioner really worked well in this house because not only were her nipples growing hard, but her legs were chilly.

"I am," she insisted, being careful not to say she was fine. "I'm good. Really, I am. You can go back to bed. I promise I'll be quiet for the rest of the night."

"You don't have to be," he said. "Quiet, I mean. If you're afraid, you can say something. I know it's not normal to go riding and have someone shoot at you. I promise you I'll find out who it was, but until I do, I plan to keep you perfectly safe."

"Oh," she said because it was all she could think of.

He thought what happened this morning was what had frightened her. Oh, how Gabriella wished it were that simple.

"It was just a dream, Tyler. I promise you I'm okay now," she said.

He nodded and turned to walk toward the door. That's when she noticed that he was only wearing shorts, no shirt, no socks, and no shoes. And she had no idea what the hell she was doing.

"You can call me if you need anything."

"Huh?" she asked when she realized he'd stopped at the door and was staring at her expectantly.

"If you wake up again or if you can't fall asleep," he said. "I'm right next door. You can call me on my cell or just come over. I don't mind."

"I won't," she replied. "Because I'm okay."

"Right. You're okay."

He gave a half smile and then a little wave of his hand before pulling the door closed behind him. The moment Gabriella heard the click of the door closing, she fell back on the bed and bit back a groan.

She had to get herself together. There was no room in her life for regrets or even memories. What happened with Austin was over and done with. She'd survived and moved on. The words seemed easier and even true when they were recited in her mind. As for her daily activities, well, that still left a lot to be desired.

Thanks to Austin's latest text messages and the dreams, Gabriella felt like she was reliving that nightmare all over again. It was so unfair. She'd worked so hard to move past this, to put herself back together after being in love with Austin had shattered her. And none of it had worked. She was still a mess. And if she didn't get her act together, she was going to show Tyler how broken she really was.

Unless…

Her mother believed in fate. How many times had Beatriz told her children about things happening beyond their control, and how sometimes those things were for the best? Too many for Gabriella to count. What if meeting Tyler was fate? What if Gabriella was meant to be in this place at this time, with this man, so that she could prove that she was finally over Austin and all that he'd done to her?

What if the physical attraction she'd felt toward Tyler from day one was fate and not just hormones?

What if she took him up on his offer and walked next door to see if that's where fate was leading her?

What…what the hell was she doing?

Gabriella turned off the light and climbed back into bed. Her mind was playing awful tricks on her. First with the bad dreams and then by adding the fantasies of Tyler into those dreams. She was here to do a job, not to get laid.

Even if she did kind of need the latter, pretty badly.

Tyler punched the pillow like it owed him money. He'd been tossing and turning for the last half hour. Sleep wasn't in the mood for him tonight, something he'd accepted hours ago when he'd finally left the office and come upstairs.

He'd paused by the closed bedroom door and stared at it for endless seconds. Then calling himself the biggest fool, he'd walked the extra steps to his bedroom and closed the door. He told himself to stop thinking about her and the fact that she could have been shot and killed today, because of him. The cold shower he'd taken had been a form of punishment for giving her a reason to stay here and had nothing to do with his hourly hard-on each time he thought about her.

This wasn't about sex. He'd put her life in danger, all because he hadn't wanted her to leave. Because he wanted to sleep with her.

The shower hadn't been punishment enough.

He'd spent the next few hours lying in bed berating himself yet again for the mistakes he continued to make in his life. Tyler knew that was normal. It was a part of growing. He'd read enough motivational books to get the picture. Do things, make mistakes, learn a lesson, stop doing things, and be a better person. That's how it worked. For some people. For him, it was more like do things, feel bad, do more things, feel worse, do the ultimate thing, and what? Get somebody killed? He'd been cursing himself and holding his pillow over his face in the hope that maybe it would stop his breathing, when he heard her scream.

It was like hearing the gunshots all over again. His heart stopped and he just took off, trying to get to her as fast as he could. To make sure she was alright. It was imperative that she was alright.

Why, he had no idea.

Or rather, he didn't want to think too hard on that particular idea.

Because it wasn't for him. He'd known that after the whole Hannah episode. Love, relationships and happy ever after weren't on the agenda for Tyler West. As for Jagger, well, he'd always won in that department. For years Tyler had thought it ironic that his father considered him the best at ranch work and Jagger hated that. While Jagger always won with the women, Tyler used to hate that.

And she was standing there, holding that pillow up like she was ready to swing it at him or whoever came into that room. She was ready to defend herself, but he'd come to her rescue. It was weird, the feeling that she didn't really need him to make sure she was okay, slapping against his guilt for putting fear in her life in the first place. He couldn't quite get a handle on it. Nor could he stop staring at the way her raised arms lifted that already short nightshirt she was wearing so that he could see the pink panties that covered her mound.

The stark fear and pain he saw etched across her face had jerked him out of the fantasy where he was pulling those panties down her long bronzed legs, with his teeth. He'd gone to her and tried to help and she'd told him she didn't need his help. So he'd left. Yet, even now, as he lay in the bed, in the room next to hers, he still felt like he was standing right there in front of her, struggling for the right words or actions that would...what? Make him the winner where women were concerned this time? Tyler groaned at the sheer stupidity of that thought.

Then he jumped at the soft knock on his door.

He got out of the bed and walked to the door, surprised once again by the sight of her when he opened it.

"You told me to come to you when I was ready. You said you would be waiting," she said.

She was standing with her shoulders squared, her hands clasped in front of her, and that wicked short nightshirt still playing a mean game of peak-a-boo with him.

"I was waiting," he admitted as he knew now that was the real reason he hadn't been able to sleep.

She licked her lips quickly and smiled. "Well, I'm here. And I'm ready."

CHAPTER 10

*T*here was no fear in her eyes. No pain etched along her face. Nothing, but natural beauty staring back at him so starkly, Tyler felt like he'd been slapped in the face and commanded to wake up from a dream.

"Are you not ready now?" she asked after he'd closed and locked his bedroom door.

"I'm trying to be sure we're both on the same page here, Gabriella," Tyler said.

He wished like hell it was as simple as saying ready, set, go and jumping into bed with her. A few weeks ago, that may have been the case. He would have gladly ripped her clothes off and thrust deep inside her without any words other than consent. Tonight, things were different.

She stood at the foot of his bed, her arms behind her back, feet bare, and hair a tangled mess haloing her face.

When he'd come back into his room Tyler had switched on the lamp on the nightstand beside his bed. So there was a golden hue surrounding her, making her appear almost ethereal. Tyler closed his eyes. He took a deep breath and released it slowly before opening them again.

"We agreed there was an attraction between us. We've spent weeks getting to know each other. You were ready first. You said you would wait for me to come to you. I'm here," she said. "I'm ready."

"What about Austin?"

The words were tough to speak because Tyler didn't know if he really wanted to hear the answer. If she told him that she was in love with another man at this very moment, he wouldn't like it. He'd live with it, but he wouldn't like it at all.

She didn't speak immediately, but the look on her face said it all. Shock, trepidation, annoyance and then resolve.

"You whispered his name when you regained consciousness," he told her before she could ask him how he knew the name. The last thing he wanted her to think was that he'd done any type of background check on her, beyond the Google search they'd both admitted performing on each other.

"Austin and I broke up months go," she stated slowly, evenly. "I don't know why I would have whispered his name."

"Are you still in love with him?"

"No. If I was, I wouldn't be here asking you to make love to me."

And he wouldn't be standing there trying to keep a tight rein on his desire.

"I know what I want, Tyler. I know who I'm with."

She grabbed the hem of her nightshirt and lifted it up and over her head.

Tyler watched the material fall to the floor and then he

looked at those white painted toe nails once more. They were the first part of Gabriella Bennett he'd ever seen. His gaze traveled upward past the bronzed skin of her calves, to the smooth curve of her thighs, and the puff of her mound covered in a wisp of pink lace.

There were no more words. No more excuses or explanations. Nothing mattered now except kissing her.

With that thought he closed the space between them cupping her face in his hands and tilting his head to touch his mouth to hers. Her arms immediately circled his neck as she returned his kiss with fervor. Damn, he loved kissing her. There was no hesitancy whenever their lips touched. Only the instant flicker to the flame that hummed constantly between them. Her blunt nails scrapped his scalp as her hands moved through his hair.

He needed more than just this kiss, this time. He needed to touch her, everywhere. His hands moved down her body, his skin singed by the heat of her skin so soft and pliant beneath his palms. He grasped the mound of her breast, groaning as his tongue continued to stroke over hers. Her nipple was already pebble hard and his dick jumped each time it rubbed against his palm. She tugged at his hair and Tyler moaned.

With her body flush against his, Tyler lifted her, her thighs parting, legs clasping around his waist. He carried her around to the side of the bed where he turned and sat on the edge. He tore his mouth away from hers only long enough to lick along the line of her neck, his tongue tracing a wet trail down her skin until the dark circle of her nipple was in his mouth. He sucked her deep, while palming the other breast. She arched her back, pressing her already damp mound against his abs.

"You taste like honey," he grumbled as he moved from one breast to the next. "The sweetest fuckin' honey."

And Tyler gorged on her, loving the sounds coming from her as well as the way her hands moved over him. From his hair down to his neck, to where her blunt-tipped nails now scraped over his back. He couldn't get enough.

He moved fast, flipping her from his lap to lay her back on the bed, then immediately lifting her legs, so that her ankles rested on his shoulders. Tyler tore that pretty little piece of pink fabric away and licked the clean-shaved curve of her mound. Her knees fell down and she opened like the petals of the prettiest blossom before him.

His mouth was on her flesh before he could think of another word to say. It didn't matter, no words would have accurately described how sweet it was to run his tongue along her plump folds, lapping the thick rivulets of her essence hungrily.

"Tyler."

She whispered his name.

He'd heard it and wanted desperately to hear it again. So he licked her faster, slipping a finger into her entrance and moaning with the delectable tightness that gripped him. She squirmed beneath him. Lifting her hips to meet his mouth, her fingers grasping the sheets. He sucked the tight bud of her clit and she bucked off the bed, his name coming in a repeated litany that was like music to his ears.

Moments later, when she'd settled pliantly on the bed, Tyler kissed the inside of her thighs. He rubbed his hands up her torso and tweaked the still hard nipples of her breasts. As he raised up over her he thought she looked like a dream lying there. Her hair spread wildly over the sheets and her body beautifully naked. That sensation in his chest started to rise again, but the pressure of his almost painful arousal demanding to be set free from the constraints of his shorts won.

Tyler stepped back from the bed and pushed his shorts down his legs. He picked his wallet up from the nightstand and found a condom inside. Coming to stand at the edge of the bed between her open legs, their gazes locked as he rolled the condom over his length. When it was done, he waited. Not sure why, but he just did not move.

Until she lifted her arms from the bed, beckoning him to her as she said once more, "I'm ready."

Gabriella wasn't ready.

Not for the instant flash of passion that burst before her eyes the moment Tyler thrust his full length into her. He'd lifted one of her legs, his fingers wrapped securely around her ankle. Holding that leg at an angle he pulled her closer to the edge of the bed and pushed inside her without speaking a word. She couldn't imagine what he could have said as a preamble to such blinding pleasure. "Get ready." "Hold on tight." "Beware."

She gasped as he stroked her long and slow. Really, he moved deliberately slow now, easing into her inch by damn inch and then pulling out in the same fashion. Her legs were trembling, cool air brushing over her nipples causing her to shiver as her teeth sank into her bottom lip.

"Please," she moaned.

"Please what?" he asked going still over her.

She looked up to see him staring down at her. His blue eyes a seductively dark green now, his hair a ruffled mess. She almost smiled as she recalled her fingers doing that. But her gaze went lower to his tapered torso and his thick length now coated with her desire, paused just on the brim of her center. It was the most erotic thing she'd ever seen, the partially ensconced penis waiting eagerly to sink deeper. Gabriella licked her lips and whispered, "More. Now!"

When he shook his head and lowered her leg to the bed, Gabriella wanted to scream, just in case he hadn't heard her instruction.

"I don't want this to go too fast," he said.

He eased all the way out of her and stretched out on the bed beside her. Wrapping his arm around her waist Tyler pulled her onto her side until their bodies touched.

"I want to remember every second of this night with you, Gabriella."

He kissed the tip of her nose, then the corner of her mouth. He licked his tongue over her lip and she shocked them both by extending her tongue to rub softly against his. Their gazes held and Tyler eased them slowly into a kiss that was more than Gabriella had ever experienced. It wasn't just hot and explosive the way the kisses she'd previously shared with Tyler were. No, this was something else. It was like a fast-acting drug, pulling her deep, down into an unfamiliar vortex. He kept his eyes open, so she did the same, but it was a struggle, because the kiss was making her languid and relaxed and safe.

In the next moments Tyler was running a hand down her side, cupping her bottom before easing her leg over his. He broke the kiss the second the tip of his sex touched the mouth of hers.

"I want you to remember every second of tonight, too. Every touch, every sensation."

He pushed into her slowly.

She moaned. "I will."

He started to move, a little faster than before, like a slow stirring of something that planned to burn long and bright.

"I want you to remember me," he whispered before licking her lips again.

"I will," she replied and knew that it was the absolute truth.

She would remember his touch, the sight of him inside her, and the feel of him filling her completely. She would never forget how warm and comfortable it felt to be in his arms and how, even though she'd been the one to come to him, there had been no mistaking that he wanted her and had been waiting for her.

That made her feel amazing. So much so that she began to move with him, giving him so much more than just her body. When his hands moved up and down her back and he dipped his head to kiss along her neck, Gabriella nipped the skin of his shoulder. She licked that spot and thrust her hips into his. When he reached down and hooked her knee in his arm and leaned her back to once again change the depth of his thrusts, she closed her eyes to the pleasure. And then when he stopped just before making her come and rubbed his thumb over her chin, staring deep into her eyes, she whispered, "I will remember you, Tyler."

He rolled her onto her back at that moment and pounded into her until they were both breathless, climbing together to reach a blissful climax.

A half hour later, after they'd taken a quick shower and

returned to the bed, Tyler wrapped her in his arms. She'd never been spooned or cuddled before. Austin was always in a hurry.

"I don't sleep with the boss," she said abruptly.

"I never sleep with clients," he replied.

Gabriella closed her eyes. She wanted to remember this feeling forever, the one where his arms were around her in the dark of night and she wasn't in the bed alone.

"And I don't share," he continued. "When I'm sleeping with a woman, I don't expect her to be sleeping with anyone else. I give her the same respect."

"I agree," she whispered.

"Then it's settled." He leaned in closer and kissed her cheek. "Let's get some sleep."

Gabriella snuggled back against him and for the first time in she couldn't even count how many nights, she fell soundlessly asleep.

"My gracious, it's three o'clock in the morning, Dessie," Clyde grumbled as he climbed down from the passenger side of his red Silverado.

"I know what time it is, Clyde. You've been reminding me every five seconds since I answered the phone."

He walked around the truck just in time to extend his hand and help his wife of thirty-one years down. She was still as pretty as the day he'd bumped into her grocery cart at the supermarket. Still as bossy too.

"Now, I don't know what's going on, but Audrey never calls me at this hour and she certainly never screams so loud through the phone that my ear drums are still ringing," Dessie said. "And you could have stayed in bed."

"Wasn't about to let you get on the road at this time of night by yourself," Clyde told her.

Plus, he had a bad feeling about this. Truth be told, he'd had a bad feeling settling in the pit of his stomach since Dessie had called him yesterday morning to say that there'd been shots fired at the ranch and that the ambulance was taking Gabriella to the hospital. Things hadn't been right since George and Verna were found in that burning truck. And Clyde was afraid they were gonna get much worse before long.

They walked through the front doors of the resort. Morena, one of the night clerks was at the front desk wearing a worried look to go with the black and yellow Westwind Resort uniform.

"Oh, Ms. Dessie. I'm so glad you're here. They're still upstairs in the room. They didn't want anyone else wandering in there, but I'm supposed to tell you to come right up. Right away!" Morena exclaimed in one breath.

Dessie walked over to her and patted Morena's shaking hand as she'd set it on the desk.

"Alright, take a deep breath. Go get yourself some water and calm down. I'm here and I'll take care of everything," Dessie promised.

She would try, Clyde thought as he walked to the bank of elevators to the left of the front desk area. There were only three floors to the resort, but it was a long building and had sixty guest rooms. Gabriella had some great ideas for expansion that Dessie was really excited about.

They stepped off the elevator on the third floor and walked down the hallway to the end. Only suites were on this floor.

They had double the space of the standard rooms below and they each had walkout patios with gorgeous views of the hills.

"Oh my Lord," Dessie mumbled as they walked.

"What?" Clyde asked while looking around because he thought she'd seen something.

"That's Gabriella's room," she said just before they came to the open door and stepped inside.

It was a mess. A horrific mess. Black paint splashed all over the walls. The curtains were slashed, pillows on the bed left in tatters. The sheets had been drenched in paint, and the mirrors were cracked.

"Ms. Dessie! Ms. Dessie!" Audrey yelled when they walked further into the room.

The thin wisp of a girl came running and draped her arms around Dessie.

"I'm so glad you're here. I don't know what happened or what to do. Willie said he was delivering room service to the room down the hall and he heard a noise down this way. When he got here the door was open but nobody was in here. The patio door was open too and the room was like this," Audrey said.

"Where's Willie now?" Clyde asked as his booted feet crunched over broken glass from the bedside lamps when he walked across the floor.

"I'm right here, sir," Willie replied. "There's black paint in the soaker tub and the water was left running so it started to flood. We've got damage to the floor and a little to the room beneath. I got maintenance down there now."

"Good job, Willie. Thanks for chipping in," Dessie said.

"Now, Audrey I need you to get your head on straight. We'll have to call the sheriff out here and let him do his thing."

"Don't touch anything else," Clyde told them. "In fact, let's just clear out and let Alvarez get down here with his guys."

"Some of Gabriella's things were still in here. Naomi came to get her clothes yesterday, but she left some stuff. You want me to gather them before Sheriff Alvarez arrives?" Audrey asked.

"That's not a good idea," Clyde said.

Dessie immediately turned to him. "That's her personal stuff, Clyde. We can't let Alvarez and his deputies start pawing through her stuff."

"It's evidence," Clyde told her. "Everything in this room is evidence now. We shouldn't even be standing in here thinking about contaminating things. So let's get on out. We'll call over to the ranch house from downstairs."

"No," Dessie said as she walked ahead of him to the door. "Those two were shot at not even twenty-four hours ago. I'm not calling and waking them up out of their sleep to give them more bad news. We'll wait until sun's up and go out there personally."

"I think that's a good idea," Audrey said. "This is gonna upset them more."

"Yeah, but they gotta know," Clyde said. "They gotta be prepared."

He didn't finish his thoughts because he didn't want Dessie to know that Alvarez was sniffing around Gabriella's past to see what he could dig up. If he wasn't already, the sheriff was going to be hot on her trail and Tyler's for that matter, the moment he saw that room. All hell seemed to be breaking loose in Hobbs Creek, and Clyde wondered who, if any of them, would survive.

CHAPTER 11

"*I* like my kale cooked in ham hocks and seasoned to perfection on a plate with a couple slices of baked ham and my grandmother's homemade baked macaroni and cheese," Gabriella said as she leaned over the counter, watching Tyler.

He was taking a handful of greens—a mixture of kale and spinach, as he'd just informed her—and dropping them into a blender.

"This twelve ounce drink will give you an energy boost unlike any of those sugar-laced drinks or any off-the-market pills," he told her. "Finish cubing those pineapples?"

"Yup!" she said with fake exuberance.

"Okay, pour them in," he instructed.

She did and he scooped out a few spoons of plain Greek yogurt. Adding that, coconut oil, lime juice, almond milk and green tea, he snapped the top onto the container and hit the blend button.

Gabriella shook her head.

"When I go over to my parents' house on Saturday mornings my mother cooks fluffy buttermilk pancakes, cheesy scrambled eggs and bacon."

"And when you're finished eating all you want to do is curl up on the couch and fall asleep," he said.

He stopped the blend cycle and lifted the top to taste his concoction.

"This is much healthier," he confirmed, before squeezing in more lime juice and hitting blend again.

"It's turkey bacon," she replied. "My dad isn't big on pork products."

"What about the ham hocks in your kale and baked ham slices on your plate?" he asked.

"That's my plate," she said with a grin. "Dad gets roasted turkey, rice and gravy and his greens are cooked in turkey necks."

After chuckling with her, Tyler poured them two glasses of the disturbingly green concoction. "You do not have that body from eating that way on a daily basis."

She had accepted the glass he offered her and was still staring down at it, when he spoke.

"No, not all the time. That's a holiday dinner. I tend to cook lighter meals and I hit the gym at least three times a week. But that's as strict as my health regimen goes."

"You drink it, Gabriella. Not stare at it," he chided and took another gulp of his drink.

He looked so good standing in that big country kitchen wearing a wrinkled t-shirt, sweat pants and bare feet that

Gabriella could almost forget what he was trying to get her to drink. Almost.

She took a deep breath and brought the glass to her lips for her first taste. He watched her closely. Months ago that would have been too closely. She would have wanted him to look away, or she would have turned away. Funny how time, and most likely, people, changed things.

Gabriella sipped the smoothie and didn't gag. She figured that was a good sign.

"You like it don't you?" Tyler asked, his grin too big and too natural for her to say anything negative.

"It's alright," she replied.

He laughed. "Just can't give me any props, huh?"

"I'm still drinking it," she said after another sip.

"Come on, let's go out on the back porch for a bit."

He had his drink in hand and Gabriella kept hers as she followed him out. She did have on socks, cut-off jean shorts and a tank top. But there was no one else at the ranch house this morning so she figured she wasn't being too unprofessional. Considering she'd spent the night in the boss's bed, she figured she'd already blown that cover anyway.

The back porch was just that, wood beams stretching about twenty feet toward the end of the house and a wood covering. It was being knocked down next week and rebuilt with sturdier wood and all new furniture. Tyler sat in one of the four rocking chairs that faced the open fields. Gabriella sat in the one beside him. For the first few minutes they rocked back and forth in the chairs without speaking.

Gabriella sipped from the glass again and watched as the sun created the perfect focal point to a lush western backdrop. Green grass stretched far and wide, with hills dipping and diving to break the monotony. The tips of trees in the distance stretched up and appeared to touch the gold and orange of the early morning sky. It was quiet, except for the occasional mooing of a cow that seemed to echo through the air.

"We used to sit out here some nights," Tyler spoke. "Me, Jagger, Mom and Dad. Of course we didn't sit in these chairs. We'd dubbed them 'old people' chairs back then."

He laughed and Gabriella smiled. She liked hearing him laugh. He didn't do it often.

"My dad would be tired after the day's work. He'd sit back with a glass of lemonade, his dark brown hair ruffled because he never paused during the day to comb it. My mom would be wearing one of her pretty dresses. She always wore dresses, except for the days she went down with the horses. And she always cooked a big dinner. I used to wonder why I wasn't fat as one of the pigs in the pen, I used to eat so much. But then getting up at four every morning and working straight through until the noon break for lunch, only to start back for another three or four hours, was plenty of exercise."

"You liked growing up on a ranch," she said.

"It was my life," he replied. "My dad said it was my future."

"But you didn't want it."

He sounded so much like her. Marvin Bennett had expected all of his children to grow up, go to college and work at his family's company. It hadn't worked out that way.

"I didn't want to risk having a family and separating them the way I felt this ranch did."

"You're talking about you and Jagger," she said.

Tyler finished his smoothie. He leaned forward and set the

glass on the porch floor beside the rocker before sitting back again.

"We used to be close," he continued. "We were brothers, only two years apart in age. We even shared a room until I was ten. Jagger packed up and moved to his own room saying he needed his space. My mom thought it was funny. My dad didn't think too much of Jagger by then, so he rarely commented on what he was doing. I didn't want to be the better brother. I just thought it was easier to do what my dad said and to do it right. Jagger was more independent I guess. He did what he wanted, when he wanted. And had a better time of it, I believe."

Gabriella drank more before deciding she was done with the smoothie. She followed Tyler's lead and set her glass down before tucking her legs under her in the chair.

"Maybe he didn't," she replied finally. "I used to think that Adriana had the best life ever. She started modeling when she was young and she traveled. My mother went with her of course, in the early years. I couldn't go because I had school. But every time I saw a picture of her I thought she was beautiful. Her smile was so big and so bright she had to be having a great time. Just a couple of years ago I learned that those times weren't all good for her. She had run-ins with some pretty mean-spirited people and she even battled with an eating disorder. I wished then that I hadn't been so naïve that I'd looked a little harder to see what was really going on with her."

"The modeling industry can be tough, especially on young girls. But I don't know that you could have done anything to change what she was going through," Tyler told her.

"Not change it," Gabriella said with a shrug. "But at least be there to help her through it."

"Yeah," he said and leaned forward again, this time resting his elbows on his knees. "I left Jagger here. I left my parents and this ranch and I didn't look back."

"You went to live your life. You don't have to penalize yourself for that." Gabriella sighed. "I spent the first years of my college life feeling so guilty every time the professor handed me a paper with a big 'ole 'C' as a grade. I thought about how much my parents were paying for me to go to school and get a good education and I was totally blowing it. But eventually I realized it was because going to a great college and getting a good education was their dream for me. It wasn't my dream for myself."

"You're a lot smarter than you look," he said.

Gabriella glanced over to find him staring at her. "Gee, thanks. Pretty girls aren't expected to be smart, huh? Thought we were years past that."

"No, that's not it. I knew you were intelligent when you walked into the equestrian center that day. I could hear it in your tone as you resisted cutting me down when I was being so rude to you. You were about your business so I assumed you'd studied well and prepared for your meeting. But to me, that's different than being smart. You get people and you react to them accordingly. I watched you do it with Brooke and then with Hannah."

"I won't call them anything other than their given names, but those two are quite a pair."

"You're so much more," he said. "So much more than either of them could ever imagine."

Her heart skipped a beat. Like it actually did some type of thump and stop action in her chest as she stared at him.

"You're more too, Tyler. More than you've been giving yourself credit for. You're keeping this ranch in the family when you have a thriving business that you should be tending to. And you're taking the time to learn how to do it right, when you could have easily returned to your business and let Stephen run the day-to-day operations here."

"I may have to do that at some point," he told her. "My manager's going crazy with the emails and Skype calls. They want me on the road promoting the sportswear line and I've been pushing off meetings to discuss the gym franchise."

"Because a part of you is still here on this ranch. It's still your home."

"I can't leave until I know what happened to them and why," he said solemnly.

"I understand." And she did. If it were her parents Gabriella knew that she would want answers to.

They fell into a comfortable silence again. It was comfortable, she realized, because she hadn't once thought about reaching for her phone to check for messages—the good or the bad. She hadn't thought about the work she needed to get done before Monday morning or even the scrambled eggs and bacon she'd been craving when she woke up. She'd been content just being with Tyler, drinking that concoction that wasn't as bad as she'd thought it would be, and sitting on this porch the way his parents had.

It was probably a quaint looking scene, one that Gabriella had never pictured for herself. But it was about to be interrupted, she thought as she heard footsteps coming from in the house.

"There you are," Dessie said as she made her way out onto the porch.

Clyde was right behind her, and the sheriff was with them too.

"Good morning," Tyler said.

His demeanor had changed. In just those few seconds, he'd stood up, his jaw set, eyes going a bit steely. Gabriella stood too and without thinking, went to stand beside Tyler.

"What happened?" she asked because from the way she and Tyler were being stared at, something was definitely going on.

"There was an incident in the middle of the night," Dessie said.

"What kind of incident?" Tyler asked.

"I'm going to need to speak to Ms. Bennett privately," Sheriff Alvarez announced.

"Not without her attorney present," Clyde stated evenly.

Alvarez frowned. "You gonna represent them all, Clyde?"

"Until they tell me otherwise, yes," Clyde replied and looked to Gabriella.

She didn't know what was happening, but her hands had already begun to shake. "No. I mean, yes, he's right. He's my attorney," she said with a nod to Clyde. "What do you need to speak to me about, Sheriff?"

Alvarez's brow was creased. He stood with his legs slightly spread, and hands on his hips. It was meant to be an imposing stance and it was. Tyler's hand on her shoulder calmed Gabriella instantly.

"I want you to tell me why someone would break into your room at the resort and tear it to shreds? You leave some secrets behind in Connecticut that might have followed you here?" he asked.

That calm that she'd felt was brief. The gorgeous landscape she'd just been marveling at, the wonderful man she'd slept with last night and spent valuable time with this morning, it all melted away. So that fear and despair could return.

Austin Sterner was here in Hobbs Creek.

Tyler slammed the door to the office.

"She is not a suspect in any of this!" he yelled at the sheriff and Clyde. "She works here, dammit! And you are not going to treat her like she's some half-witted female or some big time criminal."

"Nobody's treating her that way, Tyler," Clyde said calmly. "Let's just take a seat and talk over the facts."

"The fact is I'm sick and tired of feeling like we're in the wrong here. You call me and tell me my parents were found dead in a burning truck. Shot in the back of the head! That sounds like a hit!"

Tyler didn't keep still. He stalked across the office pushing one of the ridiculous zebra-print chairs out of his way.

"We're talking about the vandalism at the resort," Alvarez stated evenly. "That's the matter at hand."

He whirled around to glare at the sheriff whom he was also tired of dealing with. "All of this is connected. I'm not a cop and I can see it. So I'm having a hard time digesting the fact that you can't connect those dots, Sheriff."

"Now you hold on a minute, son," Alvarez chided.

He walked across the room and came to a stop at the edge of the desk.

"You don't come into my town, telling me how to do my job."

Tyler stood firm. "Then maybe you should start doing your job!"

"Let's just calm down," Clyde said, coming to stand at the other end of the desk, between Tyler and the sheriff.

"If you want to officially question my clients, Sheriff, we can schedule a time for them to come down to the station. But I'll tell you right now they won't be answering any questions that may or may not implicate them in any of these incidents. Incidents for which my clients have solid alibis."

Clyde was speaking in his official tone, which probably sounded much better than Tyler's yelling. But damn if he cared. Alvarez had looked at Gabriella like he actually thought she'd walked off the ranch and went to the resort to vandalize that room herself. It was ridiculous.

"I ain't accused either of them of anything. But I gotta say they're acting pretty guilty," the sheriff said.

"Of what?" Tyler asked. "I couldn't kill my parents when I was thousands of miles away."

"But you could have hired someone to do it for you," Alvarez countered. "You're rich enough to do so and inheriting this ranch is a damn good motive."

"Why would I vandalize the property? How would that fit into my grand plan?" Tyler asked through clenched teeth.

Alvarez leaned back on his heels and folded his arms over his chest. "Well, let's just see, when that happened you and your brother hadn't decided on whether or not you would sell or keep this ranch. So maybe your plan all along was to own this place by yourself. So you hire those same folk that did the killing of your parents for you, to come back and tear some things up. This way, your city slicker brother won't want to be bothered with the prospect of having to fend off violence on the property and he'll sell his half of the ranch to you. Which, as a matter of fact, is exactly what ended up happening."

"Then, you take Ms. Bennett out for a ride that you say nobody else knew about but the two of you. How hard would it have been to pay those same criminal folk you're in cahoots with, to stand out there and take a shot at her? Now, on the face of that I'm not sure what you have against Ms. Bennett. But then, somebody goes into the resort and tears up Ms. Bennett's room. Somebody that probably knew she wasn't there. If I ask you who knew Ms. Bennett was staying at the ranch last night, are you going to tell me nobody but you?"

Tyler's fingers clenched by his side. He wanted to punch somebody or something because everything Alvarez said made sense. It wasn't true, but it made sense.

"You don't have to respond, Tyler," Clyde told him.

"But I will," Tyler said. "You can write this down, Sheriff. I loved my parents and before they died I could care less about this ranch. I didn't know what it was worth or half the things that went on here. I hadn't seen my brother in years and hadn't spoken to him since last year on his birthday in September. And there is nothing, absolutely nothing, I would ever do to hurt Gabriella Bennett."

Sheriff Alvarez continued to glare at Tyler.

"You want to check my alibis, fine. I'll have them typed up and sent to your office. You want access to my cell phone records so you can trace who I have dealings with. I'll give you that too. Because I didn't do any of this and the sooner you realize that, the sooner you can get on to finding out who did."

"I think this meeting is over," Clyde stated. "I'll walk you out, Sheriff."

Tyler sat heavily in the chair behind the desk and turned so that he was now facing the window.

"That's fine," he heard the sheriff say. "And just to be clear, I don't think Ms. Bennett was involved in what happened at the resort. I do, however, think she may know who was. I get that you're fond of your little interior designer, Tyler. But she's hiding something. Don't you want to find out what that is before someone else is killed?"

Seconds later, Tyler heard the door closing. He swore at that moment and rubbed his hands down his face. He hated that all of this was happening and he hated that a small part of him thought Sheriff Alvarez was right. Gabriella was hiding something.

While Tyler in no way believed that had anything to do with what was going on here, the way she'd run back into the house and locked herself in the room upstairs, said she was upset. Now, Tyler wasn't a trained law enforcement expert but he had enough sense to know that's not how a normal person reacted to hearing that a room they'd been renting had been vandalized. That part he did know because it wasn't how he'd reacted when he found out his ranch had also been hit. He'd been angry and more than eager to find out who had come onto his land and destroyed his property. The look on Gabriella's face had been full of fear. And that wasn't the first time he'd seen her look that way. So Tyler was certain there was something in her past that still frightened her. Something, that maybe she thought could follow her here.

This wasn't what he planned for when he came back to Hobbs Creek. None of this was. Not becoming a ranch owner, staying in this town longer than it took to bury his parents and certainly not becoming romantically involved with a woman. A woman who he would be damned if he let anybody harm. Especially not her ex, because that's exactly who Tyler thought Gabriella was afraid of. It was who she was having nightmares about and who she now thought was here in Hobbs Creek.

But Tyler was certain Gabriella was wrong about that. There's no way her ex could have gotten onto this property yesterday morning to shoot at them. And if he had, then he certainly would have known she hadn't returned to the resort. So if he wanted her, why wouldn't he have simply come back to the ranch? Not to mention the fact that he'd had so many other chances to get to her. When she was in town shopping with Naomi. Or when she was at the resort working on the new designs there. Plenty of opportunity, he thought with a sigh.

No, this was about the ranch. It was about his parents' murder. Tyler was sure of that and was now ready to take matters into his own hands. He pulled out his cell phone and made a call. Sheriff Alvarez wasn't going to like this, but Tyler didn't give a damn. Sheriff Alvarez hadn't lost anyone he loved, and Tyler wasn't about to lose anyone else. He was scrolling through his contacts for the number when his phone rang. The number that popped up was a surprise, but he answered anyway.

"Hello?"

"Tyler? I need your help."

Thirty minutes later, Tyler pulled up in front of the hotel. He replied to a text message from Clyde and got out of his truck. He bypassed the front desk and went straight to the elevators. Getting off at the eighth floor, he walked down the hall until he saw the room number Jagger had given him over the phone. He knocked and waited.

Jagger came to the door, eyes bloodshot, shirt hanging outside of his pants.

"What the hell is going on?"

"You were right," he said, his words slurred. "You're always right."

Tyler stepped inside, pushing Jagger back out of his way and closed the door behind him. Jagger had landed against the wall, which he needed to keep from falling to the floor.

"Have you been here for the last three weeks? Sitting in a hotel room drinking?" Tyler asked after he helped his brother into the room and let him fall as gently as possible onto the couch.

"We were gonna leave when you kicked us off the ranch, but then Brooke said she wanted to look around town some more. Maybe see if we could find a place to have the wedding here. She thought with Mom and Dad being gone now, we might want to have something that family and their friends could come to," Jagger said.

His brother looked like crap. He'd leaned back on the couch, his head falling back to rap against the wall. He lifted an arm and dropped it over his eyes as he continued to speak.

"Does Brooke look like a woman who wants to get married in a town like Hobbs Creek?"

"Brooke doesn't look like the type of woman you should be marrying," Tyler answered honestly.

Jagger hadn't said what he needed help with over the phone and Tyler hadn't needed to know. Just as he'd told the sheriff, no matter what happened between them he and Jagger were brothers. They were blood. And as such, Tyler would always be there to help. But he wouldn't sugarcoat whatever fresh hell Jagger had clearly gotten himself into where that woman was concerned.

"You're right again," Jagger said, letting his arm drop down to his side.

He stared at Tyler through half-slit eyes.

"She tried to take my money," Jagger told him. "Can you believe that? Even before I could marry the conniving bitch she had her hands in my pockets."

Tyler withheld the I-told-you-so that floated through his mind.

"How do you know she tried to take your money?" he asked Jagger.

Jagger chuckled. "I got two accounts," he said, holding up all ten of his fingers.

Tyler didn't respond.

"One where my paycheck goes," Jagger said. "And another where all my bonus checks and incentives from special clients are deposited. You remember Dad telling us never to keep all our eggs in one basket."

"I remember," Tyler replied.

"So I don't keep all my money in one place. I got an offshore account too. And some bonds and investment accounts. You know that kind of stuff."

"Right," Tyler said. "That's a smart business move."

Jagger nodded. "I know 'cause I'm smart too. It's not just you." He tried to tap a finger to his temple but missed and almost poked his eye out.

"You've always been smart, Jagger. Nobody ever said you weren't."

"I went to Harvard."

"Yes, you did. And you became a very successful man. Mom and Dad would have been proud."

"No he wouldn't have," Jagger said shaking his head so hard his hair—which was in need of a cut—scraped over his forehead. "He never liked me."

"He loved you," Tyler insisted. "He loved both of us the best way he knew how."

"It wasn't good enough!" Jagger yelled. "Just like I wasn't good enough for her!"

"But Brooke wanted to marry you. She accepted your proposal and was wearing your ring."

"I took it back. The minute I got that call from my bank rep in New York telling me that a woman in Hobbs Creek, Texas walked into a branch and tried to make a withdrawal with one of my withdrawal slips. I gave her everything, man. My heart, my soul—" his words trailed off with a groan.

Tyler cursed. He believed Jagger. He'd given Brooke Radison everything but what she'd really wanted. Money. The Westwind Ranch and Resort would have given her a ton of that.

"So she tried to steal your money, you confronted her and

took back your ring. What are you going to do now? And where is Brooke?"

"She tried to blackmail me. Said she was pregnant and she was going to tell the president of our company that I was the father. We have a strict 'no fraternization' rule at the company. That's why I had to marry Brooke, because we couldn't keep sneaking around seeing each other. I had to make it right for her. I had to take care of her in the way she deserved."

"Brooke is having your baby?" Tyler couldn't believe the words he'd just spoken.

"Hell no!" Jagger yelled.

Then his brother rolled over on the couch laughing. He was clenching his side as he chuckled and Tyler tried to wait patiently until he was finished. It could have been worse, Jagger could have been an angry drunk instead of an obviously happy one.

"I had a vasectomy four years ago," he finally said between guffaws. "It was after Dad's sixty-first birthday. I called to wish him well and he had nothing nice to say to me. Didn't ask about my job or how much I was making or anything. Just talked about the ranch and asked when I was coming back. I told him never. The next morning I called my doctor and told him to set me up. I never wanted to have a child I couldn't love."

Tyler swore as Jagger broke out in laughter once more. He stood up finally and went to the couch.

"Come on, get up. We're going back to the ranch so you can sleep this hangover off."

"Nope," Jagger said. "Can't go back there yet."

"What? Why not? If you're talking about the sale of your shares, we can discuss that later. I'll sell them back to you. It doesn't have to be this way now. Not between us and not about the ranch. Now come on."

Tyler leaned down and was prepared to help Jagger up, but Jagger pushed him away.

"No. I can't go back until I help you catch her. She was my mistake and I gotta fix it."

Sighing heavily because he was tired now, Tyler stood up straight and ran a hand down the back of his head. He needed to get back to the ranch to check on Gabriella and he was still waiting for a call.

"What mistake are you talking about now, Jagger?"

"Brooke, man. She was nutso. And when I sold you my half of the ranch she really went bonkers. Talking about how it was Gabriella's fault. If she weren't whispering in your ear to save her job, the ranch would have been sold. She said she was gonna get her back."

"What? When did she say this?"

"She's been saying it for days, but that bank lady called me yesterday morning and when Brooke finally got back in here it was past three in the afternoon. I told her I caught her and took my ring back and she said she was gonna tell our boss. I told her I was gonna tell you that she had it in for Gabriella."

Tyler cursed.

"Where is she now, Jagger?"

Jagger shrugged. "Don't know. She left crying and screaming about scheming bitches. I thought that was pretty hypocritical of her. But then she came back here last night. I was totally wasted by then. She was cursing and walking back and forth talking about getting paint in her hair or something. She said she'd finally gotten some payback on Gabriella and when I heard about what happened at the resort on the news this morning, I knew it was her. But all her stuff was gone when I came out of the room to look for her."

"Dammit! So she's gone?" Tyler asked.

"Nope," Jagger said laughing again. "Her phone's got a GPS chip in it and the phone is in my name. So all you gotta do is have the sheriff put a trace on it and you'll find her."

"Get up!" Tyler said pulling Jagger by his shirt. "Get up! We're going to the police station right now."

And if Brooke Radison had already left Hobbs Creek, Tyler was going to use the private investigator he'd called earlier to find her scheming ass pronto!

CHAPTER 12

*H*er hands were still shaking. Gabriella wanted to scream. No, what she really wanted to do was pack her bags and get the hell out of this town. But where would she go? Back to Connecticut? Austin lived there. His ex-wife lived there with their two children. He worked at one of the largest real estate firms in the city and his father was a city councilman. So how was going back home going to be better?

Gabriella dropped her head into her hands and cursed. She closed her eyes and thought about everything from last June up until this point. A little more than a year, and this man had torn her life apart.

She hated the thought of giving someone that much control over her, but there it was. She'd trusted Austin. Fallen in love with him and had begun to plan her future with him. And he'd let her down. He'd hurt her physically and mentally and despite all of the daily motivational sayings she read online and prayers she whispered at night, Gabriella didn't feel like she was

160 | AC ARTHUR

anymore healed now, than she had been on the worst night of her life.

Tilting her head back, she let the tears flow in hot streaks down her face. She sat still longer than she thought she probably should have and then she sighed heavily. Opening her eyes, Gabriella climbed off the bed and found her phone where she'd tossed it into the recliner across from the bed. When she'd come up here—she didn't even know how long she'd been closed in this room—she'd intended to call Adriana and finally tell her sister everything. Adriana would understand why she'd kept the secret and why she'd thought she could handle this on her own because not only was she Gabriella's big sister and best friend, but because Adriana had gone through something horrible in her life too. Her sister had also kept a secret, for her own personal reasons. And when Adriana decided it was time, she told her story. Gabriella didn't have the luxury of time.

She was holding the phone when she heard the quiet knock on the door.

Until this moment, nobody had come to see about her. A part of her had expected Dessie, with all her mothering ways, to march up the steps and demand Gabriella stop being foolish and open that door. But she hadn't. And another part thought—or rather hoped—that Tyler would come up with a key and simply unlock the door. That he would walk into the room and lift her into his arms and carry her off into a happy ending. She chuckled at that thought because Gabriella always considered herself stronger than a woman who needed a man to rescue her. Still, when the knock came again, she wiped her face and slipped her phone into the back pocket of her shorts. She crossed the room and unlocked the door, pulling it open to see Tyler standing on the other side.

He was carrying a tray with two covered dishes, a couple of bottled waters and a glass vase with a long stemmed pink rose.

"It's dinnertime," he said, the corner of his mouth lifting into a smile. "Dessie and I thought you might be hungry. Especially since you only had that smoothie early this morning."

It was the strangest thing. Considering all that had happened today and the thoughts that had been running through her mind as each hour passed with her sitting alone in this room, it was the last possible reaction Gabriella imagined she would have to seeing Tyler. But butterflies danced in her stomach and a nervous chuckle escaped.

"I thought that smoothie was supposed to provide an unlimited energy boost."

"I didn't say you were tired, probably just hungry," was his reply.

He was too cute for his own good. And she was too smitten with that cuteness.

"I could eat," she said and stepped aside to let him in.

He entered the room and she closed the door, leaning against it with a sigh.

"I also owe you and everyone else that was here this morning an apology. I shouldn't have run away," she said.

He was setting the tray on the opposite side of the bed from where she'd sat most of the day on and he looked over to her.

"Apology accepted," he replied. "On behalf of everyone that was here this morning. Well, maybe not for the sheriff, but he was being an ass anyway."

"I'll pay for the damages—" she started saying.

Tyler was already shaking his head. "Stop. You're not a foolish woman and I'm not an ass. The person who did the damage is the person who pays. Dessie already has a crew in there working on the room. So let's not go any further with this part of the discussion."

Gabriella didn't argue. He was right. She hadn't done the damage, even if it was the room she had reserved. She'd just felt like she should offer something. Apparently, Tyler disagreed.

She cleared her throat and moved closer to the bed. "Then I guess the next topic is explaining why I left before the sheriff could ask me anymore questions."

Gabriella waited a beat to see if Tyler was going to interject and tell her that wasn't necessary either. But he did not. Instead he walked over to the recliner and took a seat. So she decided to sit too. She climbed onto the bed once more, folding her legs beneath her.

She began slowly, "Austin Sterner is my ex-boyfriend. He's a forty-four year old real estate agent in Greenwich. While I was studying for my design degree I interned with Austin's agency. When the internship was over, I was offered a permanent position with the agency. Whenever they listed a house, I was there to stage it."

Gabriella paused because she realized this was the first time she'd ever verbally gone through her history with Austin.

"We began dating three months after I accepted the permanent position. He'd been divorced from his wife about a year. They shared custody of their two children, so we often scheduled our time together around their visits and our combined work schedules. We dated for seven months before I realized it wasn't right for me."

She paused again, the pain in her chest heavy with the thoughts that followed those words.

"So you broke up with him," Tyler stated.

Gabriella knew that he was in the room. She knew he was just a few feet away, sitting in a chair, staring at her. But she'd been talking as if she were in the room alone, recounting how the beginning of her end had occurred. To her ears it sounded very innocent. Girl meets boy, they date, they don't work out, and they end it. But that was far from what happened.

"I broke up with him," she said. "I left his agency and with the help of my mentor began looking for other opportunities in the area. I liked being close to my parents, especially with all of my brothers leaving and making their own lives with their partners. I was the one who could get to my parents when and if they needed something in a hurry."

"And you were their baby," Tyler said. "I'm sure they liked having you close."

"They loved it," she replied with a chuckle. "I went to church with my mother on Sunday mornings and spent the rest of the day at their house while she cooked dinner. I watched football games with my dad."

And all the while they had no idea how much she was hurting inside.

"They were my rock and whether they knew it or not they helped me through the messy break-up," she said.

"Messy because Austin didn't want to let you go."

It sounded so simple coming from Tyler. Gabriella nodded even though she knew it was probably wrong to let him continue thinking it was that mundane.

"I moved on and he didn't. Or he wouldn't. I don't know. I

really wanted him to, but he didn't. So there were phone calls and text messages and the one night he showed up at my condo unannounced. I told him I would take out a restraining order if he didn't cut it out," she said.

"And he stopped for a while, but then when you left town, he continued," Tyler said. "Because it's one thing to be able to see you every day and satisfy his unhealthy need to be near you, but it's another entirely to have you out of sight."

She couldn't speak. His words were so on point, it was almost scary.

"I've seen stalking situations turn ugly, Gabriella. It's not your fault. Guys have fragile egos, you crushed his when you walked out of his life and he was too weak to move on. No excuses, the guy's an ass for continuing to frighten you. And if you think he's here in Hobbs Creek, I'll find him and I'll make sure he gets the message to stay the hell away from you this time."

"You don't have to do that."

"Oh yes I do," Tyler said as he stood and came over to the side of the bed where she was sitting. "Because if he does something to put that look in your eye that I saw this morning I might be the one the sheriff ends up arresting."

She looked away because she didn't want him to see the tears welling up in her eyes. His fingers were immediately on her chin, turning her head to him.

"I will not let him hurt you again," he said solemnly. "Trust me."

Gabriella didn't trust easily. She couldn't afford to because she knew how quickly that oath could be broken. And she wasn't even supposed to be in this position with Tyler West. But she was. So now what?

"Thank you," she said quickly, deciding to think about the rest later.

Because the rest was big and it was more than she'd bargained for, but at the same time she knew it wasn't something she could put off forever. Still, she just wanted this moment with him. The moment that she felt encircling them. Him looking earnestly at her, touching her with only kindness and compassion.

"I really appreciate you understanding, Tyler."

"How could I not understand when all I've done is pull you into drama and dysfunction since the day we met?"

He grinned and she smiled in return. "I guess that's true."

He laughed out loud. "You didn't have to agree with me so quickly. Come on, the food's getting cold."

As if on cue, her stomach growled. Loudly.

Tyler continued to laugh.

Fighting for at least a little dignity and because she felt partially better, she reached for the bottled water and told him, "It's not funny. You're the one obsessed with smoothies as a meal."

"Not obsessed," he said as he circled the bed and sat across from her on the other side of the tray. "They're quick and serve a purpose."

"Well, so is," she paused while lifting the cover off one of the plates. "So is this. Thank you so much, Dessie."

Gabriella inhaled the delectable scent of the cheeseburger with mustard, lettuce and pickles on her plate.

"She said that so far this was the only favorite she knew of for you," Tyler told her when he lifted the cover from his plate to reveal another cheeseburger.

"It is my most favorite meal ever," she said and picked up a napkin to set in her lap.

As her stomach had indicated, Gabriella was starving.

"Well, maybe I should tell you the news I have before you start eating. I wouldn't want to ruin your most favorite meal ever," he told her.

Her shoulders sagged instantly. "Oh no. Did something else happen? Was there some clue left in the room at the resort that confirms it was Austin?"

"No," he said. "And for the record, I never believed the person who destroyed that room was connected to you. Like I said before, I apologize for pulling you into my dysfunctional situation."

"But I just told you about Austin. He's sent me text messages since I've been here," she insisted.

"That doesn't mean he knows where you are, Gabriella. Did you tell him? Do you know of anyone who would give him that information?"

She hadn't thought about that. Adriana knew where she was and why, but Adriana lived in Miami and she had no idea who Austin was. The only other person who knew, besides her team at The Proctor Group, was Mallory, her mentor. Mallory also knew Gabriella had dated Austin and that they had broken up and that's why Gabriella left his agency. She did not know anything else and she would never tell Austin where Gabriella was.

"No. I don't," she admitted.

"It wasn't him," Tyler stated.

And she knew from his tone that there was more.

"Who was it?"

"Brooke," he said. "And before we go any further, she's in custody. The sheriff tracked her down at the airport. It's a crazy demented story of a woman that's crazy and demented and I'll gladly tell you every word of it after we eat this delicious meal."

When she was about to ask another question, Tyler held up a hand. He lifted his other arm and looked down at his watch.

"Dessie's going to be in here in about five seconds to make sure you're eating, so I'd suggest you let this conversation rest, until this plate is clean, or face her wrath."

Tyler didn't wait for her to respond, but hurriedly blessed the food and picked up his burger to take a bite.

Gabriella wanted the full story and she wanted it now. She also wanted to forego another Dessie tongue-lashing so she picked up her burger as well and took a bite.

When Tyler smiled and said, "Good girl," she could do nothing else but smile at him in return.

She was getting in deeper with him. Funny how that thought was beginning to cause just as much fear in her as the thought of Austin turning up in Hobbs Creek.

He stood over her, watching as she performed her fourth and last set of fifteen chest presses. Tyler touched her knees lightly to make sure she was keeping them tightly pressed together, feet up as she lay on the bench.

"This is going to improve your upper body strength," he said.

"Or give you a better view of my breasts," she snapped.

He kept a straight face and leaned forward, looking directly into her eyes as she pushed for the last three reps.

"I've had a great view of your breasts already," he said when she sighed heavily and let the ten pound weights fall to the floor.

It was a sight Tyler knew he'd never grow tired of and for the last week he'd seen all of her, frequently. He found himself enjoying that part about returning to Hobbs Creek above all else.

"You're getting better," he said after touching her bicep. "That's enough for today. You can shower and we can go somewhere to get a nice dinner."

"You're getting bossier," she told him as she sat up.

"Who me?" He feigned innocence. "I've never received that complaint from any of my prior clients."

"That's because the majority of your clients were probably women and they most likely wanted to jump into bed with you."

She'd stood up by then, just in time for him to snag her by the waist and turn her around. Tyler sat on the bench, pulling Gabriella down onto his lap.

"I don't sleep with clients. It's my fast and staunch rule that I make very clear on the first meeting," he told her.

She wrapped her legs around him and settled down so that her crotch—covered only by the spandex of her shorts and a sexy little royal blue thong—rubbed teasingly over his already growing arousal.

"That's a good rule to have," she replied. "Does that mean you never have girlfriends?"

His hands were on the tight cheeks of her bottom and—this

time—he had been staring down at her breasts. With that question, Tyler looked up at her slowly.

"Are you asking if I have a girlfriend now?"

"No. I assume you don't because you were quick to tell me that when you're sleeping with one woman you don't sleep with any others. I believe that about you," she said. "But lately I've been wondering why such a handsome and relatively normal guy like you doesn't have a girlfriend. Or a wife."

"Relatively normal?"

She rolled her eyes. "Those smoothies you've been introducing me to are not normal. I don't care what you say. The one this morning tasted like medicine. A very awful, foul colored, medicine."

The way she scrunched her face when she said those words caused him to laugh and want to cuddle her close. That's how she made him feel lately. If he walked by a room in the house that she was working on, he had to stop by and touch her in some way and say something to her just to hear her voice. If she was working at the employee residences or the resort, he made a point of stopping by, even if just to get a glimpse of her. And at night, she was still staying at the house, in his room, as if they were...

"I've had girlfriends," he told her. "They come and they go."

"They leave or you send them away?"

She was running her fingers through his hair, her nails scraping along his scalp. That was the equivalent of her reaching into his pants and stroking his dick. It turned him on instantly.

"It's usually mutual once we discover that I'm incapable of giving them what they need or want at the moment."

"Oh, and what's that?"

He was just about to lean in and lick the line that separated her sports bra from her cleavage, when he paused. She was asking a lot of questions which could not be good. Tyler paused and looked at her. She was staring back at him expectantly, her brown eyes warm and accepting. They'd been having a good time this past week. Even with Jagger still hanging around the house under the guise of overseeing the re-design and the sheriff still trying to find evidence to link Brooke to the shooting and the vandalism on the ranch—in addition to the crimes he'd already charged her with.

Truth be told, Tyler wasn't completely clueless. Every night he held Gabriella in his arms he knew they were growing closer. He knew and he ignored it, because that's what he preferred to do. Now, for the first time in his adult life, he might have to explain that preference.

"Dating and sex is like a mutual agreement between adults to have fun," he said.

Her hands stilled in his hair and she tilted her head as she continued to watch him.

"I mean, that's the first few weeks of any relationship. The fun part."

"Okay, I can see that. So when does it change to the part that you don't like? I'm asking so that I can be packed up and out of the way before we get to that part."

"Well, you're in luck because I'm not there yet," he said and leaned in to drop a quick kiss on her lips.

It was more to be sure she wasn't pissed at him, than to actually steal a kiss.

But when she held his head in place and licked his lips, Tyler went with it. He took the kiss deeper, moving his hands up her back and pulling her in closer.

Fire shot through him in fierce quick flames, searing his entire body. When she sucked his tongue into her mouth Tyler groaned. He grabbed the tail of her hair that was held by a black band. She gasped and let her head fall back. Tyler licked up the line of her neck. He nipped at the soft skin there with his teeth, while her fingers tightened in his hair.

He moved in the opposite direction, his tongue tracing a hot path down between her breasts as he pushed the sports bra out of his way with his chin. She arched into him and the sound she made flipped a switch inside him. With a primal groan he pulled at that sports bra until he got it over her head and her breasts dropped freely into his hands. Tyler sucked on her nipples like a child begging to be fed. She gyrated over him as he worked her breasts and his dick grew so hard he wanted to yell out in agony.

Instead, he stood them up from the bench.

"Off!" He barked the order while pushing his shorts and boxer briefs down his legs.

She moved just as quickly as he did and when he realized he didn't have a condom, Tyler cursed.

"Don't move!" he said and left her in the exercise room.

He ran down the hallway, not giving a damn if someone walked by and saw him running naked with a hard dick. He dashed into his room, grabbed a condom from the night stand where he'd put the new box he'd just purchased yesterday and headed back to the exercise room where he slammed and locked the door.

She'd listened and was still standing near the weight bench.

Actually, she was kneeling one knee on the bench, bent over at the waist, while holding a weight in her hand.

"Is this how I should properly do an arm curl?"

If he were an animal the sound Tyler made would have been classified as primal.

"Do it again," he said as he hurriedly sheathed himself with the condom and came to stand behind her.

"I like your form," Tyler told her as he stared at the plump cheeks of her bottom.

They were spread open as she stood with one foot planted on the floor, the other leg up on the bench. And when she leaned forward to lift the weight up he could see the plump folds of her sex and he felt like he would come right there on the spot.

"Really? I just want to make sure I'm doing everything right," she said coyly.

Tyler grabbed his engorged length and moved in closer while rubbing his hands up and down. "Ok. Well, let me see if I can help you."

"Oh yes," she said, dropping the weight with a loud thunk to the floor. "Please help me."

He put his hands on her first, his palms spreading over her cheeks. She had a great ass. Whether she wore those very short jean shorts or the chic dress pants that drove him insane, Tyler loved looking at and feeling on her ass. He gripped her cheeks and she dipped her back so they spread wider. His finger slipped between her crevice and he felt her already wet.

"Naughty little girl. You're not doing the curls right and you're wet without me. I wonder what I should do."

When she whispered, "Punish me," Tyler really thought he was going to come before he could sink his dick inside of her.

Instead he moved quickly, spreading her cheeks so he could see his length disappear inside her warmth. She moaned and he sighed with the pleasure that eased down his spine. He began pumping fiercely into her and she thrust her hips back to meet his every stroke.

This wasn't fun, he thought with a start. If he were truly being honest with himself, Tyler would admit that he'd leap-frogged past the fun part weeks ago. This, right here, was something else. With every stroke of his length inside her Tyler felt them joining. Like tendrils snaking through his chest and winding slowly around his heart, he felt it. With his hands on her flesh he felt as if her warmth were somehow transferred directly into him through that simple contact. And when she looked over her shoulder at him, her gaze locking with his as he continued to pump into her, he knew he didn't want that connection to break. He wasn't ready to walk away and damn sure wasn't about to let her try to do the same.

Pulling out of her quickly, Tyler wrapped his arms around her waist and guided her into his arms. He crashed his lips down over hers, thrusting his tongue into her mouth as if this kiss alone could explain everything he was feeling and thinking. She kissed him back with equal fervor, holding the back of his head and pressing into him. Tyler reached down, grabbed the back of her thighs and lifted her into his arms. He walked them to the wall and pressed into her once more. She moaned and dug her nails into his shoulders. He pumped fiercely, afraid to stop, scared that if he did stop it would end. Everything he'd had with her since the day they'd met would be over.

So he pumped harder and faster, hearing nothing but her moans and whispers of his name. He took her kisses, savoring the feel of her lips, her tongue and the moist heat of her cove. And when her legs trembled around his waist Tyler tumbled. He came with a fierce rush that shook his entire body, holding him still inside her for endless moments.

He couldn't move and couldn't think clearly. All he wanted was to stay right here inside of her, with her wrapped in his arms. Forever.

The thought frightened him and Tyler went still. Forever was a very long time.

"I bet your clients would pay top dollar for a training session like that," she said jokingly as she nipped his neck.

Tyler lowered his head until his face was buried in her neck. He held onto her and whispered, "I've never had a client that was worthy of a session like that."

She went still.

"None. Except you," he admitted.

The P&P Steakhouse was a classic old-fashioned steakhouse. With its dark wood walls and beamed ceilings, burgundy leather upholstered booth seats and high-backed chairs with a burgundy, green and brown striped pattern at the individual tables. The lighting was dim, antique green covered sconces hung on the walls, while a smaller version of the same design sat in the center of each table. The carpet, a bold floral print, in coordinating colors, brought the design together perfectly.

The waitstaff were dressed in all black, the women in short skirts and tight blouses and the men in slacks, shirt and tie. The hostesses that stood behind a high cherry wood desk wore black dresses, short and tight. Gabriella thought she was beginning to notice a theme.

"Tyler West. I called earlier for a seven-thirty reservation."

Gabriella stood beside him, still adoring the sound of his deep voice. She'd never met Tyler before coming to Hobbs Creek, but she had listened to a couple of his motivational speeches online after arriving here. In those, there was no hint of his southern upbringing. Now, at times, she could hear a bit of the Texas twang when he talked. He was settling in here and while he didn't speak about it much, Gabriella wondered how his parents' death would ultimately effect Tyler's future. Would he stay in Hobbs Creek to tend to the family ranch he'd inherited? Or would he return to his life in the spotlight of the fitness world? He could do both, she thought. It would be a compromise, but she wasn't sure if Tyler was up for compromising.

Hadn't that been why she'd brought up the conversation of relationships and where he stood with them?

The feel of Tyler taking her hand pulled Gabriella from her thoughts. She smiled and followed him as he walked behind one of the hostesses to their booth. When Gabriella had slid across the seat, Tyler nodded to the hostess and took his seat on the other side of the table.

"We'll have water and do you feature Basset Banks' Mirage?" he asked.

Gabriella looked at him in shock. She'd told him about the Basset Banks Winery in Napa Valley and that she'd attended a double wedding there. He'd said that he'd heard of the winery, but not that he was familiar with any of their wines.

"No, sir. I don't believe we do," the woman responded with a dazzling smile.

"Well, you should," Tyler said as he accepted the wine list she'd given him. "Mirage is an excellent blend of Basset Banks' cabernet sauvignon, merlot, and cabernet santo. Tell Ted I think he should definitely look into becoming one of their exclusive vendors."

"Yes, Mr. West, I will."

"We'll take the Stag's Leap cabernet. Bring us the bottle," Tyler instructed.

"Yes, sir," she said and handed them both a menu.

"I didn't know you'd actually tasted Basset Banks wines," Gabriella said the moment they were alone.

"I told you I'd heard of them. After you mentioned knowing the owners, I ordered some for the ranch. The Mirage has a nice robust taste," he said, looking down at the menu.

He wore the black slacks and an ice blue collarless button front shirt she'd watched him pull out of his closet about an hour ago. His gold watch sparkled on his wrist and his hair was combed neatly back from his face. They'd dressed together in his room at the ranch and after she'd pulled on her blue cocktail dress, he'd come up behind her and zipped the back. Just like a couple getting ready for a night out on the town.

"I agree," she said after clearing her throat. "I had a chance to taste several of their wines and the Mirage was very nice."

A few minutes passed and their waitress, Frannie, appeared to take their order. Tyler ordered steak with asparagus and baked potato, while Gabriella went with something a little lighter—the steakhouse salad.

Tyler pulled out his phone and checked his messages after

they ordered. Gabriella didn't want to look at her phone any more than necessary. She'd talked to Adriana and her mother this week and had been keeping her email box down to a manageable number. She did not open her text messages, even though she saw that she had a few. Brooke was in custody. She'd trashed Gabriella's room at the resort. Not Austin.

"The house will be finished in another week," she said abruptly because she wanted to stop thinking about Austin and whether or not he was still trying to contact her.

Tyler's head shot up and he stared at her.

"What about the employee residences and the resort?" he asked.

"They'll be a few more weeks because we had to do more construction work in both those locations. But once the structures are complete, the design part won't take long at all. So I'm thinking that by the end of the summer I should be out of your way."

"Out of my way?" he asked.

"Yes. My job here will be done and I can return to Connecticut, or wherever my next assignment takes me," she said.

He didn't look happy about what she'd just said, but he didn't respond either. Gabriella didn't know why she'd even said it. How did she want him to respond?

"Well, hello, there stranger."

The sound of the familiar female voice immediately grated on Gabriella's nerves. Seeing Hannah Palmer come over to stand beside where Tyler was seated didn't help her already tenuous mood. The fact that Tyler didn't look that happy to see her either was the only bright side to this new scenario.

"Hi Hannah," he replied. "Gabriella and I were just discussing how excited we are to taste P&P's food tonight."

Hannah never even looked Gabriella's way.

Gabriella didn't care. She had nothing to say to Hannah Palmer either. She should have slapped Brooke that night the woman thought she was supposed to put Gabriella in her place and she should have let Hannah know her childish ploys weren't going to work on her. But Gabriella had taken the high road. After what Brooke had done, Gabriella wasn't certain she was going to continue taking that path.

"I'm so glad you're getting off the ranch," Hannah continued speaking to only Tyler. "I was just telling Daddy how nice it would be to have you over to the big house for dinner. We could walk down by the lake like we used to. Oh and Mrs. Franklin from the Hobbsonian Gazette, she'd like to do a 'Where Are They Now?' story featuring us. You know since we were once prom king and queen, and because we were voted cutest couple that same year at the Valentine's Day dance."

Hannah rested her hand on Tyler's shoulder now. Her long claw-shaped nails were painted light pink, and two gold charm bracelets dangled at her wrist.

Tyler's features remained impassive, but he did reach up to take Hannah's wrist and slowly move her hand from his shoulder, while saying, "Then maybe you should tell Mrs. Franklin how the day after we were crowned prom king and queen, I found you in the back of our barn giving my brother a blow job."

Gabriella gasped but she was certain that the loud sound that several other patrons of the restaurant heard hadn't come from her. Hannah's already blushed cheeks darkened. He perfect pouting red lips formed a circle of shock and she finally snatched her arm from Tyler's grip.

"How dare you speak to me that way, Tyler West! You're in my daddy's restaurant. You will show me some respect!" Hannah hissed.

Tyler nodded. "As soon as you start showing Gabriella some respect, Hannah."

"What? Who is she? Absolutely nobody to me," Hannah continued.

"She's somebody to me," Tyler said, his gaze locking with Gabriella's across the table. "I expect you to respect that fact from now on."

For a moment Gabriella thought Hannah was going to do the right thing. She'd watched her look around the restaurant to see that people were staring at her and Gabriella was sure that this was not the type of attention Hannah Palmer craved. But the next moments proved her wrong.

"You want some respect for dating this half breed?" Hannah asked Tyler.

When Tyler's head snapped up to look at her, Hannah just shook her head. She took a step back from the table and continued as if she had absolutely nothing to lose.

"She's only half royalty, from some backwards town in Brazil, if you even count that. And she took almost seven years to complete college. She's an idiot! But then, you can't really expect much from their kind. That's how they roll in their hood," she spat.

The last was said with a fake-ass hip-hop twang to Hannah's voice and Gabriella saw the moment when Tyler decided what he was going to do next. So Gabriella stood first. She dropped the napkin she'd put in her lap onto the table and stood so that she was now only a foot away from Hannah.

"Oh, my! Look out y'all, she's about to pop off!" Hannah said. "Isn't that how you and your homies talk? Look here, missy, why don't you take yourself on back where you came from. We don't do the interracial thing down here."

"You obviously don't do too much growing up around here either," Gabriella told her. "I am here in Hobbs Creek to do a job. Once that job is over I'll be gone. But not a minute before, and certainly not because some simple-minded immature bottle-blonde who couldn't decide which brother she wanted, doesn't like that I'm here."

"You can't talk to me like that," Hannah said and took a step to close the small distance between her and Gabriella.

Gabriella wished like hell she would not have done that.

"I can do whatever I damn well please," Gabriella told her.

She hadn't realized it before but Tyler had also stood up. He was pulling Hannah back from Gabriella now.

"What the hell is wrong with you?" He yelled into Hannah's face.

"Me? You're the one running around town flaunting your little piece of black ass! Your mama and daddy taught you better than that, Tyler." She yanked her arm from him again.

"I don't even want you touching me now that you've been touching her!"

"I don't even want to be in this restaurant knowing that you're here," Tyler said. "Be sure to tell your father you're the reason he lost his account with us."

When Tyler turned away from her, Gabriella saw Hannah move to the table and grab the bottle of wine, holding it up like she was going to pour it on him. Moving quickly, Gabriella eased around Tyler and snatched the bottle of wine from Hannah.

"You may not want Tyler to touch you, so I will," Gabriella said and with her free hand pushed Hannah so hard she fell back in the booth seat.

Then Gabriella put the bottle of wine to her mouth, tossed her head back and took a gulp, before slamming the bottle down onto the table. She leaned in until she was face-to-face with Hannah.

"If you ever spout your racist bullshit in my presence again, I'll bash your head in with the next bottle of wine. You got that, Becky?" Gabriella said before standing up straight and walking away.

She didn't look at anyone else in the restaurant. In fact, she didn't even see where Tyler was at that point. She went to the truck and stood there until she heard the click of the door unlocking. Then she climbed inside the truck and snapped her seat belt in place. She did not speak another word until they arrived at the ranch.

"I think I'm going to sleep in my room tonight," she said to Tyler when she stepped out of the truck.

"Gabriella," he started.

She shook her head. "Let's not do this tonight. I've had enough."

Gabriella didn't know if it was because her voice had cracked when she spoke, or the fact that a tear had escaped and rolled slowly down her cheek. But Tyler only nodded in response. He led them into the house and locked the door behind them. When they walked up the stairs he stopped at her door and waited while she went inside and closed it behind her, before going to his own room.

Gabriella fell face-first onto that bed and cried. Not because Hannah Palmer had embarrassed her, or even really offended her. But because despite what year this was and how far they'd seemingly come, some things just did not change. And if it wasn't just the fact that racism in this country didn't change, Gabriella sobbed because her luck with men didn't seem to shift any either.

CHAPTER 13

S he was drunk.

It had only taken half the bottle of scotch she'd snatched from the bar at P&P. He watched as she swayed to music that only played in her head.

"I love to sing love songs," she was saying. "Don't you? Falling in love is like a wild roller coaster ride. You go up and down and up again and then he spins you all around."

She was spinning in circles, her feet tangling together until she tumbled forward. He caught her.

"Yesssss," she sighed, her scotch-breath filtering up to his nostrils. "That's how you're supposed to do it. You're my hero not him. Not Tyler Stupid-As-Fuck West!"

She yelled his name and he cringed inside. How many times had he called Tyler West by that same name? How many times had he wished that bastard and his brother dead? Too many to count.

"Yeah, I can be your hero," he told her. "I can be whatever you want me to be."

"You will? You promise?"

She'd clumsily tried to wrap her arms around him. He let her and they fell back onto the stacks of hay. He hated the prickly feel of it sticking into the bare skin of his neck and his arms, but he didn't complain. He wrapped his arms tight around her, enjoying the feel of her heavy breasts against his chest.

"I promise, baby. I'll be everything you need." It was the least he could do since she was going to give him something better in return.

"Oh, yes, I need so much. Tyler and that black bitch were so mean to me tonight. Making me look like a fool in front of half the town."

He almost chuckled.

She'd been going on and on about black people and white people and half breeds for most of the ride out here. She was clearly from the white privilege side of the tracks. And she thought he was too. They always did. Nobody knew his mother had been a black woman with skin as dark as the tires on his truck. His father was a white man. Looking down at his fingers as they toyed with strands of her golden blonde hair, he figured he'd gotten most of the white genes in that exchange. Goody for him.

"I don't love Tyler anymore. He's a jerk!"

"He is," he conceded. "He doesn't know what he's doing getting tangled up with her."

"No! He doesn't!"

"But we'll show him, baby. We're gonna show him!" he said and then he kissed her.

He hadn't planned that part. When he'd followed Tyler and Gabriella into the restaurant he hadn't been sure what he was going to do. He only knew that it was time to do something. Then he'd seen Hannah approach them and he knew something was about to happen. Hannah Palmer was just that type of woman. The scene had been glorifying up until the end. Seeing Tyler flustered and angry was a highlight. He knew then that Hannah was the next step.

She was a sloppy kisser. Perhaps because of her inebriated state, he wasn't sure, but he generally didn't like the feeling that his lips might be eaten off his face. Still, she was eager to please as she reached down and gripped his dick. He wasn't hard yet. It didn't usually take long to get him worked up but she wasn't his first choice as a sex partner tonight. But, he'd decided he would have sex with her, just because he could.

He pulled his mouth away from hers to catch his breath and told her to, "Take your clothes off."

"Okay," she replied giddily and pushed back off of him.

He lay there watching her. She had a nice enough body. Her tits were big even if her ass was a little on the flat side. Her waist was slim and she was shaved clean. He loved that. When she stood naked trying to pose seductively for him, he felt the first twinges of an erection. He closed his eyes for a moment and recalled watching Tyler and Gabriella earlier today. They'd been in that exercise room for hours before they'd gotten started. And even as angry as watching them had made him feel, he'd been rock hard the entire time. And when they'd come, he had too, all over his pants as he sat in that tree with his binoculars. He'd cursed afterwards, hating that he'd been reduced to dressing up like some poor construction worker and sneaking onto the

Westwind property with the crew. But since they'd gotten fancy and added all the new security measures, he'd had to figure out a new way to get close enough to do what he had to do.

Now he was here again, having stolen a security pass from the construction supervisor. It was well after midnight so Tyler and Gabriella were probably sleeping in that big bed together the way they had been doing for the past few weeks. He'd seen the bed. Had even touched it once when he was walking through the house with the crew talking about whatever crap they were going to work on next. But being here tonight was different. It was time. Finally.

"Aren't you gonna take your clothes off baby?" Hannah asked.

She didn't wait for his response but pounced on him, shimmying her body down his until she was eye level with his crotch. She unbuttoned his pants and pushed her hand inside.

"Oh?" she said and looked up at him.

He frowned. Grabbing a handful of her hair he yanked her neck back until she squealed.

"Fix it!" he yelled.

Her eyes had widened in fear at first and then she'd licked her lips and sighed, "Sure thing, baby."

He loosened his grip on her hair and she leaned forward, releasing his flaccid dick before lowering her mouth over it. He closed his eyes and thought back to the scene earlier today. It angered him to see Tyler West pumping into Gabriella. Anger that had boiled within him for what seemed like forever. But with the memory of every thrust of Tyler's hips, he thrust his own, pumping faster and faster into Hannah's mouth.

She was good. He would give her that. She took him in deep

and made him feel like he could come at any moment. But that's not what he wanted. Not like this.

After a while longer, he pulled out of her mouth and tossed her face down onto the hay. He grabbed her hips and lifted her ass up into the air and then spread her legs before thrusting deep inside of her. She was noisy. Yelling and moaning as she jerked her body around. He smacked her ass until it was angry red with his palm prints. The sight enraged him and he pumped into her harder and harder. She kept screaming and he kept pumping until he released fast, hard, and deep inside her. When he was finished she collapsed on the hay.

"Oh damn, that was good. I wish I'd known, we could have done this when I saw you weeks ago," she said.

She kept talking but by then he was tucking his dick back into his pants. He bent over and lifted his pant leg up to pull the knife from the sheath he had strapped there. When he looked down to her again she was about to roll over and he quickly stopped her. Placing his hand at the back of her neck.

"Just lay still," he whispered into her ear. "You were good, Hannah. You were very good."

For what he needed her to do for him.

Tyler knocked on her door and waited for her to answer. It would probably take her a minute because it was so early in the morning. The sun hadn't even come up yet. But he'd waited as long as he possibly could.

"Tyler?" she said with one eye closed as she peeked through the partially opened door.

"Good morning," he replied. "Can I come in?"

She hesitated and for those few seconds his heart actually stopped. When had this happened? When had knowing that they were okay, that she wasn't angry or disappointed in him, and that he could simply reach out and touch her, become such a big deal in his life?

"Sure," she said finally and opened the door.

She wore another pair of very short night shorts and a tank top that barely kept her breasts contained. But Tyler looked past that to see how tired she seemed when she climbed back onto the bed. She sat up and pulled the sheets over her legs.

"If this is about last night," she began.

Tyler took a chance and sat on the bed beside her. He took her hands in his.

"It is about last night. I want you to know how sorry I am that it happened. If I had known how truly ignorant Hannah was, I would have stopped it sooner," he told her.

"So she hid being a racist even from you?" she asked.

"Before I came back to Hobbs Creek, I hadn't seen or heard from Hannah in almost twenty years. After seeing her with Jagger that day I didn't say another word to her. And for the month and a half that I stayed here after that, I steered clear of her. Before that, she made remarks about people of different races, not just African Americans, but I never thought anything of it."

"Because you're white," she said.

He looked at her pointedly. "No. Because I didn't share her opinions."

"But you were involved with her. She was your girlfriend."

"I was sixteen and she was putting out on a very regular basis," he replied. "She does not represent me, my thoughts, or most of the people around Hobbs Creek. I mean, look at Dessie and Clyde. They're an interracial couple and they've been married forever. I don't know of anyone ever giving them a hard time about it."

She sighed. "I'm sure they have. But you know what? That's not even the biggest part of it. I knew Hannah was a bitch the first night I met her. So I'm really not surprised by her behavior."

"Then why didn't you stay with me last night?"

She slipped her hands out of his. "Because I don't know what we're doing, Tyler. What is this? We're from two different worlds. Different states. And when this assignment is over, so are we."

"Is that so?" he asked. "I didn't know we'd decided on that."

"We haven't decided on anything because we don't talk about it."

When he didn't reply right away, she sighed.

"This might be the part where it stops being fun. I didn't want it to stop. I'm just trying to be realistic."

She ran her fingers through her hair and tilted her head back. "I'm making such a mess of this. I always make a mess."

"And I always run," he said, quietly admitting something he'd always known about himself. "What if we both try something different this time?"

"You've been different," she whispered. "From anything I ever imagined, Tyler West. But honestly, I don't know."

His watch beeped and Tyler frowned.

"Gotta go down to help Stephen and the others move the cattle. We're walking the horses past the corrals today and we want to make sure there's lots of distance between them."

"Go," she said with another sigh. "I understand."

"I want to finish this," he told her. "I don't want to just walk away this time."

He didn't know what else he wanted to do where she was concerned. The words weren't forming, plans weren't instantly appearing in his mind. All he knew for certain was that he didn't want it to end.

"I want to do the right thing, for once in my life," she said and Tyler knew she was talking about more than just being with him.

"How about we get away for a few days? We could drive over to Oklahoma and let you get a taste of their barbeque since you weren't impressed with my efforts," he said.

She smiled and that simple action reached deep inside of Tyler, touching every part of him with warmth.

"Barbeque sauce cannot be healthy. If it is, it doesn't taste good," she said.

His watch beeped again.

"Go," she said. "I can get a couple more hours sleep before the crew gets here and I need to get to work."

"Think about the road trip. We could both use a couple of days away from the ranch and all that's been going on here."

She nodded. "I'll think about it."

"And I'll see you around," he said. Tyler leaned in and kissed her lightly on the lips. "You've become a part of this ranch for me, Gabriella Bennett. I look for you everywhere I turn."

He rested his forehead against hers and they both sighed.

A few minutes later, Tyler was closing the door to Gabriella's room. He'd just took the first step when he heard the beeping of the security system signaling that a door or window in the house had been opened. He jogged down the steps and walked into the foyer just in time to see Stephen and two other ranch hands come through the front door.

"What is it?" Tyler asked.

"It's bad, Tyler. It's real bad."

The moment she heard the beeping of the security system Gabriella was fully awake. Oh, who was she kidding? She was never going to fall back asleep after the tense moments she'd just shared with Tyler. As if her night hadn't already been filled with tossing and turning because of him.

She'd finally put her finger on what had been going on with her emotions for the last week. She was afraid. Because she had fallen for Tyler West. There was no denying it for her after last night. She'd just needed to figure out what she was going to do about it. But now that her heart had begun to race thanks to that incessant beeping, she'd thrown back the covers once again and was headed to the door. She'd just gotten to the top of the stairs when she heard Stephen's voice.

"It's bad, Tyler. It's real bad."

Gabriella rushed back into her room. She hurried into the bathroom and took a record twenty-five seconds to relieve herself and do a quick teeth brush before she was in the room again. Grabbing what was first in her drawer she pulled on sweatpants, a bra and a better tank top. After pushing her feet into her tennis shoes, she rushed out of the room and down the steps. Tyler's truck was still parked in front of the house which meant he must have rode with Stephen. They were somewhere on the ranch.

She got into her car and drove to the first place she could think of, the equestrian center. When she pulled up there were four other Jeeps out front and the horses were going crazy. She thought of Brown Eyes, the horse she'd ridden three times now and had grown particularly fond of. And then there was GG, Tyler's horse. Gabriella hoped they were all okay. She ran until she was through the open doors, her feet skidding to a halt as she looked down to the floor.

"No," she whispered at the familiar sight of red.

So much red, thick and running like a river. The world around her begin to spin. On shaky legs she managed to take one step and then another and another. Until she was there, seeing, smelling, feeling.

Somebody called her name. Over and over they said her name, but she couldn't answer them. She couldn't see them. Couldn't see anyone or anything but the blood. There was so much blood. Her throat was tight, her breaths coming in quick heavy pants. It was everywhere. On the walls, stuck against the strands of hay, on the floor, and on her tennis shoes. Gabriella lifted her arms in front of her face. They felt like they were weighted down, but she didn't care. She had to see. Wiggling her fingers and turning her hands from front to back she looked and she saw it, more blood.

Her stomach cramped and she pitched forward, leaning over until her head was at her knees. The putrid scent of blood was stronger and she grew so dizzy she thought she might fall to the floor.

But there was blood on the floor. If she fell it would get on her. It would be on her legs and her thighs, just like it was before. She closed her eyes and tried to wish it all away, but when she opened them again, it was still there.

Her arms and legs streaked with blood. Her chest and midsection, a bloody mess. And her face...Gabriella gasped because it wasn't her face she saw now. It wasn't her lying on the floor the way she always ended up in the dream. It was someone else, another woman with so much blood. It was...Hannah.

The first tear fell and then another, until she was screaming with the remembered pain and despair. She moved back, trying to get away. She bumped into something or someone, she didn't know. The world was still spinning and she was moving, but the blood was following her. She could see it on the ground as she moved and when she looked back the river of blood pooled after her. She had to get away. She needed to get away from it once and for all.

Run!

That's all she could think was that she needed to run, long, fast and hard! She had to run!

Jumping into her car Gabriella sped off, driving to where she didn't know. All she knew was that she had to get away from the blood and from all that pain. What had happened to Hannah? Why was she bleeding the way Gabriella had? In her bedroom and at the hospital, Gabriella recalled all the blood and the fear. It had snaked around her throat like a noose and squeezed until she'd thought she would die. But she hadn't died, not at that moment, at least. She'd spent a few days in the hospital and then she'd returned to her apartment. But the blood had still been there and no matter how hard she'd scrubbed it hadn't gone away.

Whenever she closed her eyes she saw it. If she inhaled too deeply, she smelled it. When she looked at her hands she imagined it was still there.

Tears came faster now, blurring her vision as she went through the ranch's front security gate and turned out onto the open road.

Gabriella cried for her pain and how much she'd suffered in the last six months. She cried for the agony of carrying her secret for so long. She cried for Hannah whose body had been mutilated and left like she was nothing more than an animal. She cried because she couldn't stop.

The car was moving but she had no idea where she was going or what she planned to do once she got there. And her hands were sticky. They were stuck to the steering wheel and when she tried to move them there was a gooey stickiness. She looked down to see what was going on and screamed when she saw more blood.

It was all over the steering wheel, dripping down onto her lap. Glancing up again the sight of blood pouring down onto the windshield like rain was too much for her to handle. She yanked a hand from the steering wheel to turn on the windshield wipers. That did no good, because the blood was too thick and coming down too fast. She couldn't see so she slammed on the brakes. But they didn't work.

Nothing worked!

Nothing took the memories or the pain away. Nothing stopped her from hating herself more and more every day and for making the biggest mistake of her life. And nothing was going to stop her from eventually killing herself with guilt and shame.

Nothing except the swerving of the car and the quick tumble down into a brush before the blaring of horns echoed in her mind.

CHAPTER 14

*G*abriella could still hear the horns blaring but she didn't care. She didn't care about anything else. Not anymore.

She was so tired. Her body felt week and her mind was empty. The memory had played out. All the feelings she'd kept stored had been cried out of her and now there was nothing. She was still and for the first time in too long, that felt right. It felt like what she was supposed to be doing.

As soon as she resigned herself to that fact Gabriella felt herself being yanked out of the comfort. There was pulling on her arm and then she was weightless, as if she was being carried. She didn't open her eyes. Somewhere deep inside she knew that if she opened her eyes it wouldn't be to anything good. So she kept them closed, even when she heard voices around her. They were familiar voices, but she hadn't heard them recently.

Light permeated the dark corner where she'd found solace

and she closed her eyes tighter. She'd thought she had found light before. She'd traveled to someplace new and there had found more light, but that had been wrong too. It was impossible and she should have known that sooner. She should have stopped it before she got in too deep.

"Gabriella! Open your eyes, Gabs! Come on, open your damn eyes!"

It was a male voice. He was yelling but not in anger. There was panic to his tone. Irritation and panic.

"Gabriella!"

He kept yelling her name.

"Come on Gabriella, you can do it. Just open your eyes for us. Everything is going to be okay, just open your eyes, Gabriella."

Now there was a woman. She had a firm tone, authoritative, yet caring. Gabriella knew them both. She knew them and she'd missed them. Just as she'd missed so many things in her old life.

Somebody brushed her hair back from her face. Somebody held her hand. They kept calling to her, insisting that she open her eyes. But she didn't want to. It was over, wasn't it?

"Gabs, please, just open your eyes for me. I know you're in there. You're breathing and you're alive. Gabriella, please!"

He sounded so sad. He was usually bossy with her and protective, but never sad. It made her heart hurt and she didn't like that she was the one making him sound that way.

Gabriella decided to open her eyes but it was harder than she thought it would be. She tried again and again, but it wasn't working. Why couldn't she just wake up? Because she'd thought for so long that she didn't want to wake up. She'd been walking around smiling and living as if things were as they had been before, but they weren't. She knew it and now she had to live it.

With that thought her eyes shot open and Gabriella gasped for breath. She coughed and blinked a couple of times, sure she had to be seeing things.

"Gabs! There you go! That's my girl!" he said lifting her head and shoulders up into an embrace. "That's my Gabs!"

He was rocking her back and forth and Gabriella inhaled deeply. She knew his scent. Her arms went around him and she sobbed, "Alex."

"Yes, you little troublemaker. It's me," he said with a chuckle.

He held her back away from him and smiled. "You scared the hell out of me! Twice, Gabriella! Two damn times, in twenty-four hours you've scared me to death!"

"Alex," Gabriella said again. "But how? I'm not home. I mean, I left town and he kept calling me and I didn't want to talk to him. But I wasn't home. I was...what are you doing here?"

"We can get to that later. Right now I think we need to get you to a hospital."

That was Monica. Gabriella knew that cool voice anywhere. She looked to her other side to see Alex's fiancé kneeling on the ground beside her.

"Monica," she sighed. "Oh, it is so good to see both of you."

Monica had been holding her hand and she squeezed it as she smiled at Gabriella. "It's good to see you."

"But I don't know why you're here. Or where we are exactly," Gabriella said and then tried to sit up on her own.

Alex kept his hands on her, but she managed to come to a sitting position as she looked around.

"We were on our way to see you at a place called Westwind Ranch & Resort," Monica told her.

"Then we were almost hit head-on by some maniac driving erratically," Alex said before tweaking her nose. "You almost killed all of us. What's the matter with you, Gabs? And don't you dare tell me nothing. Because I've come all this way because I know that's a big fat lie."

"We're on the road," Gabriella said, ignoring her brother's words. "I was leaving the ranch. It's back there, not too far."

She tried to stand up but Alex quickly grabbed her arms.

"Whoa, wait a minute, champ. You've got quite a lump on your head so I'm sure you're dizzy," he said.

"No, I'm okay." But she felt queasiness overtake her as she attempted to get up again. "Well, maybe not. But I will be. Just help me up."

Alex and Monica helped her up and walked her slowly to their rental car. Once they had her in the backseat and Gabriella felt like she wasn't going to vomit all over the place, she said, "Let's go back to the ranch. I have to go back there."

"Wait a minute, Gabs," Alex said. "Just hold on. You were clearly upset to be driving the way that you were. You look like you've been crying. I'm not taking you back there until you tell me what's going on."

He had come all this way to check on her. Gabriella wanted to cry again. This was love right here. Of course he was her brother, but this was the bond she wanted to one day have with someone. It was what she'd dreamed of, but had been wondering if it would ever happen for her.

"I know. I'm going to explain. I just need to go back. I need to make sure he's alright and see if I can help. I was so awful, the way I acted and then I just left and he's probably worried. I don't want him to worry."

"Oh, you mean like I've been worried since Adriana finally broke down and told me you were out of town," Alex said.

He was irritated now, his brow furrowed, lips going into a thin line.

"Alex, give her some space," Monica said. "If she wants to go back, we'll go with her."

Alex glanced over his shoulder to Monica who gave him a calm, but stern look. He shook his head as he turned back to Gabriella. "Alright, we'll go back to this ranch with you. But I promise you Gabriella, I'm not letting you out of my sight again until I get an explanation."

She tried to nod but it sent shooting pain from her temples throughout her head and down to her neck. "I know. And I'm going to tell you, I promise. Just take me back."

Alex reached over her and fit the seat belt into its holder with a resounding click.

"I'll ride in the back with you," Monica said when Alex moved from the door and walked around the car without another word.

When Monica was seated on the other side of the back seat, her seat belt in place, Gabriella sighed. She was nervous and still a little queasy, but she knew she couldn't leave like this. She shouldn't have left the way she had. She would go back and she would help Tyler with whatever was happening now and when he asked what was wrong with her this time, Gabriella swore she was going to tell him. Because this was too much and it had gone on for far too long.

Monica taking her hand again added a layer of calm to Gabriella's decision and she lay her head back on the seat, hoping the pain would stop before she arrived at Westwind.

The day wasn't going at all the way Tyler had planned. He'd wanted to get his work done as quickly as possible and then sit with Gabriella to talk about their trip. He hadn't expected to walk into the equestrian center and see Hannah's bloody body lying in one of the empty stalls.

And he definitely hadn't expected Gabriella to come running in minutes later. She'd totally lost it.

That was the only way he could describe what he'd watched happen, just about forty minutes ago. She'd run into the equestrian center, stopping quickly and staring down at the floor. Tyler had no idea what she'd seen on the floor because where she was standing there was only strands of hay and cement. But she'd looked down as if there were something there, something that absolutely terrified her. He'd walked to her in an attempt to get her to leave before she actually did see something heinous. But she pulled away from him.

She'd gone straight to the third stall as if she'd already known what she would find there. And then she'd screamed. The sound had echoed throughout the stalls, sending the horses that were already agitated into a complete state of hysteria. The ranch hands scrambled to get to them before they hurt themselves and Tyler had focused on Gabriella. She wouldn't let him touch her. Each time he'd tried, she'd move or do something strange with her arms and hands. He didn't know what was going on or how to help her.

At one point he considered just picking her up and tossing her over his shoulder so he could carry her outside. But he hadn't wanted to make whatever she was going through worse. When she'd finally backed out of the stall, he thought she was going to calm down and that he could assist her at that time, but she snapped again. And this time she took off running. He'd chased after her, but by then the sheriff and four other police cars were pulling up with sirens blaring. She jumped into her car and pulled off and Tyler told himself she would return to the ranch house to get herself together.

But when he'd finally been able to get back to the house, Gabriella wasn't there.

"What do you mean she didn't come back here?" Tyler had asked Jagger when he'd come into the living room.

"I haven't seen her since the two of you took off running out of here earlier. You could have told me what was going on," Jagger insisted.

Tyler cursed. He'd walked over to the window to look out but he didn't see her car. All he saw were police cars and flashing red and blue lights.

"What the hell is going on around here, Tyler? Nevil said Hannah's dead. She was stabbed on our property."

Jagger wore jeans and a faded blue t-shirt. That seemed to be his style lately, as he'd walked around the ranch as if he was here for the first time.

"I don't know what's going on," Tyler told him. "Stephen said when he pulled up this morning and rode past the equestrian center he could hear the horses whining and kicking against the paddock doors. So he got out and went in to check on them. He smelled the blood as soon as he got inside and thought one of the horses had injured itself, but it wasn't the horse. It was Hannah."

Tyler couldn't believe it himself. Seeing Hannah lying there like that, naked and sliced open. It was horrible and he didn't understand it. How had Hannah gotten onto the property? How had whoever had done this to her gotten onto the property? And where the hell was Gabriella?

"I gotta go out and look for her," he told Jagger.

His brother looked at him incredulously. "We've sort of got something going on here, man. How are you going to up and leave when this place is crawling with cops?"

"I can't stay here while she's out there. You didn't see her. She's upset and anything can happen to her. I just have to go!"

He headed for the doorway when Jagger grabbed him.

"Hold on a second, what are you doing? Somebody was killed and you're gonna run after her!"

"Yes I am dammit!" Tyler yelled and pulled away from Jagger. "I'm gonna find her because I don't give a damn about any of this without her!"

"Stop all that yelling and call Dr. Morrison," Dessie said as she came bustling into the living room. "Here, right here," she continued. "You can lay her right down here on the couch."

For one brief moment Tyler sighed with relief as he saw Gabriella's face. But she was limping and there was a bump on her head. A man was on one side of her and a woman on the other. Tyler jumped into action, racing over to help her.

"Gabriella, baby, what happened?" he asked as he pushed past the woman and linked his arm around her waist.

He was going to pick her up and carry her when the man beside her spoke.

"I got this," the man said. "You can get your hands off my sister."

Tyler froze. "Your sister?"

"The couch," Dessie intervened. "Get her on the couch then the two of you can exchange names, check I.D.s and do whatever else you feel like doing."

Tyler didn't leave her side and neither did the other guy. So they ushered Gabriella to the couch where she quickly lay back against the pillows Dessie had just put there. Dessie shooed both of them away and lifted Gabriella's feet up onto the chair.

"If one of you don't get a move on and call that doctor, I swear I'm gonna start swinging," Dessie yelled.

"I'll do it," Jagger said and headed out of the room.

"I'm Monica Lakefield," the woman whom Tyler had barely noticed said, as she stepped in front of him.

She held out a hand and Tyler hesitated only a second before taking it. "I'm Tyler West. This is my ranch. Gabriella is my... she's ah, she's staying here with me."

"Is that so?" the man asked as he came to stand beside Monica.

"That is so," Tyler replied. "And who are you?"

"I'm Alex Bennett. Gabriella's brother," he said sternly.

Tyler didn't waver. There would be no handshake exchanged this time.

"So Gabriella is staying with you," Alex continued. "And who are you to her? Why haven't I ever heard about you? And if she's staying here with you, why was she driving erratically on the road causing an accident?"

"I'll answer your questions out of respect for Gabriella. But don't forget you're in my house. So if there's any interrogating to be done, it will be done by me," Tyler stated evenly.

Alex opened his mouth to say something else, when Monica touched his arm.

Tyler continued. "Gabriella is redesigning and decorating the ranch and two other properties. She saw something upsetting this morning and drove off before I could stop her."

"You didn't say who you were to her," Alex interjected.

Monica tilted her head as she continued to stare at Tyler. "He's her boss. Is that correct?"

"Yes," Tyler responded tightly.

"Tell me why you're here, Alex," Gabriella said quietly.

Tyler left them standing there as he went to kneel beside the couch where she lay.

"Are you alright?" he asked and took her hand in his.

She gave him a weak smile. "I have a headache and I'm sorry for running off. But I want to hear what my brother has to say before I explain why I did."

"Always trying to call the shots," Alex said from behind Tyler.

"Are you going to answer her question?" Tyler asked without turning to look at the man that he knew was standing protectively behind him.

"We were worried about you," Alex replied after another moment of silence. "I told Mom and Dad I'd come down here to make sure you were alright."

With her free hand Gabriella touched the bump on her forehead before hissing in pain. Tyler clenched his teeth. He hated that she'd been hurt.

"Dr. Morrison's on his way," Jagger said from somewhere in the room.

The words calmed Tyler momentarily.

"I talked to Mama and Daddy a couple of days ago," Gabriella told Alex. "They knew where I was and what I was doing."

Monica came to stand at the end of the couch. She wore navy blue form-fitting pants, a white blouse and a short blue jacket to match. Her black hair was held together by a band and left to hang over her shoulder. She had brown eyes, darker than Gabriella's, and a cool stare.

"That was before the incident," Monica announced.

"What incident?" Gabriella asked.

"Maybe we should give them some privacy," Dessie suggested.

"No," Gabriella said. "It's okay. You're like my family too, Dessie."

Jagger cleared his throat.

"You too, Jagger," Gabriella said staring somewhere over Tyler's shoulder.

Tyler didn't turn to look. He didn't want to take his eyes off her, not again.

"At two-thirty yesterday afternoon Detective Cole Desdune was called to the scene of a vehicle fire," Alex said.

Tyler's heart sank as he thought of the last call he'd received about a vehicle fire.

Gabriella looked confused. "Cole's a homicide detective."

"He was called in because he's related to the owner of the car that was set on fire," Alex continued.

Gabriella gasped.

Monica reached down and touched her leg. "Nobody was in the car, Gabriella. It was in the parking garage where you parked it before you went out of town."

"My car? You came all the way to Texas because my car was on fire and nobody was in it."

"No," Alex told her. "We came all the way to Texas because when Cole questioned the residents in the building about seeing any strange or suspicious people hanging around the building, they all gave the same description of a man. One woman even knew the man's name."

Gabriella shook her head. "No," she whispered.

"Austin Sterner," Alex stated.

Tyler stood. He dropped Gabriella's hand and faced Alex. "Are you saying that her ex who has been stalking her for months set her car on fire yesterday?"

Alex raised a brow. "For months?" he asked and looked around Tyler to Gabriella. "This guy has been bothering you for months and you don't tell anybody anything about it!"

"Wait a minute," Gabriella said. "If Austin set my car on fire, he's still in Connecticut. He's not here in Hobbs Creek."

Tyler turned back to her. "No, he's not here, Gabriella. He's nowhere near you. He's never going to hurt you again."

"He hurt you!" Alex roared. "Gabriella Joy Bennett you are going to have to tell me this whole story and right now or I'm packing you up and putting you on the first plane back home."

"She's an adult," Tyler interjected.

"I wish one of you in this room would act like an adult, instead of school yard boys getting their briefs all in a bunch," Dessie stated.

She walked over, pushing Tyler and Alex out of the way.

"Dr. Morrison just pulled up. So we're all going to get out of this room and let the doctor have a look at her."

When nobody dared to speak, Dessie continued.

"Monica Lakefield, that's what you said your name is right? Okay, well Monica you and Alex Bennett can follow me upstairs. We have a guest room you can use to freshen up and get yourselves together while we wait for Dr. Morrison to finish up with Gabriella."

"Tyler, you and Jagger need to finish dealing with all the commotion out there. Sheriff Alvarez will want to speak to you both but Clyde says for you to meet him in the office so he can talk to you first."

There was silence after her commands were given and no movement.

"Go!" Dessie yelled and snapped her fingers.

Jagger moved first and Tyler looked at Gabriella. "I'll just be in the next room. I'm coming right back when I'm finished. Don't you move."

She shook her head. "I won't."

Good, he thought. That was good. And before Tyler left the room he bent down and touched his lips to hers.

"Don't you move," he whispered again.

"I won't," she replied and kissed him back.

"Alex spoke to the detective in Connecticut just before dinner. He said they're looking for Austin and don't believe he's left town. He hasn't been at work for the last two weeks. They say he's on vacation." Tyler talked while moving around the bedroom.

He was checking all the windows to make sure they were locked. He even went into the bathroom to check the small window in there before coming back to see that Gabriella was still sitting up in bed, where she'd taken her dinner about an hour ago. Tyler stayed with her while the rest of the family had eaten downstairs in the dining room.

"Great," Gabriella sighed. "He's on the loose in Connecticut and a killer's on the loose here. What kind of times are we living in that these things can happen? I mean, what is going through people's minds these days?"

"I don't know," Tyler replied. "But all I'm concerned about right now is keeping you safe. So everything is locked up tight. Jagger and Alex checked everything downstairs."

"Did Dessie leave?"

"Yes, thank God," Tyler said with a sigh. "I thought she would collapse from running around here barking orders the way she did all day.

"It's her way of helping," Gabriella told him.

She'd wanted to thank Dessie for being there for her yet again. Gabriella had meant it when she'd said they were like her family now. Dessie and Clyde, they had been seeing to her needs since the day she stepped off the plane and arrived here in Hobbs Creek. From getting her the rental car to setting up this job. And when she was prepared to leave they'd even offered to drive her to the airport and return the rental car for her. She cared about them deeply.

Jagger, on the other hand, Gabriella could only shake her head when she thought of him. Tyler's too smart for his own good brother had grown on her in this past week, especially after she'd seen how truly hurt he was over Brooke's betrayal.

He'd fallen in love with the wrong person. Gabriella could certainly relate to that.

Now her brother and Monica were here. This entire house was filled with her family. And Tyler. She clenched the sheets between her fingers and felt the weight in her chest growing heavier. Because she knew she was still lying to them all.

"Did Sheriff Alvarez leave?"

It wasn't what she meant to say, but Gabriella swore she was going to get to it. She just didn't want to freak out the way she had earlier. Causing her own minor concussion was embarrassing enough without a repeat performance.

"Yes," Tyler said when he finally sat on the other side of the bed. He bent over and was taking off his shoes. "Clyde told him we would all give our statements tomorrow. Sheriff wasn't terribly happy about that, but unless he comes back with an arrest warrant, that's how it has to be for now."

"He probably wants to ask us about the incident at the restaurant."

"Why do you say that?"

She shrugged. "It just makes sense. We have a very public confrontation with Hannah and the next morning she turns up dead, on your property."

"We're not murderers."

"No." She agreed. "We're not. We're lovers?"

He shook his head and moved over on the bed until he was sitting right beside her. "We're more than that, Gabriella. At least I want us to be."

He'd taken her hand and Gabriella looked down as he twined his fingers with hers. "I think I'd like that, too. But first, there's something I need to tell you."

"Ok, I'm listening," he said and then waited.

She couldn't look at him when she said this. In fact, she wanted to get off the bed and be as far away from him as possible. In case he needed to walk away. But when she attempted to reclaim her hand, Tyler held it tighter.

She still did not look at him, but she did begin.

"I told you that Austin had two kids and that he shared custody with his ex-wife."

"Yes, you told me that."

"Well, we um, we couldn't spend Thanksgiving together last year because he had his kids. So to make it up to me we spent the next weekend at a ski resort in Pennsylvania. The next weekend he had his kids again and then he had a big property going to settlement and I had two homes I needed to get staged. So we didn't see each other a lot in December, not until Christmas Day. Because he had the kids for Thanksgiving, his wife got them for Christmas. I hadn't been feeling well and I'd actually left my parents' house early. They were a little disappointed because they were looking forward to meeting him. Up until that point I hadn't told my family anything about Austin, but on Christmas Eve when Austin sent me a text accepting my invitation to have dinner with my family, I was excited and I told my mother I was bringing someone with me.""

Gabriella sighed and stared straight ahead at the door.

"Anyway, I didn't feel good so I went home. Austin came over to my place and he took care of me. We thought I might have a stomach virus. Two weeks later, I found out I was pregnant."

He squeezed her hand and tears filled her eyes.

"I was excited," she said. "Just like my sister was excited when she told me she was pregnant two months ago. I was going to have a baby. Austin was a great father. He loved his kids and he was dedicated to providing for them and giving them a good future. I couldn't wait to tell him."

She went quiet as she remembered that night.

"What did he say when you told him?" Tyler asked.

She cleared her throat. "He said he didn't want any more children. He said he'd told me that before and I should have made sure that it didn't happen. He wanted me to get an abortion. I told him I wouldn't. I said I could take care of my child on my own. That I didn't need anything from him, ever. And then I walked out of his apartment. He called me the next day and I made myself clear if he hadn't understood me the night before. It was over between us. He was an ass and my child deserved better."

"I agree," Tyler said.

That made her smile momentarily but she still could not look at him.

"I didn't hear from him anymore until the morning of Valentine's Day when two dozen red roses arrived at my office. He sent me a text asking me to be his Valentine. I thought he'd come around and realized how much of a jerk he'd been about the baby so I agreed to have dinner with him. I was having a hard time with morning sickness all hours of the day and fatigue, so I suggested we order in at my condo. When I arrived home from work there were more roses, all over the place. The building manager had brought them in because there were too many at the front desk."

One tear escaped and Gabriella used her free hand to wipe it away.

"Austin arrived at seven-thirty. He was always punctual. We sat down to talk while we waited for the food. I don't know how he misunderstood, or what gave him the idea that something had changed, but he thought I'd had the abortion. It was the only reason he'd reached out to me. When I told him I didn't and that I was keeping the baby, he freaked out. Yelling that I was trying to trap him, to take even more money from him than his ex-wife was. He thought I was smarter than that. He thought I had more integrity than that. He was going to tell everybody at the office that I was lying and that it wasn't his baby. I immediately felt sick. I ran to the bathroom and vomited for what felt like hours. He stayed in the living room still arguing and telling me I was getting what I deserved for not listening to him. That's when the cramps came. They were quick and potent and I immediately fell to the floor. I called out to him and after about the third time he finally came into the bathroom. I told him something was wrong. I said it over and over again."

Her chest hurt, but she kept going. She couldn't stop now.

"He called me pathetic and weak and said he could do so much better than me. So he left. I was sitting on the bathroom floor in the worst pain of my life and he left me there. The minute I heard the front door slam I tried to get up. I just needed to get to my phone to call my mother to come and pick me up. I knew I needed to get to the hospital. But I never made it out of the bathroom. I fell to another cramp and when I tried to get up again I noticed the blood. It came fast and seemed like it was everywhere. I cried because with every cramp that came afterwards I knew my baby was dying."

"The food delivery arrived and when I heard them ringing the doorbell I yelled for them to come in. They did and the delivery guy found me on the floor in a pool of blood. He called an ambulance and—"

Tyler hugged her to him. He lay her head on his shoulder and held her while she cried. Gabriella had no idea how long that lasted, but he didn't let her go.

Sometime in the middle of the night he managed to get up and take off his clothes, but when she rolled over in the darkness he was there.

"Thank you," she whispered.

"For what?" he asked groggily as they settled into their new sleeping position.

"For not saying anything and just letting me talk. I needed to get it all out."

"And you did. It's over now," he said.

"It is," she sighed into him. "It's over now."

"I'm not leaving you, Gabriella," he told her a few seconds later. "I won't leave you."

She didn't know if she was dreaming or not, but Gabriella loved hearing those words. She believed them and she trusted him because Tyler was everything Austin wasn't. He was strong and loyal, honest and caring. He wasn't going to leave her when she needed him most. She believed that, just as she believed Austin would not stop until he made her pay for leaving him.

CHAPTER 15

$\mathcal{T}$yler kissed her awake the next morning.

It was the first thing he wanted to do when he opened his eyes. He'd thought about what she'd said all night. Knowing that only distance and the fact that he needed to protect her kept him from finding Austin Sterner and beating the shit out of him. Gabriella had called him an ass. The man was so much less than that. Tyler had told Gabriella last night that they were not murderers, but the truth was, if Austin were near him right now Tyler could easily kill him and not blink an eye.

Instead, he held her close to him, loving the sound of her sigh as she opened her mouth to his kiss. His hands moved up and down her body, her arms, her thighs, her breasts, noting that her skin was softer to the touch and more appealing than he'd ever experienced. She moved her hands over his body too. Down his torso and over his chest. He loved the feel of her fingers moving over his chest. When those fingers went lower to brush over his erection, Tyler groaned. She pushed his boxer briefs down and he lifted the hem of her nightshirt.

"Are you sure?" he asked when she was naked and he was too. "I don't want to hurt you."

"I'm fine," she told him and smiled. "Really. This time, I'm fine."

She was fine, from the tip of her pert little nose to the toenails that had a color change and were now pumpkin orange. She was the most beautiful woman he'd ever seen and Tyler was sure that he'd fallen madly in love with her.

But he didn't think Gabriella was ready to hear that. So, after slipping on a condom, he eased into her slowly. He wrapped her legs around his waist and for the first time in his life made sweet love to a woman.

An hour later Gabriella was still in the bedroom. Tyler had already gone downstairs to get started with his day, but he'd advised her to take it easy. After he'd given her the best and strongest orgasm she'd ever had.

She'd showered and slipped into a simple floral print sundress and flat sandals. She'd just finished talking to Adriana on the phone, telling her sister everything she should have told her before, when there was a light knock on the bedroom door.

"Hi," she said when she opened the door to see Monica standing there.

"Good morning," Monica replied and stepped into the room. "Are you feeling better?"

"I am," Gabriella answered. And since Monica was already in the room, she closed the door. "How are you this morning?"

"I'm well. It's a little different waking up on an actual ranch, than in a Manhattan apartment," Monica said.

Monica Lakefield was one of three Lakefield sisters. Their father, Paul Lakefield had founded the Lakefield Galleries in New York. Two years ago, Monica spearheaded the expansion of her father's dream to share great art with the world by opening the Atlanta Lakefield Gallery. She was a lovely woman with a light complexion and ebony hair, which this morning was styled in a messy bun that still managed to look chic and professional. She wore a dress as well—a vibrant pink halter maxi dress and natural-colored sandals with heels that only added to her normal five foot nine stature. She was the oldest of her sisters, Karena and Deena. The more dominant and fiercely protective one. And, for the last five years she'd been engaged to Alex.

That made her family.

"I want to thank you and Alex for coming all the way down here to check on me, even though it wasn't necessary," Gabriella said when Monica seemed to be preoccupied.

Rather, she was doing what Monica always did first, assessing her surroundings. Monica was a thinker who said whatever was on her mind, when it came to her mind. That could be a good and/or bad thing. Gabriella had seen both.

When Monica finally stopped looking around the room, she took a seat in the recliner across from the bed.

"Come sit, and talk to me for a second," she said and nodded toward the bed.

Gabriella had been planning to head downstairs and get a cup of coffee before she started making calls to her crew to see about rescheduling the work that wasn't done yesterday. But, she could sit and talk...for a second.

She sat on the side of the bed closest to the recliner and waited because Monica clearly had something she wanted to say.

"First of all, don't thank family for doing what family does best—loving and caring for their own," she began. "When Renny called Alex to tell him what Cole reported about your car, we immediately drove down to Greenwich. Cole wanted to question you, to see how you were connected to Austin Sterner, but you weren't there. That drove Alex nuts not knowing where you were. When he told your parents what had happened they said you were out of town on business, somewhere in Texas. He had to call Adriana to find out the specifics. We were worried."

Gabriella sighed heavily. "I can understand that. But it's not like I didn't tell anybody where I was going. I just didn't tell everybody."

"I get that," Monica said with a slow smile. "Believe me, girl, I get it. You've found your niche and you're working it. I respect that wholeheartedly, and to tell the truth, I knew you would get there in your own time."

"Thanks for saying that," Gabriella said. It really had meant a lot to hear that somebody in her family had believed in her all along.

"Alex is still a little sore at you about leaving and not telling him, but the relief of knowing you're safe outweighs that."

"I can't believe what Austin did."

"I can," Monica told her.

"What? Why?" Gabriella had told Tyler all that had happened between her and Austin last night. And just a few minutes ago she'd relayed the same story to Adriana, who was angry and hurt that Gabriella had gone through all of that on her own. But she hadn't yet figured out how to tell Alex, her parents or her other brothers. None of them would take it as relatively calmly as Adriana had.

"Because I know his type." Monica sat back in the recliner, looking as if she were about to tell Gabriella a bed time story. There was no way Gabriella could have expected what would come next.

"I don't...I mean, I never told anyone in the family about Austin."

Monica nodded. "That's the first sign."

"I don't get what you're trying to say, Monica."

She tilted her head and stared at Gabriella a moment and then clasped her hands together in her lap. This was the most serene Gabriella had ever seen Monica look.

"His name was Yates Hinton. I found out much later that wasn't his real name, but that's what I knew him as. I met him when I was in college. He swept me off my feet and I fell deliriously in love with him. And then his wife found out," Monica spoke quietly.

Gabriella didn't know what to say.

"I broke it off with him. He grew angry and he raped me. I blamed myself, graduated from college, went home and decided to never look back. I didn't tell anyone and I did nothing to stop Yates from doing it again to someone else. Or, as it turns out, for coming after me again. Years later, he stalked me, harassed me and finally, forced me to stab him. And only after all that did I tell my story, before walking away from your brother."

"Monica," Gabriella said with tears brimming in her eyes. "I had no idea something like that had happened to you."

She nodded. "Just like no one in your family realized

anything traumatic had happened to you. But I did, Gabriella. I saw it in your eyes the moment you opened them after we pulled you out of your car. I didn't say anything because I didn't have all the facts. And I wasn't sure if this ranch had something to do with it too. But then we arrived here and I met Tyler. I saw how he looked at you and how you looked and him and my past played before me like a movie."

Monica let out a little chuckle. "My mother always said that our lessons learned should be told in order to guide someone else who might be fighting that same battle. You are where I was five years ago and Tyler is Alex, trying to love a woman who's been broken by another man. Austin is your Yates."

"You don't know the whole story," Gabriella began, but Monica stopped her.

"And I don't need to know it. Not unless you want to tell me. But Gabriella, while your details may be different from mine, the pain and despair that you've suffered is the same. I know it. I see it in your eyes right now. I feel it in my heart as I did so long ago."

Damn she was tired of crying. Lifting her hands to wipe her face, Gabriella shook her head.

"I couldn't tell," she said. "It hurt so badly and I felt so stupid, I just couldn't tell."

Monica came to the end of the chair. She reached out to take Gabriella's hands.

"That pain will pass, once you stand up to him. Don't believe that it will go away, that you can outrun it. You can't. He's sick in his mind and no rational thought will stop him, but the police tossing his ass in a cell will. Don't let him take any more of your life, Gabriella."

Gabriella, nodded. She knew that what Monica was saying was right. She knew she had to face Austin. She had to stop him once and for all.

"I won't," she said. "I know what I have to do."

Monica stood and pulled Gabriella up for a hug. "I'll stand with you if you want me to. I'll be there every step of the way."

"Thank you." Gabriella held her tight. "Thank you so much for these words and for being here today and for putting up with Alex."

To that, Monica laughed and when they broke free of the hug shook her head.

"It was a close call for us," she told Gabriella. "I walked away from him because I didn't know if I could rebuild myself after admitting everything about Yates. But I came to my senses and it all worked out. These have been the best five years of my life."

"He loves you so much," Gabriella said. "We all see it in everything he does. And when you finally marry him, it'll be such a big celebration. We'll have fireworks and a parade or something grand." She joked.

"Everybody's path in life is different," Monica said. "There are some patches that are similar, some roads that lead you around in circles, and some that drop you right into a dead end. But eventually, I believe, everybody gets to where they are supposed to be."

Gabriella took those words with her as they moved downstairs to smell the scent of breakfast cooking.

Tyler looked around the table in the dining room and for a

moment felt like he was taken back twenty-five years, to a time when his parents were alive and well and entertained friends. They would often have dinner parties or outdoor barbeques. Their closest friends would come and sometimes people that they did business with, but there would be lots of guests and laughter and a sense of home and belonging.

He didn't know when that had stopped for him, but sitting here this morning, he knew he definitely wanted to get that feeling back on a more permanent basis. Picking up his glass to finish the last of the orange juice Dessie had insisted he drink—regardless of how much sugar he told her it contained—Tyler listened as Alex finished telling a story and Gabriella laughed.

It was a rich, full-bodied sound, which had that feeling of constriction in his chest rising again. Tyler didn't bother to question the sensation this time—because he knew what it was. And when she reached out to take his hand that was sitting in his lap, he looked over to her and smiled. Aside from that bandage on her forehead that pissed him off each time he looked at it, she was as beautiful as ever, sitting beside him with her hair out and around her shoulders. This was exactly where he wanted to be and who he wanted to be with.

"Don't listen to him," Gabriella said as she continued to grin at him. "I wasn't that bad."

"She was worse," Alex added. "Everything my parents told her not to do, she did. And she did it so badly that they had no choice but to find out. Like the time she was sixteen and snuck out of the house to go to some party with her friends. When she tried to sneak back into the house at almost five the next morning, she managed to get into her room safely but then one of her friends called to make sure she was home and my mother answered the phone. Gabriella didn't know Mom was on the other line and she proceeded to talk to her friend about all the fun they'd had and how excited they'd been when the college boys showed up at the party."

"College boys?" Dessie asked with a raised brow. "Chile, I know your mother was ready to whip your behind good for that stunt. I know I would have."

Clyde shook his head. "And I would've had my gun out looking for each of those college boys that decided to attend a party with high school girls."

"I'm surprised your brothers didn't go out looking for them," Jagger added. "Ty, you remember that time our cousin Carlee, came to visit from Daytona. She had every ranch hand and supplier in the area chasing after her. Until we got the word out that she wasn't to be touched, or looked at for that matter."

Tyler nodded and smiled. He had forgotten about that summer when he and Jagger had been teenagers and much closer than they were now.

"Carlee hated us for that," Tyler said. "I don't think she came back to the ranch for a visit since that time."

"Oh believe me, Adriana and I have our share of moments when we can't stand our brothers for their overprotective nonsense," Gabriella said.

"Boys raised to be good men shouldn't be hated," Clyde said. "They should protect the women in their family at all costs."

Alex nodded and locked gazes with Tyler. "That's exactly what my dad taught us," he said.

Tyler held Alex's gaze and confirmed, "My father taught us the same thing."

The knock—or rather pounding—on the front door, halted the conversation. Everybody paused, but nobody moved. The pounding sounded again.

"It's just the door, y'all," Dessie said and pushed away from the table.

Clyde dropped his napkin on the table and got up with his wife. "Everybody sit tight."

Tyler squeezed Gabriella's hand which had gone still.

"You think any about who would want to kill that woman and leave her body on your property?" Alex asked Tyler.

Tyler had thought about it. Between that and killing Austin Sterner, he'd thought of nothing else last night. Which is why the minute he'd come downstairs this morning, he'd gone into his office to call the private investigator he'd hired.

"I'm working on a theory," he said.

"You plan on sharing that theory?" Jagger asked. "Because we're all involved now. Regardless of whose name is on the deed of this place, I'm a West and I always will be. Whatever's happening involves the both of us."

"It involves all of us," Gabriella said. "We're all here now and the killer is still out there. So it involves all of us."

Monica nodded. "I agree with her. And sometimes when more than one head is put together, solutions and answers come quicker. So, please, do share your thoughts."

Alex didn't look too pleased about what his fiancé said, but he didn't argue. Instead he sat back in his chair and again, looked expectantly at Tyler.

"Sheriff Alvarez wants to have an informal word with Tyler and Gabriella," Clyde said coming into the dining room.

"Should we leave?" Monica asked.

"No," Tyler replied. "If this is informal, we're comfortable with everybody staying. Right?" he asked Gabriella.

"Yes," she replied. "That's right."

Sheriff Alvarez had come into the room and now stood at the head of the table. He didn't look happy about the arrangement, but Tyler wasn't concerned about the sheriff's happiness.

"There was an argument between you and Hannah Palmer the night before last," he said to Tyler. "Tell me about it."

Tyler did not hesitate. "I made reservations for dinner at P&P for seven-thirty. Gabriella and I were seated. We ordered and were having a glass of wine while we waited for our food when Hannah approached us. She talked to me about us meeting up for an article in the Gazette. I turned that offer down. She then turned her attention to Gabriella and began to spew hateful racist rhetoric at her."

"Hmph."

All eyes went to Dessie who had made the sound and folded her arms angrily over her chest.

"Gabriella responded to Hannah's taunt and we left," Tyler finished.

The sheriff nodded.

"You responded with a threat to Ms. Palmer's life," Alvarez said to Gabriella.

It was a statement and not a question which told Tyler that Alvarez had spent the rest of yesterday talking to people who had been at the restaurant. Which meant, he'd been thinking of circling back to him and Gabriella all along. Tyler tried not to be angry at that fact, accepting that it made sense in the course of an investigation, considering all the facts. But damn if he had to like it.

Gabriella slid her hand away from Tyler's and sat up straighter in her chair.

"Yes, I did," she replied. "She was nasty and disrespectful. I was angry and when she tried to assault Tyler, I let her have it. With words, that is."

"What did you say to her exactly?" the sheriff asked her.

"You don't have to answer that," Clyde told Gabriella.

She shook her head. "I'll answer it. I told her that if she ever talked to me like that again I was going to bust her head with the next bottle of wine."

"And you assaulted her?" Alvarez pressed.

Clyde shook his head. "Do *not* answer that, Gabriella."

Tyler touched her shoulder and she looked over to him. She did not respond to the sheriff.

Alvarez frowned. "Where were you Wednesday night between the hours of midnight and three in the morning?"

"She was with me," Tyler interjected. "We were in bed together."

He ignored Alex's frown and prayed that Gabriella would not contradict his statement.

"Is that true?" Alvarez asked her.

"Yes," she said without hesitation. "Tyler and I were together in bed on Wednesday night."

Alvarez nodded. He also looked skeptical.

"Who else was here in the house Wednesday night?" the sheriff asked and looked around the room.

"I was," Jagger told him.

Alvarez gave a half smile. "Jagger West. Your fiancé is still sitting in my jail cell waiting for her lawyer to get there. Tell me what you've been doing here in Hobbs Creek, since she's been busy vandalizing private property?"

Jagger didn't flinch. But Tyler hadn't suspected he would.

"I had dinner alone on Wednesday night. Frozen pizza and beer. I watched some really bad reality TV shows and crashed on my bed I guess somewhere around nine. I didn't see Tyler or Gabriella but I did hear them come in," Jagger said.

That could have been true, Tyler thought, because after leaving the restaurant, even though Gabriella had been silent, Tyler had known she needed to eat. So he'd stopped at a fast food place to get them something quick, that neither of them ended up eating.

"And who are you?" Alvarez asked Alex.

"Alexander Bennett and this is my fiancé, Monica Lakefield. Gabriella is my sister. Monica and I arrived in Hobbs Creek yesterday to visit her," Alex said in a tone that almost dared Alvarez to ask him another question.

"I think we're finished here, Sheriff," Clyde said. "You've gotten all the alibis you need."

"It would have been better if these two weren't alibiing each other," the sheriff stated. "The fact is that Hannah Palmer was killed in your equestrian center between the hours of midnight and three a.m. That means we're going to question everybody who works here, who has access to this ranch or any reason to be on this ranch. And we're going to do that until we find ourselves a suspect."

"You can do your job as you see fit," Clyde told the sheriff. "But my clients have fulfilled their duty. Anything else you need to know concerning their whereabouts during that timeframe, you just give my office a call."

"We're not making no damn phone calls! Tyler West killed my daughter and I want him locked up right this minute!" Ted Palmer said as he rushed into the dining room.

"Dammit Ted, I told you to stay in the car!" the sheriff yelled.

But it was too late, Ted was headed around the table. Tyler stood before the man could reach him.

"You're gonna pay for what you did to her you pampered punk!" Ted yelled in Tyler's face and grabbed his shirt.

Ted Palmer was a fifty-eight year old man whose diet had consisted of nothing but fried and greasy foods his entire life. The paunch in his belly told that story even if Tyler couldn't see it in the pallor of his skin and hear it in the congested sound of his breathing. So pushing the older man off him barely required any effort.

Jagger and Alex had also stood, ready to do whatever the situation might call for.

"Get back outside Ted!" the sheriff yelled again. "That's an order!"

"He'd better," Clyde said. "This is private property and he's trespassing."

"I've got a security pass," Ted said and held it up in Tyler's face before he continued. "You wanted to get your piece of black ass—that was all fine and dandy. I wasn't gonna mess up my long-time relationship with your daddy and this ranch because of it. But I'll be damned if I sit quietly and let you and that woman get away with murdering my babygirl!"

Tyler snatched the pass from Ted's hand and stepped up to his face. "You can take your business elsewhere, Ted. Westwind doesn't work with bigots. Now I see where your daughter got her foolish way of thinking. Get off my land now, before I have your ass thrown in jail."

"Your daddy is tossing in his grave right now! He didn't have no blacks here except for the working ones!" Ted spat.

"That's a lie, Ted Palmer and you know it," Dessie added. "Verna was my best friend for more than thirty years. She was the sweetest woman I ever knew and she was not a racist. Neither was George."

"Get him out of here, Sheriff," Tyler said slowly. "Take him off my land before you end up hauling me in for beating the taste out of his racist mouth."

Ted lunged then, yelling at Gabriella. "This is all your fault, you little slut! All your fault that my girl's gone!"

Tyler stood firm in front of her and pushed Ted back again, this time with more force. The older man stumbled back and Jagger caught him.

"Time to go old man," Jagger said as he hauled Ted to the doorway.

Ted continued to yell profanities and racial slurs until Sheriff Alvarez followed him out threatening to cuff him and put him in a cell if he didn't calm down.

"Well," Monica said when they were the only ones left in the room again. "I think we're gonna need something a little stronger than orange juice after that performance."

"I concur," Dessie said and headed to the hutch behind the table where there were a few bottles of liquor and glasses. "I'll pour."

She'd been thinking about him all afternoon. She'd been

thinking about a lot this afternoon. Including the fact that per the sheriff, she was not to leave town because apparently she was still a suspect.

Hannah Palmer was a hateful, ignorant racist, but the police suspected Gabriella of a crime. How was that for progress?

Gabriella frowned as she walked across the grass with the sun beaming down on her bare back. Her sundress was light as she held the bottom of it bunched in her hands while she walked. She could move faster that way. And fast was definitely what she had in mind considering she felt like it was the sun's goal to bake her and anything else that happened to be outdoors today.

Tyler was where she'd thought he'd be after she'd checked everywhere else—in the east corral with GG. He wasn't riding the horse, but walked him slowly around the circle. He loved that horse, and the other ones that were now being temporarily housed in the barn. But he loved GG best. From a distance Gabriella watched and wondered what fate had in store for the two of them.

He waved at her and she stopped staring at him like a starry-eyed schoolgirl and continued her trek towards the corral. Once she was at the fence, she leaned on it and lifted a hand to fan herself.

"Still not used to the Texas heat, huh?" Tyler asked when he walked GG over to where she stood.

"It's hot, I can tell you that," was her reply.

He chuckled. "Yeah. It is. But GG doesn't like the barn too much so I wanted to bring him out for a walk before dinner."

She nodded. "I'm sure he appreciates the loving attention

you give him," she said. "What's he going to do when you decide to go back to your life in L.A.?"

Tyler held GG's reins and rubbed down the horse's neck.

"Been thinking about that," he replied. "Been thinking about a lot of things actually."

She stopped fanning herself because it wasn't working. "That makes two of us."

"So much has happened since I came here three months ago. I hadn't expected to be here that long," he said.

He wore his brown Stetson today, pulled down low, jeans and a white t-shirt. She wished she'd changed out of this dress and found a pair of shorts instead.

"You know this was my dad's horse," he continued.

Gabriella folded her arms over the railing and rested her chin on her arms. "He's beautiful."

"Yes, he is. This land is beautiful. I think I forgot that for a while. A long while."

He sounded contemplative and looked just a little sad. Gabriella wanted to reach out to him, to take his hand and assure him that despite all that was going on, things were going to work out. But she didn't. Instead, she just listened.

"I always felt so bad for being better than Jagger at everything on the ranch. I hated when my dad compared us because I knew it must have made Jagger feel awful. My mom never said much in that regard. She just kept Jagger with her as much as she could. Protecting him, I guess."

"Mothers are the best protectors of their children," she said.

"And fathers are the best at expectations, I guess."

She could have agreed with him, but something told her that

wasn't what he needed to hear right now. His mind seemed pretty made up where his father was concerned.

"That's why I didn't go after Jagger for being with Hannah. I didn't want to risk sounding like my father, even though Jagger was wrong as two left feet for getting near Hannah. He knew we were together. Everyone in town knew that," he said vehemently.

"Hannah knew it too," Gabriella said. "And considering what I knew of her, I don't put it past her to have seduced Jagger."

"He was still my brother. My blood."

"You're right. They were both wrong as two left feet," she conceded.

He gave her a weak smile.

"Seeing them together was the push I needed. And meeting that scout in the mall, she was the answer. I got out of here as fast as I could and I never planned on coming back. I feel like I was wrong for that."

As much as Gabriella hated her family's smothering tendencies sometimes, she'd never considered going away from them forever.

Tyler's hand moved further back on the horse, gliding slowly over its glistening chestnut coat.

"This is my home. It's always going to be my home. I should have come back to help out. Especially when I started to learn more about operating a business. I should have read those reports my dad sent me more closely."

"Your father sent you reports on how the ranch was doing while you were gone?"

"Every year," he replied and nodded. "When I first came back I read all of them over and over again."

"Because you saw something?"

He nodded.

Gabriella lifted her head and stared at him. "What did you see?"

"Just a few minor discrepancies at first. So I brushed them off. But then I hired D&D Investigations," he told her.

"You what?" She let her arms slide from the railing and took a step closer to where he stood. "How did you know about D&D?"

"When you told me about attending that wedding at Basset Banks Winery, you mentioned Bailey Donovan. D&D did some background checks for the company we initially used to produce my DVDs. Bailey Donovan signed off on some of those reports. So when the sheriff didn't seem to be getting anywhere finding my parents' murderer, I gave them a call."

"The detective who called my family about my car being on fire is the older brother of the other half of D&D, Sam Desdune."

"Client confidentiality," Tyler said as if he knew what she was thinking. "Besides, there's no reason they would have known to connect us. I'm contracted with the L.A. branch of D&D. But either way, Sam Desdune would not have called his brother one day and said 'hey, guess who I'm working with' and Detective Cole Desdune would not have called Sam and said 'hey, guess whose car just caught on fire'."

"But Cole did just that," she said with a shrug. "Still, I see what you're saying. They would not have known that we were together. So did they find anything else in the reports?"

"They found that for about ten years money was slowly

being siphoned from the ranch's main operating account," Tyler told her.

"But why would your father have been stealing from himself?"

"He wasn't," Tyler said. "His ranch manager was."

"Oh. Okay. So what does that mean?"

Tyler sighed heavily.

"I'd rather tell everyone at one time. I think this might be a major clue and like Jagger said earlier, we're all involved now."

Gabriella squinted in the sunlight as she looked up at him. "You think you know who the killer is don't you?"

Tyler sighed again. Then he nodded slowly. "Yeah. I think I know who it is."

CHAPTER 16

*T*he newly designed back patio area was gorgeous. Immediately after dinner they'd gone out to have a look at it.

"This is a real transformation," Dessie told Naomi and Gabriella.

Tyler had invited the ranch manager and his wife for dinner, because what he wanted to discuss afterwards involved Stephen too.

"It was so exciting to work on," Naomi chimed in with a huge grin.

Stephen had stood proudly beside his wife as she talked about what she and Gabriella had accomplished.

"So we kept the original grill, adding a new covering of Quartzite to bring the design into the contemporary western feel going throughout the house," she continued.

"That's that glossy rock stuff," Jagger had joked.

"Yes, it is," Gabriella replied with an elbow to Jagger's ribs.

His brother had undergone a transformation as well, Tyler noted. One that he was liking more and more each day.

"We used the Quartzite for the grill and the fire pit over there," Gabriella said pointing to the other side of the patio where a circular fire pit was positioned. "And for the flooring we went with Travertine tiles, with a redwood natural stain on the newly built upper deck area. This same color wraps around to the side of the house for the back deck that's accessible via the kitchen. And picks up on the new front porch for an even and consistent look to the outside of the house."

"It's gorgeous," Monica said. "I'd love something like this in our backyard whenever we get around to buying a house."

Alex agreed by wrapping an arm around Monica's shoulders and surveying the work they discussed. "I agree. I especially like this covered area with the same rock materials on the beams and the outdoor lighting. This is like its own separate space, but it's all still tied together."

He was referring to where they all stood on the deck beneath the new structure that was part of Gabriella's design. The beams on the ceiling of the enclosure met in the center with an ornate chandelier that matched the new one in the front foyer of the house. The patio furniture was a dark brown wicker that actually looked like it could pass for a wood finish, with deep burnt orange cushions and matching end tables. Gabriella said this was a way of bringing the inside, outside with a modern flare. Tyler agreed, it was a great space.

He just didn't feel safe with all of them standing out there for too long. So, after a few more comments on the space, he announced coffee and nightcaps and waited until everyone had moved back inside before stepping into the house and closing and locking the new patio doors. He pushed the button to close the automated blinds and waited until the natural colored shield was completely fitted over the door and there was no way anyone could see from the outside into the house.

Dessie and Naomi insisted on everyone moving into the living room while they went to the kitchen to get trays of coffee, tea and whiskey.

Once they were situated in the living room, cups filled with the beverage of their choice in hand, Tyler cleared his throat.

"I wanted to bring us all together tonight to discuss some things that I've learned in the past few days," he said. "For now, this is confidential information. I'm sharing it because it involves all of us on one level or another."

Naomi moved closer to Stephen who sat on one of the two matching bannister leather sofas—Gabriella had told him the name when he'd complimented the new stately-looking furniture. She'd changed the paint in this room to a cream color which did wonders to brighten up the space. A coffee table that looked like a short dark wood dresser separated the matching couches while loveseats in the same design filled the two opposite ends.

Monica and Alex sat on the couch across from Naomi and Stephen. Clyde and Dessie were on one loveseat and Gabriella had joined Tyler on the other. Jagger favored the dark brown recliner that was situated closer to the window and was the closest seat to the bar. When this was all over, Tyler was going to have a talk with his brother about the drinking part of his transformation.

"What's going on around here, Tyler?" Stephen asked. "The whole town is talking about Hannah's murder. The sheriff stopped by my house earlier today. I was still here working, but he talked to Naomi for almost an hour. And he left a message that he wanted to see me as soon as possible."

Tyler frowned. "Do you remember back to when you were a ranch hand here, Stephen?"

"Yeah," Stephen replied. "It wasn't that long ago. Two years and eight months to be exact. We were all shocked that old Jessie decided to retire. It was well known around the ranch that Jessie fully intended to croak here at Westwind, meaning we'd have to cart his dead body off the property." Stephen shook his head. "That seemed a whole lot funnier before all this started happening."

Naomi rubbed a hand over her husband's knee.

"What does Jessie have to do with this, Tyler?" Clyde asked.

"There are two names on the ranch's operating account," Tyler said. "My dad's and his ranch manager, Jessie. When Jessie left and Stephen took over the job, the names on the account were changed."

Stephen nodded his agreement to that fact.

"My dad copied me on all the yearly financial reports of the ranch, as well as all the restructuring and expansion plans," Tyler continued.

"And my mother copied me," Jagger said from his spot close to the window.

When Tyler looked up in surprise, Jagger lifted his half-full glass of whiskey in a toast to his big brother.

"I admit to not paying a lot of attention to those reports over the years," Tyler said, keeping his eye on Jagger. The slow way in which Jagger brought that glass to his lips and took a sip told Tyler his brother was guilty of the same thing. "But when I received news of my parents' death, I went through them all."

He took a deep breath and looked around the room, seeing that Monica and Alex were paying attention, but were also wondering what this had to do with the here and now.

"I noticed a few discrepancies in some of the earlier statements, but again, admit to not digging deeper into them. Not at the time. After Gabriella's room at the resort was vandalized and the sheriff still had no leads on the murder or the vandalism that had occurred on the ranch a few weeks after my parents' funeral, I was angry. So I hired a private investigator," Tyler told them.

"Always taking charge," Jagger stated.

"He is in charge now that you sold him your part of the ranch," Dessie interjected. "Now, hush while he talks."

"I gave the investigator all the financial reports I had in my possession, plus copies of some things I found in Dad's office. I also told him everything that had taken place in the past months. I talked to the investigator yesterday and was given some eye-opening news. Jessie was stealing. For almost ten years he stole a total of 3.8 million dollars from the ranch, which is why Mom and Dad felt like they were struggling for a while. But Dad finally figured out what the problem was—his longtime friend and schoolmate, Jessie. I figure that out of respect for that friendship Dad decided to let Jessie retire gracefully, instead of having him arrested for embezzlement and being embarrassed around town."

Clyde emptied his glass of whiskey.

"You knew didn't you?" Jagger asked Clyde. "You knew Jessie was caught stealing and you didn't say anything."

Clyde gripped his empty glass. "George and I discussed options. But Jessie went to school with us. We all grew up together. There was a bond, a friendship and a level of respect."

"Even though he was robbing my dad blind," Jagger countered. "Loyalty knows no bounds around this place."

"It was out of respect for Jessie's family," Clyde stated firmly. "Jessie's father used to work with George's dad. My father went to school with your grandpa and Jessie's. We're all family here in Hobbs Creek. Either by blood or by love. We all work together, support each other and take care of each other. That's how it's always been around here."

"Until somebody decided my parents had to die," Tyler said somberly.

"Jessie had a heart attack six months ago. He died before they could get him to the hospital," Dessie said.

"Guilt is a motherfucker," Jagger snapped.

Tyler didn't comment.

"When Jessie died, what happened to his place up in the hills? Who paid to bury him?" Tyler asked Clyde.

When Clyde didn't respond, Stephen did.

"Jessie's son, Noah. He came back and took care of everything for his dad. Noah had left Hobbs Creek a few years after Jagger did and nobody had seen or heard from him since. Until Jessie died," Stephen told them.

Tyler nodded. "Six months ago Noah Windmyr came back to Hobbs Creek. Three months later my parents were shot in the back of the head and burned in their truck just a few miles from Westwind. Three weeks after they were buried somebody walked onto this ranch and vandalized some property. A couple weeks after that, Gabriella and I were shot at while we rode in the early morning."

Alex cursed and Gabriella sighed beside Tyler.

"Gabriella's room at the resort was vandalized," Tyler continued.

"But Brooke did that. She was a conniving bi—" Jagger said, cutting himself off.

"Right," Tyler picked up where his brother left off. "That was Brooke. You had proof of that with the things you heard her say and the paint they found in the trunk of the rental car she was driving. But try as he did, Sheriff Alvarez was unable to find any evidence connecting Brooke to the shooting or the vandalism here. And Mom and Dad were killed before you and Brooke arrived."

"Wait a minute," Clyde said. He stood and set his glass on the coffee table. "Are you trying to say that you think Noah's behind this. Noah Windmyr that scrawny little kid that stayed to himself while the rest of you were running wild around town."

"Oh my, Lord," Dessie said with a hand going to her chest. "Noah Windmyr."

"I'm just saying that it makes sense. None of these things started happening until after Noah came back to town," Tyler said.

"But that's your only proof," Alex spoke up. "You're basing this theory on broken trust and loyal friendships. Have any of you even seen Noah Windmyr at the ranch? You have a pretty sophisticated security system here, how was it that Noah Windmyr—the scrawny loner—was able to come back to town and gain unlimited access to this place without anyone knowing? That doesn't make any sense."

Unfortunately, Alex was right.

"I don't have all the answers." Tyler admitted. "But I wanted to share what I'd found. I think its Noah."

"He was here," Jagger said. He'd sat forward in the recliner and rested his elbows on his knees, his glass cupped in both hands. "That night Dessie had the big dinner party. Noah was here, standing in this living room, talking to Brooke."

"Sonofabitch!" Tyler exclaimed. "He was."

Even with all the thoughts of Noah Windmyr today, he hadn't recalled him being at that dinner party. Not until Jagger brought it up.

"He hadn't wanted to shake my hand," Tyler added. Not that he'd wanted to shake the guy's hand either. But that had been because he was talking to Brooke, not because Tyler suspected him of killing his parents.

"So wait a minute," Gabriella said. "This guy has been on the ranch. He knows this place because he grew up here. Is it possible he could have been hiding in the wooded area all along? There's no security gate surrounding the trees, just along the roads and the entrance and exits."

"She's right," Stephen said.

"So he could have been coming and going through the woods," Tyler added. "We played back there when we were kids. There are paths we all know like the back of our hands."

"Okay, I'm convinced," Monica stated. "When do we call the sheriff?"

"In the morning," Tyler stated. "The investigator was pulling Noah's financial records and anything else he could find on him today. In the morning I'll have a full report and whether or not it points to something concrete to nail Noah to all of this, I feel like we still have a good lead to give Sheriff Alvarez. Good enough to get him off our backs."

"I don't know about that," Alex said. "As much as I hate to say this, you and Gabriella gave the police damn good reason to come after you as suspects. I mean, what were you thinking threatening this woman in a public place with all those witnesses?"

"I was thinking that I wasn't going to let her talk down to me like I should have been serving dinner or mopping up the floors in her father's restaurant instead of sitting there trying to have a nice dinner with Tyler," Gabriella snapped.

"Gabs, this is not the first time you've had to deal with racism and I can promise you that, unfortunately, it won't be the last. Especially since you're in an interracial relationship," Alex stated calmly. "I'm sure Mom and Dad went through the same thing."

"It doesn't make it right and I don't have to stand for it. I don't care who is giving people the impression that it's okay to start popping off at the mouth about their racist beliefs, I'm not going to tolerate it," she insisted.

"And neither am I," Tyler said taking her hand. "Hannah was out of line. There isn't one word about that conversation that I would change if I could. No matter how unfortunate it was that she ended up being killed on my land."

"Remind me to never put you two on the witness stand," Clyde commented.

"It won't come to that," Jagger said as he stood up. "We're going to get Noah Windmyr. Tyler and Gabriella will be cleared of all suspicion and we can get on with business as usual. You and I still have to meet to talk about a buy-back."

Tyler nodded, glad that his brother was coming home in his own way.

"With all that said," Tyler told them. "Let's get the house locked down tight for the night. Even with the sophisticated security system, I don't want to take any chances."

"That's a good idea," Stephen said. "Naomi and I will ride around and check on all the animals, make sure everything is in order before we head home.

"Thanks, Stephen," Tyler told the ranch manager. "I'm happy to have you managing the ranch. And I'd like to discuss you taking on even more responsibility during the times I'll have to fly out for business."

Tyler and Stephen had stood and Tyler extended his hand to Stephen. With a wide grin, Stephen accepted Tyler's hand and shook it enthusiastically.

"Thanks, man. I appreciate that. Westwind is my home," he said.

"And we're happy to have you as part of the family," Tyler told him.

After walking Stephen and Naomi, and Clyde and Dessie out, Tyler closed and locked the front door. He checked the security pad near the door to make sure it was engaged and then heard from Alex and Jagger that they had checked every door and window on the lower level. They turned out the lights and the five of them headed upstairs for the night.

Tyler hugged Gabriella close to him as they took the stairs and when they entered the room and closed and locked their door, he made love to her before they both fell asleep.

He touched her leg and she moaned.

His fingers brushing over her sensitive skin was just as erotic as his tongue stroking over her most intimate parts.

But he liked her thighs, often spending time touching and kissing them before doing anything else. So she rolled onto her back, spreading her legs a little wider to give him the access he desired. A shiver slipped down her spine as he grew closer to her juncture, his fingers already knew the path to her pleasure.

He stopped and she whimpered.

His next touch was to her cheek, then down to swirl a finger around each of her already puckered nipples. She arched her back, pushing her breasts upward to him, giving him whatever he wanted from her. It was how they had come to be together. Gabriella and Tyler. Even their names rung a cute little bell in her head.

She was in love.

And this time it was real.

It was unlike anything she'd ever felt with Austin. And unlike anything she'd ever imagined in her life. That's how Gabriella knew it was real. It's how she knew it was fate.

She was in love with Tyler West and every instinct she possessed told her that he was in love with her too.

Especially the way he was so tenderly touching her right now. He'd left her nipples aching and wanting more, tracing his tongue...no it was too hard to be his tongue...but it was cool and it was moving down the valley between her breasts. Cold and hard and...her eyes shot open and his hand slammed over her mouth, killing the scream before it was even born.

Tyler moved beside her and the clicking sound the gun made when the man pointed it to her head echoed in the room.

"You make a move, I blow her brains out," he said.

"Noah."

She heard Tyler whisper the name as the man pulled her out of bed, holding her back close against the front of his body. He backed up until he was near the open closet door while moonlight spilled into the room from the partially opened blinds.

"Let her go, Noah," Tyler said.

He'd eased off the bed, slowly, keeping eye contact with Noah, Gabriella guessed because he wasn't looking at her. She was shaking. The arm Noah had around her neck was strong and almost constricted her breath. But it was the nozzle of the gun rubbing along the skin at her temple that had her heart thumping wildly.

"You know that's not going to happen," Noah stated.

His voice sounded young, lacking the deep timbre of her brothers, Tyler and even Jagger's. And he was scrawny. She could feel how thin he was, but knew from the way that he was holding her that his strength should not be underestimated because of his size.

"We can talk this out," Tyler told him.

He was standing on the other side of the bed now, his hands down by his side.

"You can talk all you want, the end will still be the same. You die. Jagger dies. I get Westwind because it's rightfully mine," Noah said. "Oh, and this one here, she gets to fuck a man whose of her own race. Well, half her race since my dad seemed to have an affinity for black women too. You two shared that affliction."

"I can't let you hurt her, Noah," Tyler said. "I won't let you hurt her."

"You can't stop me!" Noah yelled. "None of you idiots can!"

He backed up again and leaned in closer to laugh eerily in Gabriella's ear.

"I've been here all along, right under your noses," he said. "You like it when he takes you from the back. Putting you on your knees like you're some kind of animal. And then you let him smack your ass like he's the stallion riding you hard until you come whining his name and stroking his ego."

Gabriella cringed at the knowledge that he'd watched them. That closet door had been closed when she and Tyler went to bed. Now it was open and Noah was hanging around it like in some way it was his home. He'd been hiding in there, watching them. She shivered with the disturbing thought.

"You like him panting over you and carting you around like a showpiece, don't you?"

Gabriella didn't respond.

"Don't you!" he yelled and lowered his hand to grab her breast. He squeezed until she whimpered.

"Noah!" Tyler called to him. "Look at me, Noah. Your gripe is with me."

Noah didn't release her breast completely but he did loosen his grip so that pain wasn't ricocheting through her body anymore.

"You're damn right, my gripe is with you. Spoiled little pretty boy!" Noah spat. "You and Jagger, the West Boys. Rich, good looking, good at sports, driving fancy new cars, getting all the girls and all the job opportunities. You both suck! I hated you when we were younger and you pushed me in the lake when you knew I couldn't swim and I hated you more when your dad told you to clean the horse shit out of the stalls and you made me do it!"

"Your father wanted you to learn how to do ranch work," Tyler said. "I was assigned to teach you."

"You were a rude bastard who treated me like the pigs you sold to market," Noah spat. "And Jagger was worse. He made me do everything he didn't want to do. He even told me to look out for you when he took Hannah back behind the barn that day. He didn't want you sneaking up on them. But you did." Noah laughed then. "That was one of the best days of my life. Watching you, watch your brother, getting his cock sucked off by your girlfriend. It was epic!"

Gabriella squirmed. She lifted an arm and tried to elbow him in the ribs, but Noah was faster. He stepped back so that her elbow only brushed over him, instead of impacting the way she'd planned. He lifted his arm, squeezing it harder around her neck.

"Keep still, bitch! Or I'll put you down right here and now," he told her. "And you!" he yelled to Tyler. "Don't you move another inch or I'll make you watch me take her before I kill her."

Gabriella's gaze shot to where Tyler had moved from the head of the bed, down to the foot, as if her were about to run across the room towards them.

Noah had extended his other arm, pointing the gun at Tyler now.

"I'll do her just like I did Hannah, making her scream my name instead of yours," Noah taunted.

Gabriella gasped at his admission.

"Yeah, that's right. I killed Hannah. It was messier than I

thought it would be, but I wanted to try it with a knife," he said and then giggled. "I'd already shot someone, or no, I shot two people. That's right. Both of them were in their shiny black F150 when they ran out of gas. And just a short distance from their precious ranch. I timed that pretty damn good."

"You piece of shit!" Tyler spat.

Noah continued to giggle.

"You sound just like your daddy did when I showed up to help them. He didn't want my help. Didn't want me anywhere near his ranch after my father had stolen his money. It was my father's money!" Noah yelled again. "My father worked here all his life. He sweat and broke bones riding those horses, falling off the fence he was made to fix all by himself. Everything that's here my father had a hand in building and if your father had just paid him what he was worth, things would have been alright."

"He stole from his best friend. That's not alright, Noah."

"Well, his best friend stole the woman my dad was supposed to marry! If that gold-digging Verna had just said yes to my father's marriage proposal, I wouldn't have been born a half breed and treated like the spawn of the devil all around town because of it!"

"What the hell are you talking about?" Tyler asked. "My parents were high school sweethearts. They got married as soon as they graduated from high school."

"And my dad loved Verna all his teenage years. He asked her to marry him the night before their senior prom and she turned him down because he wasn't a West. He wasn't going to inherit this big 'ole ranch. He could only work on it," Noah spat.

His arm shook as he continued to point the gun at Tyler.

Gabriella wanted to try to get out of his grasp again, but she was afraid he would pull the trigger and Tyler would die. She couldn't risk that. She had to think of something else.

Tyler took another step toward Noah.

"So your dad moved on. He found your mom and then they had you," Tyler said. "That's life Noah. And those decisions had nothing to do with you."

"He fucked the black bitch that had been panting after him because she was there. And you know what she did after she had me? She took all my dad's money from the bank account and ran off. She didn't want my dad, just his money. And she didn't want me 'cause I was a half breed," Noah said.

Gabriella could feel his whole body shaking as he said those words.

"Nobody wanted me!" Noah continued. "And your family treated my father like crap! Your father accused him of stealing and fired him, making him the laughing stock of the town."

"That's not true, Noah," Tyler said. "Nobody in town even knew what happened between my father and yours. They just thought that Jessie retired."

"You're a liar! Just like your daddy! You all lie and cheat. That's why I came here after the funeral and broke into those pens. Because I wanted you to leave! I wanted you to put the ranch up for sale because you were too afraid to be here! But you didn't. You stayed. So I had to do something else. Those damn birds got in my way when you were out riding. I had a clean shot of both of you until they were all swooping down around the tree getting me all confused!"

"Noah," Tyler said.

"No! You shut up! It's over! I killed Hannah to set you up,

but I don't want to wait anymore. I'm not waiting for a trial or that ass backwards sheriff to get his facts in order! It's over! I'm claiming what's mine."

With that, Noah turned quickly, tossing Gabriella to the floor and kneeling down over her. She kicked instantly, swinging her arms at him even though she knew he had a gun.

"Let her go, Noah!" Tyler yelled.

Gabriella had tears in her eyes and she was fighting to get him off of her, but over his shoulder she saw Tyler with a gun. He'd finally gotten to the gun Gabriella had seen him push between the mattresses before they went to bed.

"Let her go or I'll blow your head off right now!" Tyler told him.

Noah stopped fighting her. He rolled over on the floor and jumped to his feet, pointing his gun at Tyler. Now, they both had guns and they were in a stand-off. Gabriella quickly got to her feet.

They'd all switched positions so that now, Noah stood with his back to the door leading out to the hallway and Tyler was closer to the closet. When Gabriella stood, she was beside Tyler.

"Noah, just put your gun down," she said, her heart beating so loud she could barely hear herself speak. "Just put your gun down and we can all sit and talk this out."

She took a step toward Noah and was rewarded with a roar that sounded like a battle cry before he turned the gun to her and prepared to pull the trigger. Everything from that point on happened like a movie playing in slow motion. The bedroom door opened and Jagger ran inside, pushing Noah out of the way just as a gunshot rang out. Gabriella fell to the floor with Jagger on top of her and then there were two more shots. The room went silent after that, except for the sound of someone choking, sputtering some unintelligible words and then falling into the dresser before hitting the floor.

Gabriella immediately pushed Jagger off of her. Her feet scrambled beneath her as she struggled to stand and looked around the room. Noah was lying on the floor bleeding and Tyler...he was still standing, holding that gun, alive. He was alive.

She ran to him and he hugged her close, whispering in her ear over and over again, "I'm so sorry for getting you into this. So damn sorry for all of it. I love you," Tyler said. "I love you so much. If he had hurt you. If he had ki—"

"I'm fine," Gabriella told him. "I'm right here, Tyler. I'm fine. And I love you, too. I love you and you're alive."

She didn't know how long they stood there, but she heard when Alex and Monica came into the room. Because that was only seconds before Noah raised his arm and aimed the gun at her and Tyler as they stood embracing each other. Monica screamed and Jagger pushed the dresser on top of Noah, causing the gun to fall from his hand and clatter across the floor. Alex hurried to pick up the gun and handed it to Monica, who quickly aimed it at Noah. Alex lifted the dresser off of Noah and yelled for Jagger to find him something to tie his hands with.

Tyler sighed and rested his forehead against Gabriella's, still holding her tightly.

"It's over," she whispered. "Everything will be fine now because it's over."

Tyler nodded and kissed her forehead. "It's over," he said.

CHAPTER 17

*T*he next hours passed quickly with sirens and police cars filing onto the ranch once again. Tyler sighed because this time his house was the crime scene. Police had been in his bedroom where they'd handcuffed and arrested Noah Windmyr. They'd been downstairs in the living room as well as every other room in the house and they dusted for fingerprints to prove Noah had broken in. Tyler wasn't optimistic they were going to find any because when Noah was being lifted off the floor, the gunshot wound to his knee and his shoulder still gushing blood, a security pass had fallen out of his jacket pocket. It was a pass issued to a supervisor of the construction crew, a man who would now be questioned about a connection to Noah and the murders.

Noah had walked onto the property that night he'd vandalized the pens, but after that he'd had to find another way to get inside. And he had. Sometime last night Noah had slipped into the house and when they'd locked up, they'd unwittingly locked themselves inside with a killer. How did that happen? And how did Tyler prevent it from happening again? Because the sight of Gabriella standing with a gun to her head wasn't something he ever wanted to see again.

"It's almost over, Ty," Clyde said after clapping a hand to his shoulder.

Gabriella was in the kitchen with Alex, Monica and Dessie. Sheriff Alvarez was talking to Stephen in the office and Naomi was fixing coffee, going around the house making sure everyone had a full cup. It was almost dawn and the house was full of people like it was an afternoon gathering. Tyler stood in the den, next to the mantle over the fireplace that he'd told Gabriella not to touch in her redecorating. She hadn't and the West family photos still stood proudly on that mantle looking on to the next generation.

"He just wanted to carry on the family name," Tyler said as he looked at his parents' wedding photo. "And she wanted to make it bigger and better, to bring it into the 21st century with the glamour and style it deserved."

"Now it's up to you," Clyde told him. "You and Jagger. They loved and were proud of both of you. I know that George had a funny way of showing his pride and appreciation toward you boys, but that was just the way he'd been brought up. His father wasn't affectionate toward him and so George did what he'd learned. You boys had Verna. Her light shines in both of you."

"Noah said Jessie proposed to my mother," Tyler stated slowly, the words still causing him pain. "Is that true?"

"Yes," Clyde replied. "I'd forgotten about that it was so long ago. But the day before prom Jessie walked right up on Verna's front porch and asked her father if he could speak to her. Verna's dad had seen Jessie around town with George so he hadn't thought anything untoward was going on. He sent Jessie in the house where Verna and her sister, June, were. Jessie went in there and got down on one knee, asked her right there in front of her sister. June told us later that Verna turned him down in the nicest way possible, but that Jessie left the house spitting mad."

"Why did my dad hire him at the ranch if he knew that Jessie was in love with his wife?" That was like Tyler asking Austin to come work for him at Ty-Fitness.

"Jessie had been following me and George around since we were young boys. Right after Jessie's father went to jail for burning down three buildings in one weekend, Jessie started acting strange. Rumor was, his father was looking for a black man who he said had stolen from him, so he followed the man and burned down every place he thought he'd seen him. Everyone in town knew that Windy, that's what they used to call Jessie's father, was a little touched in the head. Anyway, Jessie was about ten when that happened and he started acting strange kicking cats and breaking stuff for no good reason. That's when George decided we should keep an eye on him. From that point on we just kept Jessie real close because we thought it would help him get past what his father had done and that bad reputation."

"And then his son grew up to murder my parents, the ones who only tried to save his father," Tyler said quietly.

The grief was heavy and powerful as it weighed on him. For his parents and for Hannah who, no matter how simple-minded she could be, did not deserve to die.

"You will move past this," Clyde told him. "We all will. The world keeps turning, no matter what."

"It does," Tyler said with a nod. "And things just keep changing."

"Change isn't always a bad thing. Dessie would say it's necessary and I agree with her. You and Jagger have a new chance at a meaningful adult relationship. Both of you have business experience that George and Verna never possessed. This is your time here at Westwind. I hope you don't waste it," Clyde said.

"I won't," Tyler told him. "I plan to carry on the family name with the sense of pride and loyalty that my parents instilled in me. Thanks for being their friend and for helping us through this, Clyde."

Tyler extended his hand to the man who had always been like an uncle to him. Clyde shook his hand but then pulled Tyler in for a hug.

"You're a good man, Tyler. I always knew you would be and I'm glad to have you home."

Home.

Tyler was home and that finally meant everything to him.

The minute that front door closed Alex gave a sigh of relief. It had been a grueling five hours. And it had reminded him of another time—two other times to be exact. Third time was the charm.

He walked into the living room where everyone had convened just as they had last night. They all sat in similar locations, but Monica stayed close to Gabriella, sitting on the loveseat with her while Tyler had stood to fix them a drink. Alex did not stop, but walked right across the room and grabbed

Monica's arm. When he had her standing directly in front of him, her face affixed with shock, mouth open ready to ask what the hell was wrong with him, Alex kissed her.

He touched his lips to familiar ones and closed his eyes as he poured his heart and soul into a kiss that was going to change his life. There'd been a time when Roland Summerfield and his daughter were so focused on revenge that they'd been willing to kill anyone in the Bennett family to get it. Shots were fired, but Alex's family had remained safe and alive. Alex had been truly grateful for that fact. A couple years later, he found himself in a parking garage facing another lunatic who was hell bent on killing the woman Alex loved because she was no longer in love with him. Alex had stood staring at the gun Yates Hinton had pointed at him and then watched Yates crumple to the ground when Monica stabbed him in the neck. More death and grief had struck around his family and his friends in the years following and in the world in general. Mass shootings, police brutality, government corruption, racially charged protests and more, seemed to be getting out of hand. The country they lived in seemed to be burning down around them and Alex felt the need to grab whatever happiness he could in the time he had.

He broke the kiss and stared into Monica's still surprised face.

"I want to marry you Monica Lakefield. Not later, now," he told her earnestly. "You proposed to me five years ago and then asked me to wait until you were one hundred percent sure you could be a wife and a mother. Well, you've been the best fiancé I could have ever hoped for in those five years and while I love you with every breath in my body, I am not willing to wait another five years, or even five months. I want to marry you now, Monica. I want you to be my wife as soon as we can possibly make it happen. Do you understand what I'm saying to you?"

Alex hadn't realized until that moment that everyone in the room was quiet and staring expectantly at them. And he didn't care. All that mattered was Monica and the words that would come out of her mouth next.

"I love you, Alex," she started. "You've been my strength for these past five years. And anybody who knows me, knows that I don't lean on anybody else, ever. But you, you've been everything I've needed at every moment I needed it. For these past years I kept telling myself I wasn't ready, that we were fine with our relationship the way it was, and that may have been true yesterday and all the years before. But I hear you, Alex. I hear what you're not saying and I agree. Our time is now. It's right now."

He cupped a hand to her face, letting his thumb run over her smooth skin. "Say it," he told her. "Say the word and we'll do it."

She was nodding rapidly, her eyes filling with tears. And if Monica Lakefield crying wasn't a sight for all to see, the words she spoke next were what Alex and so many others had been waiting so long to hear. "Yes, Alex. Let's do it. Let's get married!"

Applause erupted around them and Alex pulled Monica into his arms once again. He spun her around, closing his eyes and recalling all the time he'd been with her and all the nights he'd wondered when or if they would ever really get married. Well, he had his answer. They were getting married and he couldn't be happier.

"Beautiful!" Dessie cheered. "Just beautiful! Now, I know you city slickers won't be getting married here in Hobbs Creek but I'd love for you to send me pictures of the big day. I know it's going to be a spectacular event."

"What are you talking about Ms. Dessie," Monica said when Alex finally released her. "You and Mr. Clyde are definitely on the guest list. So you'll just have to come on up to the big city and celebrate with us."

"That's right, Ms. Dessie," Alex said. "We'll even show you and Mr. Clyde around town when you get there."

"No," Jagger intervened. "I'll show Clyde and Dessie around New York when they come. And you're both staying in my condo while you're there."

"Well," Dessie said with a big grin. "Then I think I'll get on into this kitchen and start fixing us a celebratory breakfast. Come on Naomi, you can help me while Stephen checks on the ranch hands and the morning work around here."

"I call waffles, Dessie. And those buttermilk biscuits you make," Jagger chimed in.

"Then you'd better get your butt in this kitchen and help," Dessie said.

Alex chuckled at Jagger's mock frown. They reminded him a lot of his family, the way love still shined through in the end, despite their differences. Monica had taken Alex's hand and was leading him into the kitchen, but he told her to wait a second as he turned to see Gabriella still sitting on the couch and Tyler still standing by the bar. They looked so far a part, not just in the space of the room, but in their relationship and even though she was his little sister and he'd never planned to watch another man steal her heart, Alex wanted happiness for her.

260 | AC ARTHUR

"No," Monica said when he'd started to go to her. "Let her be. She's going to find her own way, in her own time."

"But will her way make her happy?" Alex asked as he continued to watch Gabriella staring down at her hands folded in her lap.

"Gabriella knows what she wants and she knows what she needs to do to get it," Monica told him. "Her happiness will come, you just have to let it come when she's ready for it."

Alex hoped Monica was right.

"Well," Tyler said when they had been alone for a few minutes.

The silence had instantly become deafening causing Gabriella's thoughts to echo loudly in her head. She'd been thinking for hours now, since the moment Noah had pulled her off that bed.

She'd thought of her life up until this point. The decisions she'd made. The things she should have done or said. She considered her situation with Austin and the child she'd lost because of it. She pictured Adriana becoming a mother and how happy Parker would be to become a father. She wondered about her job and what would happen after the company heard about everything that had happened here in Hobbs Creek. Especially the fact that she'd fallen in love with her client. One of the biggest taboos in a professional setting.

And then she'd thought of Tyler.

Slowly, she lifted her head to look at him.

While they'd waited for the police to arrive he'd slipped into sweat pants and a t-shirt. She'd pulled on a pair of jean shorts and one of Tyler's t-shirts. She wore only socks on her feet and had no idea how her hair looked at this moment. And she really didn't care.

Tyler looked tired. His normally neat beard was scraggly, his bright blue eyes, shadowed. He had bed hair, which always made her want to run her fingers through the thick dark brown strands again and again. And his shoulders slumped a bit. She wanted to go to him, to wrap her arms around his waist and hug him tight. But she remained still while thoughts continued to run through her mind.

"Should we get into the kitchen to help Dessie?" he asked.

Gabriella watched as he finally put down the glass he'd been holding. She squared her shoulders and replied, "No. I think we should talk first."

He didn't say another word, but came to sit on the love seat next to her. He didn't touch or look at her, he just sat. And she continued.

"My family and I have wondered for five years if Monica and Alex were ever going to get married. I think it's ironic that another one of my mess-ups was the catalyst for that to finally happen," she said.

"This wasn't your mess up. It was Noah's," he stated seriously.

She sighed. "I know. I'm not at all taking any of the blame for that. But I am owning up to the mistake I made. The misjudgment and the decision to keep it all a secret. That was on me."

"Everybody decides to deal with a situation in their own way," he said. "I didn't have to leave and stay away from here. I could have come back and continued to be connected. I chose not to."

"What are you going to do about that now?" she asked him.

"I'm going to make it work," he replied. "I'm going to move back to the ranch primarily, but I'm also going to work with Stephen on taking more managerial responsibilities for the times that I have to be away on Ty-Fitness business."

"That's a good plan," she said with a nod. "My dad always says it's good to have a plan."

"Do you have one, Gabriella? Is that what you want to talk about?"

She waited a beat and then extended her arm across the space between them until she could lace her fingers with his. He squeezed her hand and she looked down at them sitting on the leather love seat. Black and white. Man and woman. Lovers and friends.

"I love you, Tyler. I meant that when I said it. And I know that I don't have a glowing track record in the area of love, but I know what I feel. And this, what I've felt in the time that I've been here with you is unlike anything I've ever experienced or imagined."

"But?" he said the moment she paused.

"But I have to go," she told him. "I have to go back to Connecticut and deal with Austin."

"You can let the police deal with him," Tyler said.

He squeezed her hand again until she looked over at him. "Stay here with me. Move into the house that you've helped to make a home with your innovative design and your enthusiastic presence. We can both travel for work and—"

"Stop," she said, using her free hand to reach up and cover his lips. "Don't say anything else. Don't ask me to do anything. Not right now."

Looking into his eyes and telling him she was leaving may have been the hardest thing Gabriella ever had to do. But she knew it was necessary.

"I'm going to fly back to Connecticut with Alex and Monica. Naomi can supervise the last days of the project. And I'll be sure to report that she did to the Proctor Group. I'm going to go back and deal with Austin. Because if I don't, it will never be over with him. He won't stop unless I stop him," she said.

"Then I'll go with you," Tyler said over her hand.

Gabriella smiled and moved her hand from his mouth to cup the side of his face.

"No. I got into this on my own. I tried to handle it on my own once before. It's only fitting that I go back alone and fix it."

"But you're not alone anymore, Gabriella. I'm with you. I told you I would never leave you. I love you," he said.

Gabriella eased over to him. She leaned in to drop a soft kiss on his lips. "I love you so much Tyler. That's why it's so important that I do this. I don't want to come to you with all this baggage. And you're not leaving me," she said with a tentative smile. "I'm technically leaving you."

"And I'm not dealing with it too well," he said. "Gabriella, please reconsider."

"It's better this way," she said and sat back against the couch again. "This way, when I come back—because Tyler, I definitely plan to come back to you—I'll be whole and renewed and completely healed. And then we can start our future, on new and solid footing."

"I don't like this idea," he said with a mock frown. "But I understand that you need to do this for yourself. I respect that you want to do this for yourself."

"And for us," she told him. "I want there to be an 'us', Tyler. Please don't doubt that."

He smiled. "No. I don't doubt it. I just don't want you to forget it."

"I won't," she said. "Here, get your phone out."

She'd slipped her phone into her back pocket and she pulled it out while Tyler released her hand and retrieved his from the side pocket of his sweat pants.

"Pull up your calendar. We're going to set a date," she said.

He chuckled. "Okay. But what are we setting a date for?"

"For September the first at three o'clock in the afternoon. That's when we'll meet back here at the equestrian center. The place where we first met," she said after she finished typing it into her phone.

She leaned over to make sure he'd typed the same thing into his phone and smiled when he hit the save button and returned his phone to its locked screen.

"September the first," Tyler said while gazing into her eyes. "At three o'clock sharp I'll be at the equestrian center with GG and Brown Eyes waiting for you."

"I'll be there," she promised.

"Don't make me wait a second longer," he whispered as he moved in closer.

"Not one second longer," she stated just seconds before they sealed their deal with a kiss.

CHAPTER 18

2 weeks later, August 31st
Greenwich, Connecticut

"A toast," Alex said. "To Gabriella. A fierce and determined young woman who took no crap from Austin Sterner as he stood in the courtroom and tried to deny all that he'd done to her."

Although she hated being the spotlight of tonight's family dinner, Gabriella lifted her glass and accepted the toast to herself. She deserved it for everything she'd endured in the last two weeks.

When she'd returned home from Hobbs Creek, Gabriella hadn't been certain how she was going to deal with Austin, she just knew that she had to do something. So, after going to the police station and filing a formal complaint for harassment, she'd gone to the office where she used to work with Austin under the pretext of returning some literature that belonged to them which she still had in her home office.

Faran Beulsky, the lead agent at the firm happened to be at the front desk when she'd arrived.

"Hello, Gabriella. It's such a nice surprise to see you again," Faran had said.

He'd always been very nice to her and so Gabriella had smiled at him genuinely. "I'm only back in Greenwich temporarily, Faran. Just wanted to drop these materials off to you."

"Ah yes," he said taking the stack of pamphlets and papers from her. "I heard that you were working for the Proctor Group now. I'm sure they have you traveling a lot."

"Yes. As a matter of fact I've just returned from a project in Texas."

"That's wonderful," Faran said. "No. That is a lie. It's not wonderful. I wish you were here still working with us."

"Why thank you, Faran. I did enjoy my time here with you and the other agents. It just became too uncomfortable after Austin and I broke up," she told him.

"What? You mean that rumor was true?"

"What rumor is that, Faran?"

"The one where you and Austin were involved in a relationship that you eventually ended. When I confronted Austin about it, he told me it was a lie. That you'd probably said that because he hadn't been satisfied with your work on the last project and suggested you find another position. I told him I would have liked to talk to you about your position and I would have liked to see that project that he was so unhappy with. But he brushed it off saying that he'd handled it and it was over."

Gabriella kept her smile in place. If she had been feeling any measure of guilt for intending to come to his job and tell Austin's employers what a sick bastard he was, she definitely wasn't now.

"I assure you, Faran, we definitely had a relationship. I have the text messages, emails and doctor's bills to prove it," she quipped.

Faran immediately began shaking his head. "No. Don't tell me he was abusive. I will not stand for such a thing. Not at my firm."

"Oh no, Faran. Austin never laid a hand on me. I'm talking about the baby I lost because Austin wouldn't take me to the hospital when I begged him to," she said and while there had been a pinch of sadness and pain at her words, the look on Faran's face was enough to make it better.

By the time Gabriella left, she felt confident that Faran was going to call Austin and tell him that she was back in Greenwich. That was what she'd wanted when she decided to go there. Now, all she had to do was wait for him to come to her.

And he did, not three hours later.

He knocked on her apartment door and Gabriella had answered it ready for whatever was about to happen. At least she thought she was before she saw him.

Standing at six feet even, Austin Sterner was one fine black man. His clean-shaved head and muscled chest only accentuated how brilliant he was in the real estate market. He wore gray slacks and a gray dress shirt with the first two buttons left open. The shirt was fitted because Austin liked to show off all the work he put in at the gym.

"So you returned," he said as he walked into her apartment without an invitation.

It was fine. Gabriella had let him in. If she didn't want him there, he wouldn't be.

"I have."

"And you're running your mouth about me already. Look Gabriella, I told you I wanted you back. We could have worked this out, baby. You didn't have to go running to Faran feeding him a bunch of lies," Austin said.

Gabriella folded her arms over her chest and stood with her back against the door.

"Oh, they were lies? I thought for sure that I'd spent three days in the hospital earlier this year because of a miscarriage."

Austin shook his head. "I told you to deal with that situation well before that time. It's not my fault you waited," he told her.

She nodded. "You're right. It was my decision to continue with the pregnancy. But it was your decision to leave me on that floor bleeding when you knew I needed to go to the hospital. It was your decision to tell me that bullshit about not wanting another child when you barely ever remembered to use a condom when we were together. Now, true, that was my fault. I should have never trusted an ignorant bastard like you. But I'm cool with my mistakes now, Austin. I've come to terms with them and I'm ready to move on."

He took a deep breath and held out his arms to her. "It's about time," he said. "Now, come here and give me a hug, girl. You standing there looking all fine in those jeans and that shirt. Got yourself a little tan too. Makes you look more Cherokee than Brazilian, but you know I've always loved your exotic look."

When she didn't move, Austin came to her. He was in just

the right position for her to pull her knee up and slam it into his groin. When he stumbled back, speechless from the pain, Gabriella walked toward him.

"You're a spineless coward, Austin. I know you set my car on fire because I wouldn't take you back and I know you told Faran that I lied about our relationship and that I messed up on one of my projects that's why you wanted me out of the office. You're a liar and an ass and if I never see your face again it will be too soon," she said.

Austin still couldn't speak and she'd backed him up until he was close to the couch. He was bent over and holding his stomach while he gasped for air. She started to push him, just to see him roll onto the floor. But she stopped. It was enough and she'd already won. Seeing him in pain was just the icing on the cake. Gabriella went to the table by the front door and picked up her phone. She dialed a number and said, "I'm ready."

In less than five minutes, Detective Cole Desdune and his partner came through the door. The next words Gabriella heard were, "Austin Sterner, you are under arrest."

That had been a day that Gabriella knew she'd never forget.

Earlier today, Austin had been in court for a bail review. It ended with him being remanded back to jail and held without bail because Faran and Gabriella testified that he was a flight risk and posed an existing danger to her. Austin yelled every name he could think of at her in the courtroom and Gabriella held her head up high as she stared him eye-to-eye and waved goodbye.

Now she sipped her champagne and enjoyed the feeling of accomplishment.

"She was fierce, Mama. You should have seen her," Adriana said.

Her sister was now six months pregnant, with a bump that resembled a basketball tucked beneath her shirt. She and Parker had arrived in Connecticut two days ago as a surprise to check-up on Gabriella.

"No. I just did what I had to do," Gabriella said, casting a thankful glance at Monica who was sitting on the other side of the table.

"Not every woman can do that," Beatriz told her youngest daughter. "You should be proud that you stood up. Not only for yourself but so many of those who could or cannot stand for themselves."

Gabriella nodded. She understood exactly what her mother was saying, without looking at Monica again.

"Well, since we're celebrating and Gabriella is leaving us again tomorrow, Eva and I have an announcement to make," Rico told them.

"Oh my," Marvin spoke from the head of the table. "I don't know if my heart can take anymore announcements or admissions from my children."

His comment was meant for Gabriella. Her father had been extremely hurt when she told him and her mother about the baby and her time in the hospital. He'd said over and over again how he'd raised his children to trust him and to always know that they could come to him no matter what. She'd let him and her mother down, Gabriella knew that, which was another reason why she'd wanted to come home and deal with all of this personally.

"It's okay, Dad," Rico continued. "This is good news."

Eva sat back in her chair and rubbed a hand over her very flat stomach. "It's very good news," she said.

It only took another second for clapping and cheers to erupt as Marvin and Beatriz realized they were now going to be blessed with two grandchildren. Tears stung Gabriella's eyes for a moment, but she breathed deeply until they subsided, then stood up to go and hug her brother and sister-in-law. She was happy for them, just as she was for Adriana and Parker and for Monica and Alex for setting a wedding date.

"So, while we're all on a good note, I'm going to head back to my apartment," Gabriella told them. "I have an early flight tomorrow."

She was going back to Hobbs Creek to meet Tyler and she couldn't wait.

"Oh honey, I wish you could have stayed home a little longer," Beatriz said as she came around the table to hug her daughter.

Gabriella hugged her mother tight. "I know, Mama, but I'll be back to visit real soon. I promise."

"You'd better," Marvin said as he came to stand beside her.

Marvin Bennett was a tall and burly man who could be imposing and downright scary when he wanted to. But to Gabriella he was just her dad. When he wrapped an arm around her she immediately lay her head on his chest and let him hold on.

"You take care of yourself out there, little girl. And don't you dare keep another secret from me like the one you just did," he told her.

"I won't, Daddy. I promise," she said just before the doorbell rang.

"Who in the world can that be at this time of night?" Beatriz asked.

"I don't know," Marvin said. "Gabs, why don't you go and answer the door since you were getting ready to leave anyway."

"Oh, okay, Daddy," Gabriella said and left the kitchen to walk down the long hallway toward the front door.

She grabbed her purse from the table closest to the door and was prepared to tell whoever it was—probably a lost delivery man or something—to be on his way and then head out herself. But she stopped in her tracks when she opened the door and saw Tyler standing on the other side.

He looked spectacular dressed in black denim and a crisp white chambray shirt. His boots were new and matched his hat. And the flowers in his hand were gorgeous.

"Am I late for the family dinner?" he asked.

"What? How did you know we were having a family dinner?" she asked in return.

"Of course you're not late," Beatriz said as she came up behind Gabriella. "Come on in, Tyler. I'm Beatriz. We spoke on the phone."

"Yes ma'am," Tyler said. "It's a pleasure to finally meet you in person. These are for you."

Gabriella watched him hand her mother the flowers. Then she looked at the rest of her family that had assembled in the hallway.

"What's going on here?" she asked them all, needing somebody to answer her quickly. "Tyler, what are you doing here? I thought we were scheduled to meet at the equestrian center tomorrow."

He looked around and after a nod from Marvin, reached up

and took off his hat. He had hat hair now and Gabriella's fingers instantly itched to reach up and touch it. But she didn't because she was still trying to figure out what was going on.

"I could not go another day, Gabriella. Not one more second," Tyler said.

He reached out and took her hands in his, holding them between the two of them with everyone watching.

"I've learned the hard way about waiting too long to say what I have to say and do what I need to do," he continued. "I cannot change the way things turned out with my parents and I know that they both loved me as much as I loved them. But there was so much time wasted and I don't want to do that ever again. I love you, Gabriella Joy Bennett. I love you today. Tomorrow. For Always. Will you please do me the honor of becoming my wife?"

His words had come so quickly Gabriella didn't think she'd heard them correctly. This had to be a joke. But her heart had started to beat faster, her eyes blinking to keep her tears from falling.

"What are you doing?" she asked and then looked around at her family. "What's happening?"

They were all smiling. Her mother, Adriana, Monica, Eva and Bree. Her brothers didn't smile, but they weren't brooding like they were ready to jump on Tyler and beat him senseless either. And her father, well, he was standing next to her mother with his chest poked out as if he were proud of her, or this moment, or all of the above.

She turned back to Tyler just in time for him to release her hands. He dug into his side pocket and pulled out a black velvet box. Gabriella gasped. She covered her mouth with one hand

and began shaking her head. When he went down on one knee and opened that box, extending it up to her, Gabriella dropped her arm to the side and whispered, "I thought we were just going to meet up at the ranch. I didn't know this was going to happen."

Everyone around her chuckled. Tyler smiled as he said once again, "Will you marry me?"

With tears freely flowing now and her family already clapping their approval from behind her, Gabriella was nodding before the words could fall from her mouth.

"Yes! Yes! Yes. I love you, Tyler. I love you for always."

WILL THE ICE QUEEN TURN INTO BRIDEZILLA?

Find out in the next Donovan Friends book,
THE WINTER WEDDING
Coming Winter 2018!

"I'm so excited for you, Monica!" Cheyna exclaimed. "You and Alex are one of the greatest couples I know."

"Thank you," Monica replied. "And since you did such a fantastic job with the gallery anniversary party last month, I'd like to hire you to help me plan my wedding."

Cheyna wanted to jump up and down, maybe do a few cartwheels, a back flip and then yell "Yes! Yes! Yes!" over and over again. But she refrained. She sat back in the guest chair and looked Monica Lakefield directly in the eye before responding, "I would be happy to help you, Monica. Have you and Alex set a date? When would you like to get started?"

Monica opened a side desk drawer. She pulled out two white binders. Handing one to Cheyna and keeping the other on her desk, she opened to the first page. Monica looked up to see Cheyna staring at her in anticipation of an answer to her questions, and raised one elegantly arched brow. Cheyna quickly opened the binder.

"The date is December 21st," Monica stated. "It's the first day of winter and will be the first day of me and Alex's married life together."

Cheyna had seen that printed in gold script on the white sheet of paper that marked the first page of the binder. She swallowed and looked up to Monica once more. "That's two months from now."

"Yes it is. Will that be a problem for you?"

"No," Cheyna quickly replied. "No. That won't be a problem at all."

"Good. Then let's get started. We have a lot to get done in a short period of time. And everything has to be perfect." Monica flattened her hand on the book and for the first time since Cheyna had come into her office, Monica Lakefield smiled before saying, "I'm getting married."

THE DONOVAN FAMILY TREE

Download the Donovan Family Tree:
http://www.acarthur.net/download/3056/

1ST GENERATION

Elias (d) & Gertrude Donovan (d) – Children: Rowan (m. Adeline) and
    Charleston (m. Cora)
    Rowan (d) & Adeline Donovan (d) – Children: Isaiah (m. Dorethea), Aaron [d] (m. Sondra), Abraham (never married) and Bridgette a.k.a. Birdie (never married)
    Charleston (d) & Cora Donovan (d) – Children: Cephus (m. MingLee), Joanna (m. Johnathan Bowers), Katherine (d) (m. Myles Denton), Della (m. Robert Sats)

2ND GENERATION

Isaiah "Ike" (d) & Dorethea "Dot" Donovan (d) – Children: Albert (m. Darla[d]), Henry (m. Beverly), Bernard (m. Jocelyn), Everette (m. Alma), Reginald (m. Carolyn) and Bruce (m. Janean)

    Aaron [d] & Sondra – Child: Gabriel (m. Maxine)

    Abraham "Abe" Donovan – Child: Margo (m. Klevon Whitfield)

    Bridgette "Birdie" Donovan – No Children

Cephus & Ming Lee – Children: Charles (m. Brenda), Wen (m. Hugo Norton)

    Joanna & Johnathan Bowers – Children: (twins) Loretta (m. Billy Ringgold), Lorraine (m. Jerry Seavers)

    Katherine "Kay" (d) & Myles Denton (d) – Children: Myles, Jr. (m. Alice)

    Della & Robert – No Children

3RD GENERATION

Albert & Darla – Children: Brock (m. Noelle), Brandon (m. Amber) and Bailey

    Henry & Beverly – Children: Lincoln (m. Jade), Trenton (m. Tia) and Adam (m. Camille)

    Bernard & Mary Lee (x) – Child: Keysa (m. Ian)

    Bernard & Jocelyn – Child: Brynne

    Everette & Alma – Children: Maxwell (m. Deena) and Benjamin (m. Victoria)

Reginald & Carolyn – Children: Savian (m. Jenise), Parker (*x* Jaydon (d)) (Adriana), and Regan (Gavin)

    Bruce & Janean – Children: Dion (m. Lyra) and Sean (m. Tate)

    Gabriel & Maxine – Children: Roark, Ridgely and Suri

    Margo & Klevon – Children: (triplets) Alexis, Adonna and Amelia

    Charles & Brenda – Children: Cadence "Cade", Dakota

    Wen & Hugo – Child: Xia

    Loretta & Billy – Children: Maria, Morganna & Hannah

    Lorraine & Jerry – Children: Kendra & Cecile "CeeCee"

    Myles Jr. & Alice – Child: Myles, III

4TH GENERATION

Brock & Noelle

    Brandon & Amber – Child: Serene

    Bailey & Devlin

    Lincoln & Jade – Children: Torian & Tamala

    Trenton & Tia – Child: Trevor

    Adam & Camille – Children: Josiah, Jordan

    Dane & Zera

    Keysa & Ian – Child: Madison Lee

    Brynne & Wade

    Maxwell & Deena – Child: Sophia

    Benjamin & Victoria – Child: Aria

    Savian & Jenise

    Parker & Adriana

    Regan & Gavin – Child: Raleigh

Dion & Lyra – Child: Ilyssa
Sean & Tate – Child: Briana

******Key: m = married; [d] = deceased; x = divorced

THE DONOVAN SERIES

The Seniors are listed in order by birth and their children are listed below them (also in order by birth)

Senior – Albert Donovan

Brock & Noelle — Book 4: FULL HOUSE SEDUCTION

Brandon & Amber — Book 13: IN THE ARMS OF A DONOVAN

Bailey & Devlin — Book 14: FALLING FOR A DONOVAN

* * *

Senior - Henry & Beverly Donovan

Lincoln & Jade (Children: Twin daughters, Torian & Tamala) — Book 1: LOVE ME LIKE NO OTHER

Trenton & Tia (Child: Son, Trevor) — Book 3: DEFYING DESIRE

Adam & Camille (Children: Sons, Josiah and Jordan) — Book 2: A CINDERELLA AFFAIR

* * *

Senior – Bernard & Jocelyn Donovan

Keysa & Ian — Book 6: HOLIDAY HEARTS

Brynne & Wade — Book 15: DESTINY OF A DONOVAN

* * *

Senior – Everette & Alma Donovan

Maxwell & Deena (Child: Daughter, Sophia) — Book 5: TOUCH OF FATE

Benjamin & Victoria (Child: Daughter, Aria) — Book 9: PLEASURED BY A DONOVAN

* * *

Senior – Reginald & Carolyn Donovan

Parker & Adriana — Book 11: EMBRACED BY A DONOVAN

Savian & Jenise — Book 12: WRAPPED IN A DONOVAN

Regan & Gavin (Child: Son, Raleigh) — Book 10: HEART OF A DONOVAN

* * *

Senior - Bruce & Janean Donovan

Dion & Lyra (Child: Daughter, Ilyssa) — Book 7: DESIRE A DONOVAN

Sean & Tate (Child: Daughter, Briana) — Book 8: SURRENDER TO A DONOVAN

THE DONOVAN FRIENDS

The Desdunes

Lucien & Marie Desdune

Lynette & Brice (Child: Son, Jeremy) — A CHRISTMAS WISH, part of the *Under The Mistletoe* Anthology

Cole & Loren — ALWAYS MY VALENTINE

Samuel & Karena (Child: Son, Elijah) — SUMMER HEAT

Sabrina & Lorenzo (Children: Daughters, Delia & Desirae, Son, Daniel) — GUARDING HIS BODY

* * *

The Bennetts

Marvin & Beatriz Bennett

Alexander & Monica — WINTER KISSES

Ricardo & Eva — ALWAYS IN MY HEART

Lorenzo & Sabrina (Children: Daughters, Delia & Desirae, Son, Daniel) — GUARDING HIS BODY

Adriana & Parker — Book 11: EMBRACED BY A DONOVAN

Gabriella & Tyler — FOR ALWAYS

* * *

The Lakefields

Paul & Noreen Lakefield

Monica & Alexander — WINTER KISSES

Karena & Samuel (Child: Son, Elijah) — SUMMER HEAT

Deena & Maxwell (Child: Daughter, Sophia) — Book 5: TOUCH OF FATE

THE DONOVAN SERIES & THE DONOVAN FRIENDS BOOKS IN READING ORDER:

Book 1: LOVE ME LIKE NO OTHER

(Lincoln Donovan & Jade Vincent)

Book 2: A CINDERELLA AFFAIR

(Adam Donovan & Camille Davis)

Donovan Friends #1:

GUARDING HIS BODY

(Lorenzo Bennett & Sabrina Desdune)

Book 3: DEFYING DESIRE

(Trent Donovan & Tia St. Claire)

Book 4: FULL HOUSE SEDUCTION

(Brock Remington & Noelle Vincent)

Book 5: TOUCH OF FATE

(Maxwell Donovan & Deena Lakefield)

Donovan Friends #7:

FOR ALWAYS

(Tyler West & Gabriella Bennett)

ALSO BY AC ARTHUR

OTHER CONTEMPORARY ROMANCE

The Office Series

Book 1: OFFICE POLICY

Book 2: CORPORATE SEDUCTION

* * *

The Indecent Series

Book 1: INDECENT PROPOSAL

Book 2: INDECENT EXPOSURE

* * *

Rules of the Game Trilogy

Book 1: RULES OF THE GAME

Book 2: REVELATIONS

Book 3: REDEMPTION

* * *

The Carrington Chronicles

Book 1: WANTING YOU - Part One

Book 2: WANTING YOU - Part Two

Book 3: NEEDING YOU

Book 4: HAVING YOU

* * *

The Rumors Series

Book 1: RUMORS

Book 2: REVEALED

* * *

The Royal Weddings

Book 1: TO MARRY A PRINCE

Book 2: LOVING THE PRINCESS

Book 3: PRINCE EVER AFTER

Book 4: TAMING THE PRINCE

* * *

The Taylors of Temptation

Book 1: ONE MISTLETOE WISH

Book 2: ONE UNFORGETTABLE KISS

Book 3: ONE PERFECT MOMENT

* * *

OBJECT OF HIS DESIRE

UNCONDITIONAL

LOVE ME CAREFULLY

HEART OF THE PHOENIX

SECOND CHANCE, BABY

SING YOUR PLEASURE

DECADENT DREAMS

EVE OF PASSION

~

PARANORMAL ROMANCE

The Shadow Shifters

Book 1: TEMPTATION RISING

Book 2: SEDUCTION'S SHIFT

Book 3: PASSION'S PREY

Book 4: SHIFTER'S CLAIM

Book 5: HUNGER'S MATE

Book 6: PRIMAL HEAT

Book 7: A LION'S HEART

* * *

The Damaged Hearts Series

(Shadow Shifters Spinoff)

Book 1: MINE TO CLAIM

Book 2: PART OF ME

Book 3: HUNGER FOR YOU

Book 1-3: DAMAGED HEARTS BOX SET

* * *

The Wolf Mates

The Alpha's Woman (Available as part of the GROWL Anthology and
CLAIMED BY THE MATE VOL.1 Duology)

Her Perfect Mates (Available as part of the WILD Anthology and
CLAIMED BY THE MATE VOL.2 Duology)

Bound to the Wolf (Available as part of the HUNGER Anthology and CLAIMED BY THE MATE VOL.3 Duology)

CONTEMPORARY SMALL TOWN ROMANCE (W/A LACEY BAKER)

The Sweetland Series

Book 1: HOMECOMING

Book 2: JUST LIKE HEAVEN

Book 3: SUMMER'S MOON

YOUNG ADULT PARANORMAL (W/A ARTIST ARTHUR)

The Mystyx Series

Book 1: MANIFEST

Book 2: MYSTIFY

Book 3: MAYHEM

A Mystyx Novella: MUTINY

Book 4: MESMERIZE

ABOUT THE AUTHOR

Stay in touch with A.C. on the web!

Be the first to know when A.C. Arthur's next book is available! Follow her at BookBub to get an alert whenever she has a new release, preorder, or discount!
www.bookbub.com/profile/a-c-arthur

Visit the "Contact" page on her website, www.acarthur.net, to sign up for her monthly newsletter.

"Follow", "Friend" and/or "Like" her on Facebook (AC Arthur's Book Lounge), Twitter (@ACArthur), Pinterest (acarthur22), Instagram (@acarthurbooks), Tumblr (acarthurbooks), Google Plus and GoodReads.

Made in the USA
Middletown, DE
20 August 2024

59462378R00168